Marina Oliver lives in Shropshire.

A DISGRACEFUL AFFAIR

Sylvie Delamare's great-uncle Sir George sends her a mere £20 — claiming it to be a whole half of her inheritance — and she's infuriated. Her parents had been wealthy, so she wants to go and confront him in Norfolk. Meanwhile, she is invited to visit Lady Carstairs, her friend's aunt in London, to be presented. However, Sir Randal is suspicious of Sylvie, after seeing her with Monsieur Dupont, who he suspects is one of Napoleon's spies. Then when Sir Randal follows Dupont, he meets Sylvie in Norwich on her way to see Sir George. And when he offers her a lift — he becomes embroiled in her affairs . . .

MARINA OLIVER

A DISGRACEFUL AFFAIR

Complete and Unabridged

ULVERSCROFT
Leicester

First published in Great Britain in 2008 by
Robert Hale Limited
London

First Large Print Edition
published 2009
by arrangement with
Robert Hale Limited
London

British Library CIP Data

Oliver, Marina, 1934 –
 A disgraceful affair
 1. Great Britain- -History- -George III, 1760 – 1820- -
Fiction. 2. Love stories. 3. Large type books.
 I. Title
 823.9′14–dc22

 ISBN 978–1–84782–823–1

Published by
F. A. Thorpe (Publishing)
Anstey, Leicestershire

Set by Words & Graphics Ltd.
Anstey, Leicestershire
Printed and bound in Great Britain by
T. J. International Ltd., Padstow, Cornwall

This book is printed on acid-free paper

1

Sylvie Delamare blinked at the letter in astonishment, then read it again. Slowly her numbness gave way to fury; she cast the bank draft down on the bed, jumped up and began to stride back and forth in the tiny room. Two steps one way from bed to the small window, swing round, three steps to the door, two steps back to the bed. Oh, if only she could sprout wings, she would by now be on her way to Norfolk and the curmudgeonly skinflint who was her great-uncle.

Reaching the door of the room again she leant against it, resting her head on her arms, and tried to calm down. She had to plan sensibly. Another wave of fury swept over her and she banged her fists against the door.

'Sylvie? What is it? Why are you making this noise? Can't you open the door?'

Sylvie gave a stifled laugh. 'Celia? I'm sorry. Did I disturb you?'

'Not really. But what's the matter?'

She stepped back and opened the door. 'Come in. My only surviving relative has condescended to write to me and, belatedly, congratulate me on my coming of age!'

1

Celia Mannering, a delightfully pretty, fair-haired, blue-eyed, fragile-looking girl, her best friend at the Bath seminary, came in looking worried.

'Your uncle? Sir George? Well, the posts are unreliable. You can't blame him.'

'I can! Sir George Clayton is a despicable, miserly, crooked, fraudulent knave! I won't recognize him as connected to me!'

'Sylvie, calm down and tell me what he's done to put you in such a pother.'

She pushed Sylvie who collapsed on to the bed. Celia sat beside her, and picked up the discarded bank draft. 'Here, don't tear this up. It looks important.'

Sylvie thought for a moment of doing exactly that, then her sense of humour returned. 'Oh, no, I mustn't do that. Celia, that twenty pounds is precisely half my total inheritance, according to that — that worm!'

Celia stared at her. 'Twenty pounds? But you always told me your mama had been an heiress, with a London town house and a big estate in Cambridgeshire. And your father was a wealthy jeweller. What has happened to all the money?'

'That, Celia, is what I mean to find out. Great-uncle George wasn't my only trustee, but first I mean to go and confront him and find out why my inheritance has dwindled to

2

almost nothing. And what's more,' she added, growing heated again, 'he has the kindness to inform me that this half is mine, to help me become established as a governess, and he will retain the other half either until I marry and have a husband able to control it for me, or he dies. How he expects me to marry respectably if I do become a governess, I haven't the slightest notion!'

Celia looked shocked. 'Oh, no, you simply can't be a governess. Though Mrs Shaw would employ you; you've been teaching French to the girls here for years.'

'Which is one very good reason why I won't contemplate doing it for the rest of my life. Oh, I've been grateful to her, keeping me on as a teacher so that I could earn my keep when that old skinflint refused to pay my school fees after I turned eighteen, but not any longer.' She shuddered. 'Can you imagine such a tedious life? Never going to London, no parties, dull schoolmistressy gowns, endlessly reciting irregular verbs to chits who couldn't care less whether they spoke correctly or not?'

'What will you do?'

'Go to Norfolk and demand to know where my inheritance is. I'd better go through London. At least with this money he's sent me' — she waved the draft — 'I can afford the fare on the public stage, and pay for a night's lodging in London. What was that hotel your aunt said was the only respectable one for ladies on their own?'

'I don't think she meant it was suitable for young unmarried ladies,' Celia said doubtfully. 'But why don't you come and stay with me? Aunt Augusta is sending her coach and her maid to escort me to London next week. She'd love to have you to stay in Berkeley Square.'

Sylvie hesitated. It would be far preferable to travelling on her own. 'It seems rude, to inflict myself on her without so much as an invitation,' she said slowly.

'You've stayed with me before, and she loves having guests. Oh, do come, Sylvie!'

'I've stayed with her in Oxfordshire once, during the summer holidays, four or five years ago, when you'd just come to Mrs Shaw's and were homesick. Your parents had just gone to India. That was different.'

'No it wasn't. She liked you, and said you were to come with me at any time.'

'I'm sure she didn't mean to London when the Season's just about to begin, and she's bringing you out.'

'Why not? You could come to some parties and perhaps a very rich man would fall in love with you and then your lack of fortune wouldn't matter!'

Sylvie laughed. 'Celia, you are a romantic! Besides, I will not even consider marrying a rich man just for his money. When I marry it will be for love, and I intend to bring my own fortune into the marriage.'

'You're the romantic. Most marriages are business arrangements, to bring estates together, for instance. But it would be nice to love your husband,' she added wistfully.

Sylvie grinned at her. 'I'm not going to look for a husband, but I'll stay just one or two nights until I can buy a seat on the mail to Norfolk. Thanks, Celia. I'd better go and tell Mrs Shaw she'll need to find a new French mistress.'

⋆ ⋆ ⋆

Mrs Shaw, given an edited version of the truth, smiled sadly at Sylvie.

'We shall miss you, my dear. You've been here for ten years!'

'Eleven. Since my parents died, and my guardian did not know what else to do with me.'

'Sir George Clayton, yes.'

'He's my trustee — one of them, not my guardian. That was my godmother, an elderly lady who would not have been able to give me a home. She died last year.'

5

'Even so, I'm surprised he did not send for you when you turned eighteen, but I understand he is a rather reclusive gentleman. He suggested that I might find you a post as a companion to a lady here in Bath, since he would not pay the fees to keep you here for a few more years. That would not have been suitable; you are — shall we say — too lively to be an old lady's companion! So fortunate that your dear father was French, and you speak the language fluently, so I could offer you a post here instead.'

To save the old miser the trouble of paying the fees, Sylvie thought bitterly. She had trained herself not to dwell on thoughts of her parents, killed so tragically when the friend's yacht they were sailing in had been in a collision with a fishing boat and sunk. Mrs Shaw's words brought it all back — the shock when she had been told, the gradual realization that she would never again see her pretty mother or dashing father, the wrench of being taken from her home and dumped here in Bath with strangers.

It had not been an unhappy few years once the first anguish had abated. Mrs Shaw was kind, she'd quickly made friends with the other girls and, as she was naturally clever with her needle and light on her feet, she had won the praise of the teachers for her embroidery and dancing achievements. Mrs Shaw had a good library, and though she did not encourage the girls to spend too much time with books, warning them they risked being regarded as blue stockings, she had permitted Sylvie greater laxity, saying that if she lost herself in those old stories of the Ancient Greeks and Romans she would pine less for her dead parents.

'You've been very good to me,' Sylvie said, suddenly reluctant to leave the only home she'd known for so long.

'It has been a pleasure to have you with us,' Mrs Shaw said. 'We'll miss you, Sylvie, and if ever you are in need come back to us here in Bath. You will always be welcome.'

Sylvie nodded. It was comforting in a way to know she had this refuge, should she ever need one, but she was determined to discover what had happened to her inheritance. There had been her father's business, which had been one of the most highly regarded in London.

Then there was her mother's fortune, her houses and land, and other investments. How could they all have vanished? She meant to find out, and if, as she suspected, the great-uncle she was becoming convinced would prove to be a crook who had cheated her out of her inheritance, he would be forced to give it back to her.

★ ★ ★

Sir Randal Fortescue handed the reins to his tiger, jumped down from his curricle, and strode briskly through the imposing portals of the Ministry. Soon he was closeted with a senior official.

'Have you any news from Leicestershire?' Mr Sinclair asked.

Sir Randal shook his head. 'Only negative. They have found no traces of French agitators there. Someone has been stirring up the mill workers, in the same way they have been doing in Manchester, but no one knows who it is. Our information must have been incorrect.'

'Or deliberately misleading.'

'Possibly.'

'And Lincolnshire? There has been a great increase in smuggling since Holland allowed American ships into her ports. They find it easier than landing on the French coast. Napoleon's blockade is faltering, everyone wants to trade.'

'I've found little evidence of increased smuggling from either Lincolnshire or East Anglia.' Randal shook his head. 'Being a stranger there did not help. The locals are suspicious.'

Peter Sinclair steepled his fingers on the

desk. 'We know they operate mainly from the south coast, but our revenue officers there have been achieving some successes lately. They will have moved their operations elsewhere, and the east coast is the obvious place if they are going to Holland.'

'We'll keep on looking. So what has been happening here while I've been away?'

'We're starting to look at a Frenchman who has been living in New York, and came to England six months ago.'

'An interesting combination. Because of his intimates here? Are there any suspicions about them?'

'Marc Dupont is said to have supported Paine back in America. He is known to consort with a variety of radicals here. Some are followers of Burke and supported the Jacobins. But he disappears for two or three weeks at a time, and without sparing the men to follow him, we cannot discover where he goes.'

'So you think he may be helping to stir up the mill workers, to damage our trade?'

'Or is organizing smuggling, perhaps financing it. Being both French and American we cannot be sure where his sympathies lie. They may be with the French, or he may be an angry American disputing our policies over the blockade and impressment of men who hope to escape it by serving on American ships.'

'Is there no one able to get close to him and discover it?'

'That, my dear Randal, is where you can help.'

'I?'

'He's become friendly with young David Carstairs. Cavalry man, wounded at Corunna last year and on extended home leave. I believe you know Lady Carstairs?'

'Enough to visit. She and my mother are friends. But she's done little entertaining since her husband died. I actually have a small estate in Oxfordshire which runs with theirs. It was left me by a distant cousin a year ago, and there are things I need to discuss with Sir David.'

'Convenient. But I think you'll find Lady Carstairs will be entertaining this year. Her sister is out in India, and she's bringing out the niece. The chit's been at some Bath seminary. So you must get on her visiting list. It shouldn't be difficult. These hostesses are all eager to invite plenty of young men.'

Sir Randal frowned. 'So I have to do the pretty and get put on her invitation list, do I? To watch Dupont?'

Sinclair laughed. 'The girl's an heiress. All the young sprigs will be begging for invitations. If Augusta Carstairs has any sense — which is not obvious from what I knew of her years ago — she'll welcome you with open arms. You've an obscenely large fortune of your own, but you're not on the catch for a schoolgirl, however wealthy she is. She won't have to worry about protecting Celia Mannering from your attentions.'

'Who knows? I might decide that a peaceful life with a complaisant wife, on one of my country estates, is preferable to chasing possible agitators or smugglers!'

★ ★ ★

'My dear Sylvie, you can't possibly rush off to Norfolk the minute you arrive!'

Lady Carstairs, fair and pretty in a rather faded way, clasped Sylvie's hands and gazed into her eyes. Sylvie saw the appeal there, and sighed inwardly. It would be rude of her to dash off after such a friendly welcome. Lady Carstairs had greeted her so warmly, assuring her she was delighted Celia would have a good friend with her when she made her first entrances into Society, that Sylvie, much as she wanted to confront Sir George, felt unable to refuse compliance.

'A few days, then, Lady Carstairs,' she agreed, 'but then I must make arrangements to see Sir George.'

'Of course, you will want to see your only relative, after so many years in Bath. The poor man's an invalid, isn't he? He never comes to London now, though I can remember him here when I made my own come out. It was rumoured he was crossed in love and retired to live in the country, and never got over it. He is much older than I am, of course,' she added, giggling. 'Let me see, it was his sister Charlotte who was your mother's mother, wasn't it? She was married to Sir James Betteridge, who owned hundreds of acres in East Anglia. Or was it Cambridgeshire? Is that East Anglia? I'm never sure. A very good match, I believe, as she came from only minor gentry. But I'm told she was remarkably pretty. As your own dear mother was. She had dark curls just like yours, and the same green eyes, but I think your features are a little finer. The nose and the chin are sharper, just like your father's. Oh, what a commotion there was when she ran off to France to marry a tradesman! A foreigner at that.'

Sylvie, who had been trying to stem this tide of reminiscence, broke in ruthlessly at this.

'My father's father was a count, but he chose to become a master goldsmith, ma'am. He made jewels for the royal family and all the French aristocracy.'

12

'And he managed to bring out his wealth when they came home, I understand.' She laughed delightedly. 'How much more convenient jewels and gold are to carry away than big estates would have been, when those wretches started their horrid revolution. You were just a baby, I think.'

Sylvie nodded. 'I was born a few months earlier, but my father thought I and my mother would be safer in England. He wanted to go back, but my mother persuaded him it was not safe. I'm glad, I knew him for a few years, and he taught me French, which has been of great use to earn my living at Mrs Shaw's.'

'So odd, dear, that Sir George forgot to pay your fees. I wonder if the poor man is losing his wits?'

Sylvie shrugged her shoulders. She had begged Celia not to reveal to her aunt the true state of affairs. She had known from her earlier visit to their Oxfordshire house that Lady Carstairs was an inveterate gossip, and would never be able to resist imparting this titbit of scandal to all her equally empty-headed cronies. Sylvie had no wish to be talked about by the *ton*. First she needed to discover the true situation and, if possible, recover some of her fortune. It could not all have vanished. Her father had opened a workshop in London, saying he needed to invest his own fortune profitably so that he did not live on his wife's. He had not worked there himself, apart from very special occasions when he made some unique setting for a favoured client, but it had been profitable, and should have continued to be so after his death. He had employed one of his former Paris workmen, as skilled a craftsman as he was himself, as manager, and the profits should have been adding to Sylvie's inheritance during the past eleven years. She would find her way to the workshop while she was in London, before she confronted her great-uncle. She could discover what had happened to the town house in North Audley Street at any time while she was staying with Lady Carstairs, but to get to the City she would have to elude her hostess.

Lady Carstairs was still chattering, detailing all the parties she meant to take them to, and what entertainments she was planning herself, but Sylvie had ceased to listen. She was absorbed in making her own plans.

★ ★ ★

Sylvie had thought it would be easy to escape from Carstairs House while Lady Carstairs was escorting Celia to purchase the many gowns she would be needing. The following morning she would slip out, take a hackney and go to the workshop located near St Paul's in the City. If it still existed, she reminded herself.

Her plans were frustrated when, at breakfast, Lady Carstairs announced that she meant to present Sylvie with some new gowns.

'I am holding a small party tonight, just an informal one for a few friends, and I know you will have nothing suitable from that dreary seminary of yours. Celia told me how Mrs Shaw insisted that everyone, even her teachers, wore plain and dull gowns.'

'I — I can't permit you to buy me gowns, Lady Carstairs.' Sylvie was horrified. She had no intention of spending any of her precious twenty pounds on finery she would probably never wear again, unless she recovered her inheritance, and she could not permit her hostess, who was being generous enough just housing her, to buy clothes for her.

'Nonsense, child. You've just had a birthday, your coming of age birthday, and from what Celia has said even Mrs Shaw did not give you a present, and all you had was a small locket from Celia, the only thing she could afford from that ridiculously small allowance her father gave her while she was at school.'

'It was only a small locket,' Celia put in. 'I have a simply enormous allowance now, Sylvie. Papa said I'd need it now, and he isn't mean. Do let me buy you something else. A shawl, or a fan. And you must have suitable gowns for the parties. You can't offend Aunt Augusta by refusing.'

Sylvie felt betrayed. Celia knew her true circumstances, knew she could not afford to waste money on gowns, and shoes, and shawls and the many other essentials a young girl just entering Society would need. She must escape as soon as possible from this stifling generosity.

'I shall be offended if you don't permit me to equip you suitably just for this one party,' Lady Carstairs put in, and Sylvie knew she had lost.

'You are very kind,' she murmured.

'Where are your mother's jewels?' Lady Carstairs suddenly demanded. 'She had a fabulous collection, naturally, since your father was such a clever jeweller. Are they in a bank vault somewhere?'

'I expect so,' Sylvie said, and wondered in whose name the bank held them. No doubt they had vanished along with the rest of her fortune, she thought grimly. Another black mark against Great-uncle George!

With Lady Carstairs apologizing that there was not enough time for her own modiste to make the necessary gowns, Sylvie and Celia soon found themselves in a discreet establishment where the proprietor assured them that any alterations could be made immediately.

Lady Carstairs declared she deplored the insipid white which most debutantes wore, and Celia, with her delicate blonde colouring, should favour pretty pastel shades, while Sylvie could wear darker colours.

Sylvie recognized that her hostess was in her element, and gave up protesting. Lady Carstairs was unstoppable, and Celia whispered to her that her aunt was wealthy enough not to notice, and was delighting in having two girls to clothe, as she had only a son herself.

Celia was enchanted with a high-waisted, narrow-skirted gown in a delicate shade of pink, trimmed with appliquéd rosebuds and embroidery in a deeper shade. It had tiny puffed sleeves, edged, as were the scooped neckline and ankle-length hem, with embroidered roses. While that was whisked away for minor alterations Sylvie was persuaded to try on a gown in deep primrose. It had narrow bronze ribbons threaded through the neckline, wider ones at the hem.

'It suits you, with your dark hair,' the proprietor said judiciously. 'It needs no alteration. You are tall enough not to need the hem taking up.'

'We'll take it, and now for morning gowns, and a walking dress. Sylvie, that delightful poke bonnet would go beautifully with this walking dress. It's exactly the same shade of rose pink, and we can match the dark green ribbons with these gloves, and find matching shoes. And for you, Celia, the pale blue, I think, with the scalloped edging, and dark blue gloves and bonnet. Now for some evening sandals.'

★ ★ ★

Celia was upstairs with her aunt, trying on her new gowns, when Sir David Carstairs burst into the library. Sylvie had been renewing acquaintance with some of her favourite poets, and was curled up comfortably on a sofa, with her shoes kicked off. She dropped the book of Elizabethan love poems and sat up straight, trying to rescue her shoes as she did so. She'd never met Sir David, but his fond mama had told her he was expected back from a visit to Newmarket that day, and she assumed this was he.

He had slightly long hair, and wore riding

clothes, with a coloured cravat tied loosely round his neck. Though the clothes were of the most expensive materials, and had clearly been made by a good tailor, there was something dandyish about the whole. Sylvie could not quite decide why. Perhaps, she thought, it was because the coat was slightly too waisted, the breeches too pale a colour, and the cravat of too violent a pattern.

He was very like his mother, fair-haired and fine-featured. He was almost effeminate, but Lady Carstairs had praised, lavishly, his valorous deeds in the cavalry and, even allowing for a mother's partiality, it had seemed that he'd acquitted himself with honour. He had been wounded at Corunna, and sent home to recover. According to his mother he was fretting to be allowed back to the Peninsula, where Wellington was slowly turning the tide against Napoleon's troops, but the army surgeons were being cautious, as one of his wounds was not healing satisfactorily.

Sylvie barely had time for these thoughts before she became aware of another man entering the library in Sir David's wake. He was, she judged, ten years or more older. Tall, with dark, slightly waving short hair, ice-blue eyes and an expression of disdainful amusement on his handsome face, he was just the sort of man she had taken care to avoid in Bath. He was elegantly dressed in a blue superfine coat, so superbly tailored it seemed like a second skin, and pale buff pantaloons. His cravat was intricately tied and a single diamond pin nestled in the folds. The contrast with Sir David was plain. This man was no dandy.

Even in the seminary they were not totally cut off from society, as Mrs Shaw had deemed it her duty to introduce the older young ladies in her care to the customs of the polite world. Once a month she had held decorous dances, the young men she invited being, in Sylvie's opinion, the most boring, wimpish and unadventurous scions of local families. Occasionally a visitor had infiltrated this select gathering, thinking that with a roomful of nubile girls he had ample opportunities for dalliance. Mrs Shaw had been prepared. If they put one foot wrong they were shown the door, politely but firmly, and never readmitted. She smiled to herself as she thought of how Sir David's friend would not have permitted Mrs Shaw to dictate to him. He was taller than most, dark-skinned, hawk-eyed, with a determined chin and athletic figure. But then, she told herself, he would never have allowed himself to be drawn into some insipid affair at a seminary for young ladies.

Sylvie, however, had been granted wider opportunities of meeting people. As a teacher she had occasionally been sent on commissions into the town, and had become adept at avoiding the attentions of sprigs of fashion who haunted the environs of the Pump Room and Assembly Rooms. Not that anyone as handsome as this stranger had ever attempted to strike up an acquaintance with her.

She realized she was permitting her attention to wander, and forced herself to listen to Sir David.

'I'm sorry, I didn't know anyone was here. Who are you? Are you staying with Mama?'

Sylvie explained.

'Oh, that's capital. I'm David Carstairs, in case you hadn't realized, and this,' he added, turning to the silent man who stood behind him, surveying the scene with barely hidden amusement, 'is Sir Randal Fortescue. His mother and mine are great friends. He has just inherited an estate in Oxfordshire which adjoins mine, and we think there could be mutual profit in exchanging some of the fields. Now, where did I put those maps?' he said, moving to one of the cabinets. 'Here, I think,' he added, his voice muffled as he delved into a cupboard. Then he swung round, a dusty roll of papers in his hands.

Sylvie, unable to locate one of her shoes, stood up and offered her hand. 'Your mother has been so kind to me, Sir David. I'm on my way to visit relatives in Norfolk, and she asked me to stay for a few days. I was at the Bath seminary with Celia, your cousin. I'm Sylvie Delamare.'

Sir Randal looked interested, the first animated expression Sylvie had seen on his face. He raised a quizzing glass and surveyed her through it. 'A French name?' he enquired.

'Yes, sir,' Sylvie replied. She flushed at his scrutiny, lifted her chin defiantly, and vouchsafed no more. She had on more than one occasion suffered suspicions from people who regarded everyone French as traitors.

Sir David broke in. 'Where's Mama? I must tell her Randal is coming to join us tonight.'

'She's with Celia, upstairs. I'll go and tell her,' Sylvie offered, and giving up all pretence of decorum, bent down and retrieved her errant shoe from its hiding place under the sofa. Smiling brilliantly at the two men, she stooped to slip it on her foot, and then walked with as much dignity as she could manage out of the room.

2

The maid Lady Carstairs had engaged to look after Celia came to help Sylvie dress her hair. At the seminary she had allowed it to grow long, but Phyllis persuaded her to have it cropped, and when she had finished and arranged Sylvie's curls, with a gold ribbon threaded through them, Sylvie felt completely different.

The new gown helped. It was by far the finest she had ever possessed, and Celia, giggling, said it made her look quite regal. Her only jewellery was the locket Celia had given her for her birthday, but her friend had insisted on buying her a fan with pictures of flowers painted on gold gauze. Sylvie felt she could hold her own with anyone tonight.

Most of the guests were young ladies about to make their debut into Society, with their mamas and a judicious sprinkling of young and, Sylvie judged, respectable men whom Lady Carstairs considered might be presumed to make good husbands.

The one exception, so far as she could see, was Sir Randal Fortescue. He was older than most, in his early thirties, and looked far more serious. He was the most elegant man in the room, probably because of his greater age and experience of society, Sylvie decided. He wore a silvery grey waistcoat with his evening clothes, and a single emerald ring, which made the younger men look flamboyant with their fancy waistcoats and multitude of fobs and jewelled pins.

Instead of joining in the lively banter he stood to one side, leaning against the drawing-room wall, and watched with what she considered a sardonic gaze. While she sat on a sofa listening with half an ear to the gossip of two overdressed and over-painted mamas, who flirted shamelessly with the young men they were supposed to be introducing to their shy, retiring daughters, Sylvie watched him. Only a couple of the young damsels had ventured to approach him, and after a few words which had been received with calm but unwelcoming politeness, they had retreated, discomfited. The others, perhaps too shy to attempt conversation with an older man, had carefully avoided him.

She was intrigued, and when one of the mamas began to quiz her on her family and fortune, she deftly turned the conversation to him.

'I met him with Sir David this afternoon,'

she said easily. 'Is he a friend of the family? He seems rather old to be one of Sir David's intimates.'

'Oh, Randal Fortescue is intimate with few,' one of them said, sniffing. 'Don't set your cap at him, my dear. You'll be disappointed. He's a cold fish, has raised the hopes of several chits only to treat them with indifference a week later.'

'Wealthy as Golden Ball, and terrified he'll be courted for his money,' the other mama said.

Sylvie nodded, and when, some time later, one of the mamas moved and Sir Randal came to take the seat beside her, she looked enquiringly at him.

'You are French, I believe, Mademoiselle Delamare?' he said without any preliminary remarks.

'My father was French, sir,' she replied coldly. 'My mother was as English as you are.'

He raised his eyebrows. 'You know the entire history of my family, do you?' he asked.

'No, but I judged by your tone that you are not a friend of the French. My father, sir, left France when the Bastille was stormed. He wanted to protect my mother and me. He had no sympathy with the *canaille*.'

'And you? Have you relatives in France still?'

'We lost touch with my father's family, apart from hearing about a brother who perished on the guillotine. I have none left that I know of, though I fail to see what concern it is of yours, sir!'

He smiled, and Sylvie had to admit he had a most attractive smile. 'Just a friendly interest,' he said calmly, and somehow Sylvie felt at a disadvantage.

Perhaps she had been too sharp in her defence of her father. Over the years many people had asked her whether he had fought on behalf of King Louis and against the mob, and she had grown tired of explaining he was a craftsman, not a soldier, and had considered his first duty to be the protection of his wife and child.

As to that, why was Sir Randal not in the army? But as she opened her mouth to ask him, Lady Carstairs appeared, bringing Celia with her, and began to introduce them.

Sylvie slipped away, grateful she had not permitted her hot temper to lead her astray. Maybe she was too sensitive, too ready to leap to the defence of an honourable man who had needed no excuses.

To her relief, the party was soon over and she could escape to her bedroom. She would slip out of the house early in the morning, she decided, and make her way to the City to see what had become of her father's workshop. Sighing, she turned over and prepared for sleep, but to her disgust images of that handsome face kept appearing before her, and it was hours later before she had cast the wretched Sir Randal into the oblivion he deserved, and she was able to fall asleep at last.

★   ★   ★

Randal went to the Ministry early the following morning.

'Tell me more about Marc Dupont,' he asked Peter Sinclair. 'And how can I become acquainted? I'd prefer to have at least seen him before I meet him at Carstairs House.'

Sinclair fetched a file which he opened on the desk in front of him. 'Let's see, now. Born in Paris in 1780, parents of the merchant class. They emigrated to America three years later, after American Independence was formally recognized. They opened a shop in New York, and sent him to school where he was a good scholar. He was their only child and they doted on him. They both died a few years ago and left him moderately rich. He'll never have to earn his bread. I'm not sure how that squares with his avowed revolutionary principles.'

27

'He appears to have met Thomas Paine some time after 1802, when Paine returned to America. He'd be at an impressionable age, and we know he was influenced by Paine's writings. Our man there, who first alerted us to his visit to England, says he has copies of all Paine's books and essays. He would support the revolution, and America's independence. He's a republican, possibly an atheist, though as far as we are aware he keeps these views to himself, unless, we assume, he's with friends who have the same beliefs. It was when Paine died last June that he first made plans to come to England. Paine was in New York, and it's almost certain they met there.'

'So he could be working for France or America, even both. How can I meet him, or at least have a quiet look at him? Has he any known haunts where I might go without rousing comment?'

Sinclair laughed. 'He's been seen in a few places where the gambling is deep, and often suspect. He's been to prize fights, and he frequents a certain bawdy house in Seven Dials. I don't think you would blend in there.'

Randal grinned. 'Doesn't the fellow do anything respectable?'

'He often goes to the theatre, and one of his favourite plays is on tonight. He's not missed a performance so far. I'll send Richards with you. Dupont doesn't know him.'

★ ★ ★

Sylvie woke with a start when the housemaid brought in her morning chocolate. She yawned. It had been a late night. Then she recalled her intention to visit the city early that morning and groaned. It would be far too late now. She would have to wait another day.

The morning was occupied with more fittings, Lady Carstairs insisting on giving Sylvie some of her own dresses.

'Since you will not permit me to buy you more, child,' she said. 'I have so many, and I am as tall as you, and not a great deal fatter, so my gowns can easily be altered to fit you.'

They received several callers in the afternoon, people who had been at the party and came to say thanks, and others who had heard Celia was in town, and wished to pay their respects to her because they knew her parents.

'We'll dine quietly at home tonight, we don't want you girls to be done up before the Season proper starts,' Lady Carstairs decreed.

David joined them, and he and his mother soon became deeply involved in a discussion about changes he wanted to make at Lowmoor.

'It makes sense to give Sir Randal those fields which run down to the river,' David said. 'They are surrounded by his land, and we find it difficult to use them, but if instead we have the ones Randal's cousin enclosed, nearer to the village, they could be added to the Home Farm, and it makes that more compact, easier to manage.'

'Yes, I see that,' Lady Carstairs agreed. 'Does Sir Randal agree? After all, it is a minor estate for him. Most of his land is in Somerset.'

'He still takes an interest in it, and is agreeable to what I have suggested. We really do get the better of the deal, Mama, since those fields are often flooded, and only useful for summer grazing. The ones I am acquiring in exchange are good wheat-growing fields, and with the price of corn so high, we will gain from selling it.'

Sylvie, who had until now regarded David as somewhat immature, was intrigued by his grasp of farming realities. When his time in the army ended, she suspected he would settle down contentedly as a country squire, with a pleasant wife and several hopeful children. She wondered whether Celia would be that wife.

David then began to detail what he wanted to do to the house, and here found his mother opposed to many of his suggestions.

'I am fully aware I have no right to oppose you,' she said, 'but I beg of you not to put in train building works until you can be there to supervise. I have no desire to spend months in the country making sure that builders do what they have been told.'

'You don't like my plans for a new front,' he said, and Sylvie detected a trace of boyish sulkiness in his voice. 'I tell you, the Egyptian style is all the rage.'

'I have no wish to live in the Dower House and look out over mock tombs of Pharaohs,' his mother said with unusual asperity. 'Please, David, wait until you have a wife who might have her own opinions. Celia, don't you think Lowmoor would be spoilt by what David suggests?'

Celia looked embarrassed. 'I know so little of architectural fashions,' she said at last. 'It's for David to decide, but you've lived at Lowmoor and loved it, you must know what would be suitable there.'

The discussion went on, over minor details, until it was time for bed, and Sylvie retired wondering how obvious Lady Carstairs could be in her constant appeals to Celia for her opinions.

31

★ ★ ★

The hackney driver denied all knowledge of a
jeweller named Delamare, but he drove to the
address Sylvie gave him. She walked slowly
along the whole length of the short street, but
there was no business of that name. There
were other jewellers in the street and Sylvie
walked along again, trying to decide whether
one of them might have been her father's
workshop. She had only visited it occasionally
as a child, and could not be totally certain
where it had been, except she thought it was
located somewhere in the middle, and on the
shady side. But children remembered things
oddly. She'd visited friends in Berkeley
Square, and her memory of it had been of a
much vaster place. Of course, the workshop
could now be in different premises. Had it
been absorbed into another business, and the
name changed?

She tried to recall the name of her father's
French manager, but could not. Perhaps one
of the businesses had a French name. She
stepped back to look up at a name engraved
on an upper floor window, and collided with
a solid body.

'Ah, *mademoiselle, votre pardon!*'

'*Pas du tout, monsieur*,' Sylvie replied
automatically. 'I'm sorry, it was my fault. I

should have been looking where I was going.'

'You speak the French perfectly, as if you had been born there.'

She looked at the Frenchman with interest. It was the first of her compatriots she had met for many years. He was small, only just her height, slight and dark. She judged he was about thirty years old. His hair was cut in a short and neat style, brushed back severely. He carried a gold-knobbed cane, which he seemed to lean on heavily. His coat, though looking new, seemed slightly too large for him, and his pallor made Sylvie wonder whether he had been ill and lost weight.

Sylvie smiled. 'Well, I was, though I did not spend more than a few months there.'

'But you are alone? Where is your maid? A young lady should not be permitted to wander about the streets of London without an escort. Please, may I procure you a hackney to take you home?'

'I am trying to find a jeweller who may have a French name,' she explained, 'but I don't know what it might be. It has clearly changed the name since I was last here.' She was wondering if perhaps he might be able to assist her, if he knew the area.

He shook his head. 'I do not know London well, and I fear I have had no dealings with the jewellers. It is chance I am in this street where so many of them seem to have their business premises.'

There was nothing more she could do, Sylvie decided, short of invading every jeweller's in the vicinity and demanding to know their history. When she saw Sir George she would discover the truth.

She allowed the Frenchman to hail a cab for her. She gave the driver the Berkeley Square address, and turned to shake hands with the Frenchman before stepping into the cab. As he bowed over her hand she was afraid he was about to raise it to his lips, and firmly suppressed a smile. It was too like a stage Frenchman. Then, glancing over his shoulder she frowned. A tall gentleman turning aside into one of the shops looked familiar. She thought she recognized Sir Randal Fortescue.

She told herself not to be ridiculous. She had the man on her mind after their conversation the previous day, and the way he seemed to challenge her, but it was most unlikely such a fashionable creature would be up and about, and in the City at that, so early in the morning. She hoped to be back in Berkeley Square before Celia or her hostess rose from their beds.

★　★　★

Sir Randal hovered in the doorway until Miss Delamare's hackney was out of sight. All the while he kept an eye on the Frenchman, who had been pointed out to him the previous night at the theatre, but that gentleman stood watching the hackney equally intently. Then he turned and walked swiftly away towards Finsbury Square, and Sir Randal strolled, apparently aimlessly, after him.

Chance had brought him to the City, to witness that meeting. He had come to consult with his man of business about the proposed exchange of land with Sir David Carstairs, and to draw up the necessary papers. He might as well take the opportunity of observing Dupont when he was unaware of surveillance. Where was he going now? Was it connected with any of his suspected dubious activities?

His thoughts swung back to the short conversation he had held with Miss Delamare. Had the meeting with Dupont been contrived? In any case, what the devil was a girl like Sylvie Delamare doing in the City so early in the morning, and alone, if it had not been to meet with the suspected man? Was he a paid agitator, working for the French? The meeting had looked accidental, but these people were careful. They never met twice in the same place, or at the same time. This was necessary to protect their anonymity. The authorities knew of several different suspicious contacts of Dupont's, but they would not have managed to identify all of them. Sylvie was not on the list Sinclair had shown him the previous day. Then he remembered, she had only come to London a day or so ago. That could easily be checked. Celia Mannering was too young to be involved, and had no reason to have sympathy with the French. She was herself above suspicion, and if she confirmed that Sylvie had been at the same seminary for years, how had the girl become entangled in the plots he was attempting to unravel?

★   ★   ★

Sylvie slipped back into the house without Celia or Lady Carstairs being aware of her morning expedition. The footman who admitted her told her they were in the breakfast-room, so Sylvie hastened upstairs to change her shoes and leave her shawl. When she came down again she found them deep in plans for entertainments the next few days, starting with a drive in the park that afternoon and attendance at a ball being given by the parents of another debutante that evening.

Sylvie began to say she had no suitable

gown, so must beg to be excused, but Lady Carstairs smiled at her and waved her to silence.

'Celia said you might try to avoid it, but we won't permit that. My maid is altering one of my own gowns for you, Sylvie,' Lady Carstairs said firmly. 'Celia tells me you have dancing slippers, as you were taught to dance at your seminary, so I will accept no excuses.'

There was nothing she could do but accept gracefully. As they drove round the park later, while Lady Carstairs was busy greeting acquaintances and introducing Celia and herself to them, all the time bewailing the fact that London was woefully thin of company, Sylvie was wondering how soon she could escape from this stifling hospitality and start to discover what had happened to her mother's fortune and her father's business.

The evening gown which had been altered for her was a delightful shade of green, like new leaves on beech trees. It was far too young a colour for Lady Carstairs, Sylvie thought privately, and these thoughts were confirmed when Lady Carstairs, surveying her critically while they were waiting for dinner to be announced, laughed and nodded in satisfaction.

'I can't think why I ever ordered such a gown,' she said. 'It suits you to perfection,

Sylvie, with your dark hair. What a pity you don't have your mother's emeralds here. As I recall, the necklace was a most intricate, delicate filigree pattern. The emeralds were not great vulgar stones, but dozens of tiny chips which caught the light whichever way she moved. But no doubt your uncle will pass them on to you now you are of age.'

'I hope so,' Sylvie said. 'That one sounds enchanting.' For a moment she wondered whether Lady Carstairs would know what had happened to her father's business, but decided on caution. She needed to know more before talking about her family affairs. 'Lady Carstairs, please don't think me ungrateful, but I ought to be making plans to visit Norfolk soon. Sir George will be wondering why I have not paid him a visit to discuss my future.'

'Is he your guardian? Oh dear, if so, why did he not make arrangements himself for your journey?'

'He is not my guardian,' Sylvie said hastily, silently congratulating herself on this fortunate fact. 'That was my godmother, but she died six months ago and no one else was appointed. I don't know how these things work, but I imagine as it was so close to my birthday and no one even thought of it immediately, they decided it was not worth the trouble. But I ought to pay my respects to him, and I know he wishes to tell me how things are left.'

'Of course, my dear, but do spare us at least a few more days. We must take you to the theatre, or the ballet. Which do you prefer? And,' she went on, not waiting for Sylvie to reply, 'there is a soirée at Lady Fortescue's tomorrow evening. That's Sir Randal's mother, she's very learned, reads both Latin and Greek. At this affair all we have to do is listen to the poets and pretend to enjoy their verses. And no doubt she'll have one or two singers. And her refreshments are always most superior. I used to think blue stockings didn't care about their food, and certainly when the Misses Galbraith held their evenings, I came away as hungry as when I had started.'

Fortunately for Sylvie's gravity the butler announced dinner, and the ladies went into the dining-room. Lady Carstairs began to fret about Sir David's absence.

'Of course, he often prefers to dine out with his friends, but he promised to be here to escort us tonight. I do hope he has not forgotten.'

'I expect he'll come before we are ready to set out, Aunt Augusta,' Celia said quietly.

Lady Carstairs smiled at her. 'You are such

a comfort, my dear. How I wish I had been given the gift of a daughter like you. But I suppose I shall have to wait until David brings home a bride.'

Sylvie bit her lip. Lady Carstairs seemed determined to promote a match between her son and niece. She caught a fleeting look of panic in Celia's eyes, then her friend took a deep breath and smiled brightly. Had she previously entertained any notion of these hopes?

Sir David, from what little Sylvie had seen of him, was a typical, high-spirited boy. He may well have spent several years in the army, but he was by no means ready for the responsibilities of a wife and marriage. Celia, however, was well able to take care of herself and resist any pressure her aunt might exert. Sylvie had no time or energy to spare for her friend's concerns. She needed all her attention for her own, far more desperate situation.

★　★　★

Sir Randal, who rarely danced, stood leaning against one of the pillars at the entrance to the ballroom, watching the animated scene. Lady Carstairs had just arrived, accompanied by her son and the two young girls. Then he frowned. Following them, clearly one of the party, was another young man he knew very well, his cousin Aubrey. He hadn't known the young man was in London, believing him to be at his Cambridge college.

He watched as the younger people settled Lady Carstairs amongst the dowagers, and then Sir David led Celia into the set just forming, and Aubrey followed with Sylvie.

Idly speculating whether his volatile cousin had been sent down, or left college without permission for a few days in town, Sir Randal surveyed the scene. He really did not know why he had agreed to come, but so far the Season was not in full swing, and until they had further information on the possibility of French agitators, or news of increased smuggling from the east coast, there was little he could do.

Suddenly his eyes narrowed. Marc Dupont had just entered the room. Sir Randal rapidly ran through what he had discovered about him since that morning. He lived on the fringes of the *ton*, but he had managed to ingratiate himself with many hostesses who cultivated personable young men. He was accepted by all but the highest sticklers, but invited mainly to the large parties where hostesses wanted spare unattached men to partner the eager debutantes. He appeared

41

to have no close intimates, though he consorted with some known radicals. He travelled out of London frequently, to undisclosed destinations. He wished, he had apparently explained, to see as much of the country as possible since he expected to return to New York in the near future. Following him that morning had been a profitless exercise, since the man had merely visited a book-seller and purchased a volume of Lord Byron's poetry.

As Dupont strolled towards the dowagers' corner, Sir Randal moved after him discreetly. Dupont paused, just as the dance came to an end and the dancers left the floor. How, he wondered, would Dupont and Sylvie Delamare react when they came face to face?

Dupont ignored her, speaking instead to Sir David, who greeted him as an old acquaintance. Sir Randal frowned. For how long, and how closely, had the two men known one another? Had Dupont, knowing of Sir David's recent service with Wellington in the Peninsula, deliberately sought his company? David Carstairs was a very junior officer. It was unlikely he knew much about the army's plans. Yet, Sir Randal told himself, for a Frenchman who might have ties with Napoleon, perhaps any slight item of information might be useful. He'd been told Dupont was a republican. Would he support a self-made emperor?

Sylvie had stared closely at Dupont when she first saw him, then turned away to speak to Aubrey. When Sir David touched her arm to draw her attention and introduced her to the Frenchman they met as strangers. Interesting, Sir Randal thought, and moved closer to join the group.

★ ★ ★

Sylvie braced herself. If the Frenchman who seemed to know David mentioned their meeting this morning she would have to confess to her clandestine expedition, and perhaps Lady Carstairs would be offended. She could explain, but her hostess might well take it amiss that she had gone alone, and in secret.

To her relief, apart from a quizzical look in his eye, he greeted her as a stranger, not even commenting on her French name. After a few moments David asked her to dance, and they moved away. Celia was partnered by Aubrey, and Marc Dupont wandered away into one of the rooms set aside for cards.

After this dance both Sylvie and Celia found themselves in demand, and their dance cards were soon filling. Aubrey Fortescue reappeared and waited patiently while Sylvie chatted with her latest partner, then stepped forward as the other man moved away.

'Sylvie — Miss Delamare,' he began, only to be ruthlessly interrupted by Sir Randal.

'Miss Delamare, I trust you will grant me one dance,' he said, taking Sylvie's card from her hand. 'Ah, good, I see you are free for the supper dance.' Smiling, he scribbled his initials in the space.

'Randal, I was about to ask Miss Delamare for that dance,' Aubrey said, flushing.

'Really? Then you must give way to an older cousin. I wasn't aware that the Cambridge term had ended yet?'

Aubrey grimaced. 'It hasn't, but there was a silly fuss. Some people can't take a joke.'

'And you've been sent down?'

'Yes,' Aubrey admitted. 'Just until the end of term. It really was the silliest affair, and just because old Johns was in a filthy temper over something quite different, he took it out on us.'

'If you are to enter the diplomatic service, Aubrey, you need to learn not to offend people in a temper. I will see you in a short while, Miss Delamare,' he added to Sylvie, and bore away his young cousin, still protesting volubly that it was nothing really.

Sylvie smiled. She had had little to do with young under-graduates, having met only a couple of brothers visiting their sister at the seminary in Bath, but she recognized the air of fragile sophistication, the attempt to appear up to snuff, and the mortification at being in the wrong. Then she began to speculate on the relationship between Aubrey and Sir Randal. When David had arrived in Berkeley Square just in time to escort his mother to this ball, he had only briefly introduced his friend, since his mother had been full of demands to be told why he was so late, and what had he been doing, and Sylvie hadn't caught the full name. So he and the enigmatic man who, in some strange way, made her feel shiveringly uncomfortable, were cousins.

She tried to dismiss them both from her thoughts and concentrate on what her present partner was saying. As the movements of the country dance drew them apart every few seconds, it was difficult, and in the end she confined her responses to nods and the occasional murmur of agreement. It seemed to satisfy him, however, and Sylvie smiled inwardly. One of the teachers at the seminary had drilled it into the girls that men did not like being argued with, much less contradicted, and all they looked for in a wife was agreeable complaisance. If that is so, a much younger Sylvie had decided, she would never find a husband, since she could never refrain from expressing her opinion if she disagreed with anything.

★ ★ ★

Sylvie's next partner was Marc Dupont. As soon as he led her on to the floor she took a deep breath.

'Thank you, sir, for not mentioning our meeting this morning,' she said hurriedly. 'I — as I told you, I was trying to find the workshop where my father once had his business. He was a goldsmith,' she explained.

'But surely, mademoiselle, your so kind hostess would be able to discover that for you?'

'There are reasons,' Sylvie began. 'Oh, it is nothing disreputable,' she said, trying a light, carefree laugh, 'but I do not wish to trouble her. I thought I could make a quick visit myself to see whether it was still there.'

'Your father, he is perhaps dead?' Dupont asked cautiously. 'If so, please accept my condolences.'

'He died a long time ago,' Sylvie said. 'He and my mother were drowned in a boating accident. I — I have to visit my trustee soon, and I wanted to see whether the business was still being run under my father's name.'

'Delamare? I think I have heard the name. He was famous, was he not, before the revolution? Did he not design necklaces for *la pauvre* Marie Antoinette? I think I once heard my own mama bemoaning the fact that she could not afford one of his exquisite pieces. That, of course, was before my family fled to New York. Afterwards, we would have heard no more about him. I understand he came to England?'

'Yes, my mother was English, and had a house here.'

'And you have had trustees looking after it for you? Forgive me, a lady does not like having her age mentioned, but your charming little friend tells me that you have recently come of age and into your inheritance? You are to be congratulated.'

I hope Celia didn't tell him how small this inheritance is, Sylvie thought. The man was too forward, too eager to learn about her family. Did he think she was a great heiress? Then she reminded herself she had always been told the French were more direct and practical than the English when discussing money and possible marriage alliances. Besides, it was ridiculous to imagine that on the strength of two brief meetings the man could have any possible interest in her. If he were eager to find a rich wife Celia would be

47

a far better proposition. Celia, a niggling inner voice insisted, had a careful aunt and cousin to look after her interests. If Marc Dupont were an adventurer she would be well protected. Sylvie was alone and would have to care for herself.

3

Sir Randal appeared at Sylvie's side and after speaking briefly to Lady Carstairs, took her hand to lead her into the set just forming. Her fingers trembled in his, and he wondered why. Was she aware of his connection with the Ministry? Had Dupont somehow become aware of it and warned her to be on her guard? Few people did in fact know of the work he did, the unofficial tasks which no one else had time for, but which kept him from the boredom he would otherwise have found in a relentless social round. It was always possible that some minion in the office relayed information in exchange for money. If Dupont and Sylvie Delamare were working together he would have warned her.

He made a few innocuous remarks, to which she responded with some reserve, and rather to his relief the dance soon ended and he led her into the supper room and found a small corner table. He went to fetch food from the lavish buffet, and on his return deterred with a single sharp glance a couple of young men who had been proposing to draw chairs up to the table.

Sylvie, to his surprise, laughed. 'You have a most daunting look,' she told him. 'They were telling me, very earnestly, what good friends they are of Sir David's. I gathered their friendship was confined to the card tables and racing stables, as Newmarket featured rather prominently in the conversation.'

'Probably. I've seen them there several times. Which does not indicate that gambling is a major passion of mine, in case you infer it is,' he replied, and she chuckled. 'They can go and be friendly with him. Tell me, you were at the same seminary as Miss Mannering, I believe? Yet I understand you are some years older than she?'

She frowned and he wondered what had upset her.

'Why is everyone suddenly so concerned about my age?' she demanded. 'I was not made to repeat my studies because I was backward!'

So that was it. He grinned at her and she looked startled. He sighed inwardly. He should have remembered his older sister's advice, never to smile at a woman, for they all fell for that crooked grin. He had no desire to make any woman attracted to him, least of all an elderly schoolgirl who might also be working for a French agitator.

'Somehow I did not imagine your wits were deficient.'

'I'm sorry, that was rude of me,' she said softly. 'I had to stay there until I was of age, so I helped to teach French.'

'Your father was a goldsmith, I understand.' He had spent part of the day investigating her background. She nodded, but did not volunteer any more information. 'So that was the reason you were in the City this morning.'

To his satisfaction he saw she was startled. She looked round swiftly as if to make sure no one had overheard.

'I wondered if it was you I saw. I didn't realize you had seen me.'

'You met Monsieur Dupont,' he said, and she flushed. He decided her reactions to his barbs were so open he might discover more by a direct attack than by more oblique methods.

'I bumped into Monsieur Dupont by accident, literally, when I stepped back to try and read the name above one of the shops,' she said curtly. 'I did not then know who he was, until we met again here this evening.'

'It was rather foolish of you to go to such a place on your own, was it not? Have you no maid? Lady Carstairs would have sent a footman with you had you but asked.'

'I did not wish to trouble Lady Carstairs on what was purely my own business,' she snapped. 'And, sir, it ill becomes you, who are a stranger to me, with no authority over me, to criticize my conduct. I don't answer to you.'

With which she laid down her fork, stood up, and with barely a glance at him, swept past and out of the room.

He sat back, considering. Was she telling the truth? Had Dupont been a stranger to her that morning? Her indignation at his questioning had seemed genuine. It would be easy to check up on her story about her father's place of business. But he still did not understand her reluctance to admit Lady Carstairs into her activities. From what he knew of the lady she would do all she could to assist any young friend. Well, he would discover nothing by remaining here, and there were some reports on smuggling activity from Lincolnshire to read. He would leave the problem of Sylvie Delamare until another time.

★   ★   ★

The three ladies were having a lazy breakfast the following morning when one of the footmen, barely hiding a grin, came into the breakfast-room bearing in front of him an enormous arrangement of flowers and greenery.

'For Miss Delamare,' he said.

'For me? What in the world have I done to deserve this?'

Lady Carstairs gestured to the footman to put the floral offering on a side table, which he did and then swiftly retreated.

'Look and see whether there is a note,' she advised calmly.

Sylvie approached the table slowly.

'It won't bite,' Celia said, stifling a giggle. 'Go on, do tell us who the generous admirer is.'

Sylvie plucked out a sheet of paper in a shade of pink more vivid than any of the flowers, and opened it. 'Oh, no! It's Aubrey Fortescue,' she said, and chuckled. 'And an exceedingly bad verse which is meant to say, I think, he is swearing undying devotion and will slay any dragons I care to point in his direction.'

'How — er — charming,' Lady Carstairs said. 'I'll send for some flower vases. Do you think half a dozen of the largest will be adequate?'

Sylvie groaned. 'I did nothing to encourage him,' she protested. 'Besides, he's just a boy, probably not even my age. He's still at Cambridge!'

'He's two and twenty,' Lady Carstairs said. 'He's a very wealthy young man. All the Fortescue family are indecently well off, but

53

most of his fortune came from his mother. His father was a younger son. Brother to Sir Randal's father. How did you find Sir Randal last night, Sylvie? It was much remarked that he singled you out to dance. He rarely does dance.'

She was about to reply that he was impertinent, inquisitive and intolerable when she remembered she could not explain why. 'He was all right,' she said lamely. 'Lady Carstairs, I am so grateful to you for having me here, but I really must make arrangements to visit Sir George soon. I feel so unsettled until I know how my situation is, about my mother's fortune, and my father's business. May I send one of the footmen to speak a place for me on one of the coaches in a day or so?'

'Of course, my dear. I do understand how you feel, though it has been such a pleasure to have you with us, and you must promise to come back if you have to return to London. I hope you will visit us again in any case, soon. But you will be here for Lady Fortescue's soirée tonight. Now, what do you both intend to wear? I think that pale blue will suit you best, Celia dear.'

Sylvie breathed a sigh of relief that she had obtained her way. She sent off one of the footmen to find her a seat on a coach to

Norwich, from where she would hope to hire some sort of conveyance to take her to her great-uncle's house. She would take the minimum of clothing, and if she had to ride, for she had little expectation that she would be able to find even a country trap, she could carry it all with her. Within a few days she would be able to confront Sir George and discover exactly what he had done with her inheritance. As she began to select the clothes she would need, she knew this was an encounter she was looking forward to.

★ ★ ★

Celia decided she needed some new gloves, so she and Sylvie set off for Bond Street. This, Sylvie decided, gave her the ideal opportunity of visiting her mother's London house and trying to discover what had happened to it, whether it had been sold for some reason. If she, through the trust, still owned it, the income from letting it each year would come to far more than the miserly sum her great-uncle said was the total of her inheritance. Lady Carstairs would not be concerned if they were out of the house for a long time, for Celia had said she wanted to visit the subscription library, and normally they could be depended upon to linger there.

Celia was perfectly willing, even eager, to choose a book quickly and then walk to North Audley Street. When they reached the Delamare house, though, they were disappointed. The shutters were up and the knocker taken down.

'Oh, no one's at home,' Celia said. 'How disappointing.'

Sylvie was not prepared to give up easily. 'There must be a caretaker,' she said. 'I remember Mama always left a married couple in charge.'

She hammered on the door, and after a while they heard slow footsteps approaching.

'What d'ye want? There's nobody home.'

Sylvie smiled at the elderly man who stood glaring at her.

'This used to be my own home,' she explained, 'and I wondered who lived in it now, whether I might know them.'

He looked at her suspiciously, then shrugged. 'Family by name o' Tempest,' he said eventually. 'Know 'em, do ye?'

'Are they the Tempests from Cambridgeshire?'

He chuckled. 'They might be now, they used ter be the Tempests from Shoreditch. Merchant, he was, traded wi' India before he made a pile and bought his way into the gentry.'

The way he said this encouraged Sylvie to think he was not overfond of his employer. 'Did he buy the house?' she asked. 'Is it perhaps leased?'

'I wouldn't know, I only took this job a few months back, and it's not my business.'

'When will they be back here?'

'Why'm you so eager to know?'

'They might be the people I used to know, from Cambridgeshire, and if so I'd like to pay my respects.'

'They'm wi' some friends, or relations, I don't know. They'll be back soon, tryin' ter nab rich husbands fer the daughters.'

'Daughters? Then they do sound like the Tempests I know. Is one of them called Margaret?'

He frowned. 'I don't think ye know 'em at all. Anne and Mary, they be.'

'Mary, of course! So they'll be back soon, you think? Thank you so much. I'll come back later and try to see them.'

'What name shall I say?' he asked, suddenly remembering his function.

Sylvie, pressing a small coin into his hand, affected not to hear as she thanked him effusively and turned away.

She and Celia walked as far as Grosvenor Square without speaking, then Celia sighed in frustration.

'That hasn't told you whether the house was sold or not,' she said.

'No, but at least I know the names and can call again, if I don't find out from Sir George what has happened. Come, we'd best go home, or your aunt will be wondering where we are. Even I cannot pretend to stay for so long choosing a book.'

★　★　★

Lady Fortescue was not the typical blue stocking Sylvie had expected. She was a stately brunette, with not a single grey hair in her elaborate coiffure. She was wearing a fashionable gown of shimmering amber silk, and a parure of excellent diamonds. She greeted Lady Carstairs as an old friend, smiled at Celia and wished her a happy time for her debut, and then turned to Sylvie.

For a moment she appeared startled, and looked puzzled. Then as Lady Carstairs presented Sylvie her look of puzzlement went.

'That explains the resemblance. I knew your mother, child, years ago. She was much younger than I, of course, but she and my youngest sister were great friends, and your mother often stayed at Brystone Court with us. I was so shocked to hear of her death.'

Sylvie warmed to her. She had expected Sir

Randal's mother to be stern and aloof, as he was, but she was totally different. He must have inherited his own cold nature from his father, she decided, and then she forgot him. They had moved on into the room where the entertainment was to take place, which was furnished with many sofas and chairs, and her attention was taken by Aubrey coming up to her, an anxious look on his face.

'Oh, good evening, Aubrey,' she said. 'I must thank you for those beautiful flowers you sent me. So kind!'

'You didn't think they were too many?' he asked, and she hadn't the heart to say yes.

'I enjoyed arranging them,' she said instead, refraining from mentioning that it had taken her much of the morning, and she had on several occasions roundly cursed him for choosing blooms which seemed determined not to stay where she wanted them to.

His face relaxed. 'Oh, I'm so pleased. Randal said I ought to send you just a posy, which you could wear tonight if you wished, but that did not seem enough to, well, to express my sincere regard for you!'

So Sir Randal had seen that superabundance of floral offering, had he? Sylvie wondered what he had thought, and then told herself she did not in the least care what the aggravating man's opinions were.

At that second she saw him approaching. He suggested to Aubrey that the ladies might enjoy a glass of champagne, and when the boy had gone greeted Lady Carstairs and Celia. Then he turned to Sylvie. 'I see you have not worn my cousin's posy,' he said, and she choked with sudden laughter. 'Was there not a flower or two or three — of a suitable colour?'

'There were too many for me to make a selection,' she replied, her voice demure. 'I feared that by choosing one I would make the others jealous. It was very sweet of your cousin to think of me.'

'Sweet. H'm. Yes. Ah, here he comes. I will no doubt speak with you later. Forgive me, ladies, I have to make sure the musicians have all they need.'

To Sylvie's surprise the entertainment was of an exceptionally high standard. She had expected it to be of the same mediocre quality as she had endured in Bath when Mrs Shaw had arranged what she called culture for her boarders. The musicians could not only play without wrong notes, they played with real feeling. The singer, a deep rich contralto, filled the room with her glorious voice, and at the end received the compliment of a moment of appreciative silence before the audience burst into a storm of applause. Even the poet, a thin young man with overlong hair, read verses which, Lady Carstairs declared, were quite as good as those of Lord George Byron, whose under-graduate effusions had created such a stir a few years ago.

Then it was time for refreshments, and Lady Carstairs eagerly led the way into the room where a buffet was laid out. It was as lavish as she had promised. Aubrey came and found seats for the ladies, then went off to fetch food for them. Waiters handed round more champagne, and Lady Carstairs heaved a sigh of contentment.

'What a pity David had a prior engagement. He would have enjoyed tonight, even though he maintains such affairs bore him. How he can possibly prefer playing cards with the same men night after night, I'll never understand. But his dear father was the same. After our first year he could rarely be persuaded to accompany me to any but the most important social occasions. But that is the way of the polite world. Husbands who sit in their wives' pockets are laughed at. Such a pity,' she added wistfully, and Sylvie remembered that her husband had died just a few years after their marriage. It seemed as though it had been a real love match, on her side at least. As a rich young widow she would have had many opportunities for a second marriage, but she had apparently remained true to her first husband's memory.

Would she ever marry, Sylvie wondered? Unless she recovered the inheritance she had expected to be hers, it would be unlikely. She had met few men, and so far none had attracted her as she imagined a man who might become her husband would appeal. How did girls know? What did they look for? Mrs Shaw had, she thought with a sudden laugh, omitted to teach her pupils some useful aspects of life. Perhaps she thought they would all be guided by parents, who would naturally know what was best for their daughters. Girls like herself, without either parents or guardians, would presumably need to rely on other instincts. She wished she knew what these were.

'What is so amusing?' Celia asked, and Sylvie came out of her reverie and grinned at her friend.

'I was wondering how one knew the right man to marry,' she said. 'Will you accept whoever Lady Carstairs tells you is the right one?'

Celia blushed. 'I suppose I will have to be guided by her,' she replied slowly, 'but I believe she will take my views into account. She has never been stern, with me or with David.'

Sylvie recalled her suspicion that Lady Carstairs intended to marry Celia to David. 'Do you like him? David, I mean. You've known him all your life.'

'Yes, and he's been like a big brother. Even though he's five years older, when I stayed with them at Lowmoor during holidays he used to allow me to trail after him when he went off rabbit shooting. And he taught me to skate on the lake there. I missed him when he went into the army.'

She sounded fond of him, but did not, Sylvie was sure, regard him as a possible future husband. Well, time would show. Celia was pretty, lively, and rich. She would have plenty of suitors and could make her own choice. In the end Sylvie doubted her aunt would force her into anything distasteful, even if she did all else in her power to bring about the marriage she wanted.

It wasn't her business, Sylvie reminded herself. Celia was strong enough to look after herself, and would not accept a match she did not want just to please her aunt.

She began to think about her own next moves. She had secured a seat on a coach leaving two days later. She might have to remain for one night in Norwich, if it was too late to reach Sir George's house near the coast that day. Perhaps it would be better to wait, and not arrive late in the day, weary and dishevelled from a long journey.

Lady Carstairs had greeted this news with some concern. 'My dear, I feel I ought to send a maid with you. It was remiss of me, but I hadn't fully appreciated you meant to travel on the public stage, all alone. It isn't right.'

'I will be perfectly safe, Lady Carstairs. If I have to become a governess in the end, I will have to get used to it. I'm going to my uncle's house, after all. What could be safer?'

'A governess? Oh, no, surely not. You must be funning, child. Both your parents were wealthy, you will find you are quite an heiress.'

Sylvie inwardly cursed her unruly tongue. Lady Carstairs did not know about her real situation. She forced herself to laugh. 'Of course. But until I actually have the money I need to be careful. One thing I always recall my papa saying was that one should never get into debt. Of course he did not mean the sort of debt I owe you for being so kind to me these past few days. I have enjoyed being with you.'

'And we still have tomorrow. Would you and Celia care to ride in the park in the morning? And it's my At Home in the afternoon, and we are to go to the theatre in the evening. We must make the most of your last day.'

Lady Carstairs had hired hacks for Celia and Sylvie, and David accompanied them on their ride. Sylvie had ridden every day at Danesfield, her mother's country home near Cambridge, until she was ten, but only occasionally had the opportunity since. Lady Carstairs lent her a riding habit, laughing and saying she had not worn it in over ten years. Tight waisted, with close-fitting sleeves, it was a dark green with paler green reveres, and there was a dashing, tall-crowned hat to go with it. Sylvie found it was delightful to be back on a horse, even one so staid and unexciting as this one. She longed for a fast gallop, but had to content herself with a mild canter, and then a sedate walk as they met and greeted many of David's acquaintances and he introduced the girls to them.

Soon they were joined by Aubrey Fortescue, who turned his own showy black to accompany them. Celia and David went ahead while Aubrey anxiously demanded of Sylvie whether she had enjoyed the entertainment the previous evening.

'My aunt has a reputation for excellence in everything she does,' he said morosely. 'That's where Randal gets his notions from. I don't see why, when one has to endure

Cambridge, one has to work there too. What does it matter whether one can write Latin poetry or not? English poetry is bad enough!'

Sylvie laughed. 'What would you prefer to be doing?'

'I mean to join the cavalry, like David, as soon as I come down. Randal wouldn't allow it before I finished Cambridge.'

'Is he your guardian? I thought you were of age?'

'I am, and he is, or he was. But I can't have my money until I'm five and twenty, so I have to do what he says or he'll stop my allowance.'

He sounded like a petulant boy, but Sylvie had sympathy with him. However, judging by his clothes and his horse his allowance was an ample one. She encouraged him to describe his home, a large estate near Lichfield in Staffordshire, but he confessed he rarely went there.

'Randal installed an agent, but until I have full control I don't want to have to argue every point with him. I spend vacations here in London or with friends. We go on walking holidays in the summer. It's a pity we can't go to France or Switzerland, but the country round the Lakes in Cumbria is pretty good, if you like mountains.'

'Will you be going there this year?'

'No, I'll join the army as soon as I can. The others are going to Scotland, but that's too bleak for me. Sylvie,' he hesitated, 'will you come for a drive with me tomorrow? I've just bought a new pair, a really good-looking pair of greys, and I want to try them out.'

'I'm sorry, but I'm going to visit an uncle tomorrow,' Sylvie said, and frowned as she thought of the reason.

'Oh. Then the day afterwards?'

'He doesn't live in London, I shall be away for several days.'

'Well, never mind, I'll see you when you get back. You'll still be staying with Lady Carstairs, I expect.'

'Yes,' Sylvie agreed. What she did after she'd seen Sir George remained obscure. But she fully expected she would have to return to London, if only to try and discover what had happened to her father's business.

⋆   ⋆   ⋆

Sir Randal saw his cousin in the distance, and frowned. Aubrey seemed to be living in that girl's pocket. He was riding as close to her as he could, bending attentively as if to catch her every word. He was far too young to be caught in some female's toils. He had to sow his wild oats like any young man, but he

67

should know better than to tangle with a girl of good family unless his intentions were serious. He was too young to marry, and in any case could not afford marriage unless he, Randal, increased his allowance, and he had no intention of doing that. When his cousin reached the age of five and twenty, Randal hoped he would have learned more sense, and be fit to take on the responsibilities of marriage. He would have no control over the boy then, and judging by Aubrey's current behaviour, little influence either.

Sylvie was of good family, at least on her mother's side, and her father had been of the minor French nobility, even though he had defied convention by setting up as a goldsmith. After the guests had departed on the previous evening he had persuaded his mother to tell him all she knew.

'Jane Betteridge was a very pretty girl, had several offers in her first Season,' Lady Fortescue told him. 'She was a great friend of your Aunt Eliza, often stayed with us. She had a substantial fortune and could have married an earl, but as soon as this French goldsmith appeared she had eyes for no one else.'

'Her parents agreed a match with a mere craftsman?' Randal asked, raising his eyebrows.

Lady Fortescue shook her head. 'He had a good pedigree,' she said. 'He was the son of a count, and his father owned land somewhere in the south. He was the second son, and would have inherited a château and considerable land, but apparently he cared for nothing but designing jewellery, so he took his patrimony and set up a workshop in Paris. He became quite famous at Louis's court, I believe. In some ways it was fortunate, as he could bring out his wealth, which he did when the Bastille fell. He set up here in London, and was doing very well, I believe, when he and Jane died.'

'So Sylvie Delamare is a wealthy young woman? She has both her mother's fortune and his?'

'I heard her country house was sold some years ago, and I have no idea what happened to her father's business. I imagine that was sold too, and it was all invested in the funds by her trustees.'

Randal rode on thoughtfully. If Sylvie were independently wealthy, in control of her fortune, and Aubrey were really smitten, he might commit the imprudence of marrying and living on her money. Somehow, he had to prevent this. The boy was far too young to know his own mind. He needed to become acquainted with the girl.

4

Aubrey was the first to arrive at Lady Carstairs' At Home, and after chatting for a few moments to her and Celia, he took the opportunity, when more guests were announced, to move to a stool drawn up beside Sylvie's chair.

Sylvie listened to him tolerantly. She'd had little to do with young men, apart from the few brothers of girls at the seminary, but she recognized the shy yet eager boastfulness of a young male wanting to impress a female, but with little understanding of what really interested them.

Aubrey was relating the story of a visit he and some under-graduate friends had paid to a fight some miles outside Cambridge, and his own skill at forecasting the winner of the main bout, when all his friends had scoffed at him and backed the loser. 'I pride myself on knowing something about the art,' he said, and then gulped nervously. 'Oh, confound him!' he added, under his breath.

Sylvie, who had been listening with only half her attention, looked up at this and saw Lady Fortescue and Sir Randal entering the room. She frowned slightly. Why did the appearance of his cousin discompose him so much? She was aware that Sir Randal was displeased with Aubrey for his being sent down from Cambridge, but surely, after the first display of irritation, his disapproval could not cause the younger man the sort of dismay he was now exhibiting? They had seemed on good enough terms the previous evening.

After greeting their hostess, Sir Randal made sure his mother was comfortably ensconced in a chair beside Lady Carstairs, and then strolled across the room towards Sylvie.

Aubrey reluctantly rose to his feet. 'I didn't know you were used to doing the pretty,' he said rather truculently.

Sir Randal greeted Sylvie, and then turned to his cousin. 'You don't know me at all well, do you, Aubrey? But I can assure you, I always mean what I say. Now, go and talk to my mother while I make Miss Delamare's better acquaintance.'

Frowning, Aubrey hesitated, then walked away to stand behind his aunt's chair, glaring at Sir Randal who sank down beside Sylvie.

'How long do you stay in town?' he asked.

'I leave tomorrow,' Sylvie told him, and was surprised to see a gleam of relief in his eyes.

'To visit friends? Or do you go home?'

Sylvie told herself he was merely making polite conversation, such as hundreds of people who knew one another only slightly would do. Yet his voice held a note of urgency she could not understand. This was no idle query, she was sure. The answer mattered for some inexplicable reason.

'I visit my great-uncle,' she said.

'Do you have far to go?'

He was being too inquisitive. 'No,' she replied briefly. Let him wonder. He would not have the impertinence to enquire further, she was sure.

With a fleeting smile that made her even more uncomfortable than his questions, he changed the subject to what she had thought of the entertainment the previous evening. In enthusing about the performers she lost her reserve and became animated, so was quite unprepared for him when he rose to his feet, held out his arm and told her she must come and talk to his mother.

Sylvie found herself unable to snub Lady Fortescue. For one thing, the lady spoke so kindly of her mother Sylvie found her eyes filling with tears. When she was asked if she intended to visit her old home she shook her head.

'I have to see my great-uncle first,' she said. 'He is my trustee, and I do not know until I have seen him how my affairs stand.'

'Your mother's uncle? Sir George Clayton? I have not seen him for many years. I'm told he is a recluse now, and never leaves his house. Near Norwich, I believe?'

'Twenty miles away, I understand, a village near the coast, though I have never been there before. Not that I recall. I may have been taken to visit when I was a child, but I have no recollection of it.'

It was too easy to talk to Lady Fortescue, Sylvie realized. She had revealed more than she had intended saying to anyone. Then mentally she shrugged. Why was she making a mystery of it all? Soon the whole world would know her circumstances, if they cared about it. She wanted to find out for herself first, though, so that she could absorb the shocks there were bound to be before having to face the world, with her forty pounds, all that appeared to be left of the fortunes her parents had owned, and which they would presumably have left to her.

★   ★   ★

At the theatre that evening Sylvie began to think she was haunted by Sir Randal Fortescue. He was with a party in a box opposite their own, and immediately bowed,

73

acknowledging Lady Carstairs' party which consisted of the three ladies, David, Aubrey and an old acquaintance of Lady Carstairs. This was a retired general who had, throughout dinner, reminisced about his activities in the American Wars of Independence forty years before, with detailed comments about what the politicians at home and the generals in America should have done to bring about a different result.

Aubrey, having seen his cousin, muttered under his breath and retreated to the back of the box. When, during the first interval, he saw Sir Randal rise to his feet and leave his own box, he swiftly made some excuse and went away. Was he afraid of meeting his cousin, Sylvie wondered? She was puzzled by their attitude towards one another. Then she forgot her speculations as the Frenchman, Monsieur Dupont, entered the box.

He bowed to the ladies, raised Lady Carstairs' hand to his lips, and took a seat beside her. Soon he was chatting about a forthcoming ball, and turning to Celia and Sylvie, said he hoped to see them both there.

'Sylvie may not be back,' Celia said, and then had to explain she was going out of town to visit a relative who lived near Norwich.

Dupont expressed his regrets, and said he

74

hoped to meet Sylvie again when she returned. She smiled, but did not reply. Soon afterwards he took his leave, and it was time for the second act.

Aubrey slid into the box as the curtain rose, and whispered to Sylvie, 'Did Randal come round?'

'No. Shush.'

She heard him breathe a deep sigh, but he sat back and appeared to be paying attention to the stage. However, when the curtains closed again he muttered another excuse and once more left the box, not waiting for the refreshments Lady Carstairs had ordered.

Sir Randal was not in his own box, nor did he pay them a visit. Sylvie told herself she was not disappointed. She was uncomfortable in the man's presence, that was all. It was just that not knowing where he was, and what he was doing, made her nervous for some odd reason.

Aubrey slid back in and sat behind her, in the shadows of the box. 'Randal isn't in his box,' he muttered. 'What's he doing? Where can he have gone? If he's with a party it's unlike him to leave however bored he might be. He has such good manners.'

Sylvie soon forgot Aubrey's peculiar behaviour when she was back in Berkeley Square. She finished her packing and went to bed, for she had to be up early in the morning to catch the coach to Norwich.

* * *

Sir Randal left the theatre before the play ended and made his way to the Ministry. A message had been brought to him during the second interval, requesting an urgent consultation.

Peter Sinclair was waiting for him. 'Sit down, Randal. We've just heard there's a French boat cruising off the Norfolk coast, near Cromer. It made rendezvous with one of the fishing boats we suspect of smuggling.'

'Was the fishing boat taken?'

'No, the fools let it get away. They claim a sea mist came down so that they lost sight of it. But that is not why I sent for you. Our friend Dupont set out an hour ago, riding a fast horse. We think that's where he's off to.'

'How do you know?'

'I've put a couple of fellows to watch him.'

Randal raised his eyebrows. 'What has changed? I thought you could not spare any men to watch him.'

'We had a description from one of our men in Manchester of a man who had been seen talking with some of the leaders of the disturbances there. It fits Dupont amazingly closely. I can now make out a case for keeping watch on him. But the men we have in Norwich don't know him. We can't send someone to follow openly. I need you to go and point him out to them.'

'He was at the theatre tonight. I saw him during the first interval. He must have left immediately afterwards.'

'After proving he was there. Just time for one of the men watching him to get here and for me to send a message to you. Can you get there?'

'Why can't one of your tails go?'

'They are small beer. I'd prefer you to go in case we have to take action to restrain him. If he tries to leave on that French boat we'll have to arrest him. If he's guilty we don't want him getting away. I didn't want to show our hand quite so soon, but at least if he is acting suspiciously we have a reason for questioning him.'

'He won't ride all night.'

There was a discreet knock at the door and a small man who looked like a groom slid into the room.

Mr Sinclair nodded to him. 'Well?'

'He hired the horse as far as Epping. Said he'd sleep there and set off again first thing.'

'Good. Thanks, Will. Go home now, we'll follow him.'

The man slid out as quietly as he'd arrived.

'Dupont's shadow?' Sir Randal asked.

'One of them. At least we know he's going in that direction. If you follow you can alert the fellows we have stationed at Norwich and they can take over. I don't want anyone to know you're involved unless it's unavoidable.'

'I'll take the curricle, and start early. If he's riding I should be able to catch him up. Fortunately I keep my own cattle on the Newmarket road, so I can be sure of good ones to begin with.'

'If he doesn't try to leave, let the locals deal with it, just observing what he's up to, and report back to you. I need you back here soon. There have been some other disturbing reports from Lincolnshire, but they can wait until you get back. I'm expecting more information in the next day or so.'

Sir Randal nodded and went away to his rooms. He sent a message to the stables to have his best pair and his curricle at the door by six in the morning, and packed saddlebags with a change of linen and some clean shirts. As he made ready for bed he suddenly recalled that the Delamare chit would be travelling the same road soon. His mother had not discovered how she was travelling, nor when, and he wondered whether he would encounter her on the way. It no longer seemed to matter. She was not a penniless fortune-hunter as he had feared. According to Lady Fortescue her mother had been a considerable heiress and her father a wealthy jeweller. Such a girl would hardly consider Aubrey, young for his age, as a husband. She would be looking for someone older and with more knowledge of the world.

★   ★   ★

Sylvie had a corner seat, much to her relief. She had been driven to the coaching inn by Lady Carstairs' coachman, at what seemed the middle of the night, and once they were on their way she collapsed thankfully against the seat and closed her eyes. Soon the rocking of the coach sent her to sleep, and it was the first change before she woke. It was still dark outside, and she felt no desire to rush into the coffee room to try and swallow some scalding liquid in the few minutes allowed them. When they set off again she sank back into slumber.

Two hours later she ate some breakfast. By then it was light, she could sleep no more, and began to take notice of the countryside. It was flat, with only gently rolling hills, quite unlike the ones she had been used to near Bath. It was like the countryside of her childhood, and she felt a deep nostalgia for those lost, happy days. Would she ever recover her old home? She cared less for the town house. That held fewer happy memories, and she could not imagine herself living there on her own, whereas she would be perfectly content to live always at Danesfield.

It would take most of the day to reach Norwich, and Sylvie knew she would be so shaken and sore from the rattling about in the coach there would be no point in setting off for Sir George's house that day. Besides, it would be dusk again. She would have to find a room for the night.

To her relief, when the coach drew up at the Norwich inn, there was a room available. Her story, to account for her travelling alone, was that she was a governess on the way to a new post, and the landlord seemed to accept it. In the future, she thought wryly, it could even be true.

She was too tired to eat and went straight to the tiny room under the eaves. Within minutes she was in bed and asleep, her last thought that she must find a means of reaching her uncle's house first thing in the morning.

She woke early, just as the first rays of dawn crept past her uncurtained small window. She lay there, knowing she ought to make the effort and get up, but unwilling to face what the day might bring. She had looked forward to this day ever since she had received Sir George's letter in Bath. She had relished the thought of the confrontation to come, but now it was almost upon her, she knew she dreaded what she might hear. How had her inheritance withered away to almost nothing? Had Sir George or his fellow trustees cheated her of her fortune? If so, how could she ever prove it?

Somehow, she would, she told herself firmly, and the thought was sufficient to drive her out of bed. She rang for hot water, suddenly hungry and eager to set off. Half an hour later she went down to the coffee room to find something to eat, and walked in, hesitating briefly as she saw a man already there. He was seated at the only table, a many-caped driving cloak cast negligently across a chair beside the fireplace, where a struggling fire failed to warm the room. Sylvie shivered and clutched her shawl closer to her.

The man turned round, rose to his feet, and Sylvie took a step back. 'What are you doing here?' she demanded.

Sir Randal Fortescue smiled. 'Good morning, Miss Delamare. May I pour you some coffee? Do come and join me. This is quite a tolerable breakfast.'

She needed food to warm her, so sat down

in the chair he held out. They were silent while she sipped the welcome coffee and he helped her to some slices of ham.

'I understand you are on your way to visit Sir George?' he said, as she began to eat. 'Is he sending some conveyance for you?'

Sylvie hastily swallowed some ham. 'I — no! How do you know what my movements are? And what business is it of yours, sir?'

'I make it my business when I discover the daughter of a woman my mother held in some esteem is traipsing about the countryside quite alone,' he replied smoothly. 'It is neither seemly nor safe.'

'I am not traipsing! As to what is seemly, I will be the judge of my own conduct! And it is perfectly safe. Hundreds of girls on their own travel the country when they have no other option.'

'Country girls, servants, not young ladies who have been brought up to behave with decorum. And if it became known that you are an heiress, there is always the temptation for rogues to kidnap you in the hope of ransom.'

Sylvie almost laughed. 'Whether I am an heiress or not is doubtful,' she said, unable to keep the bitterness out of her voice. 'If you or any prospective kidnappers believe it, they are better informed than I am myself.'

He raised his eyebrows and she bit her lip. Why had she admitted even so much?

'Certain knowledge may not be necessary before they take action,' he murmured.

Sylvie decided to ignore this. 'I mean to hire a horse and trap. My great-uncle is not expecting me, or he would have sent someone to fetch me,' she said firmly, fully aware this was probably untrue. The only hope she had of confronting Sir George was to catch him unawares so that he could not avoid her, which she had convinced herself he would do if he had the chance.

★   ★   ★

Randal left Sylvie at the inn while he went to meet the two men who would take over watching Dupont. When he had described the Frenchman to them yesterday they assured him they could soon discover the inn he was staying at.

'Not many Frenchies hereabouts,' one of them said.

Now he met them by arrangement at a small hostelry near the cathedral and they told him they had found Dupont. He had ridden on northwards only ten minutes or so past.

'The Cromer road?'

'Aye, sir, though he made out he was only going as far as Aylsham.'

'Where is that?'

'Halfway. Shall we follow him?'

'Yes, but not too closely, and perhaps travel separately. If he sees two following he might panic. Don't stop him unless he's getting into a boat. If that happens bring him back to me here in Norwich.'

Feeling restless that there was nothing he could do, and he'd have to kick his heels all day, Randal went back to the inn. Sylvie Delamare would set off for her great-uncle's house soon. That was near Cromer. The fact both she and Dupont were on the same road suddenly seemed highly significant. His earlier suspicions about her had been lulled when it seemed she could not have known Dupont before she came to London, but now they surged back. He wanted to follow her, but feared he might hamper the other men if he did. He hadn't told them about her, and now it was too late. Then he turned into the taproom to see Sylvie talking to the innkeeper. Perhaps it was not too late after all.

★ ★ ★

Sylvie stood with her small valise at her feet, angrily facing the innkeeper.

84

'That's outrageous!' she said. 'It's far more than that scrawny horse and miserable trap, which is falling to pieces, are worth.'

'Ah, yes, miss, but consider the inconvenience if I has to wait till next market day to buy another horse. And traps like this one are not easy come by.'

'I'll bring the wretched trap back. It's not worth stealing.'

'That's what you say, miss, but I don't know you from Adam — or Eve, perhaps I should say,' he added, chortling so that his fat, jowly face grew red.

'I'm visiting my great-uncle, Sir George Clayton, at Clayton Court. Isn't that a good enough reference?'

'Sir George who? Never heard of anyone o' that name.'

Sylvie stamped her foot, ready to scream with frustration and fury. If she had the money he was demanding as a deposit against hiring her the horse and trap, she'd have paid it, but it was more than she possessed. He had already refused to hire a horse, saying he had none in the stables that would tolerate a female on their backs.

She seized her valise. There was nothing for it, she would have to walk, and hope she might beg a lift from some carter going in that direction. She favoured the innkeeper with a pithy catalogue of his failings, his greedy snatching of pennies, his lack of human charity, and for good measure the inadequacies of his kitchen, for the bread had been stale, the coffee stewed, and the ham too salty. Then, with a toss of her head, she swung round and almost collided with Sir Randal Fortescue, who was standing in the doorway smiling appreciatively.

'You!'

'Yes, I. Do I understand you are in need of a suitable conveyance to take you to Clayton Court?'

'This — this skinflint is trying to charge me more than the value of the trap, and has the audacity to suggest I may want to steal the wretched thing!'

'Then you will permit me to drive you there.'

Sylvie's first instinct was to refuse. She did not want to accept favours from him. But it was an answer to her problem. 'What business is it of yours, sir?' she asked.

'I am making it my business, on my mother's behalf. Don't flatter yourself I followed you here. I had business in Norwich, but as that is dealt with and I have to kick my heels here for a day or so, I am free to help you.'

'I can walk,' Sylvie said, making a belated

bid for independence. 'I need no help!'

'That is debatable. Whatever you think, it is what I mean to do, whether you want my help or not. Now, landlord, pray send to the stables to have the horses you promised me put to,' he added.

Sylvie, despite herself, giggled at the sudden change in the innkeeper's manner. She didn't want to be beholden, but knew she was defeated. The wretched man was quite capable of hurling her into a carriage and carrying her off, and she was tolerably certain no one would make any attempt to stop him. Besides, a sneaking thought had crept into her mind that Sir George might be less willing to turn away such an obvious man of fashion as he might to disown her. She had not found any solution to the problem if he refused her admission to Clayton Court.

★ ★ ★

If she and Dupont planned to meet, Sir Randal thought, his presence would prevent it. Her anger had been genuine. She had desperately needed that horse and trap, but was she really heading for Clayton Court? His driving her gave him the perfect cover for being in the area should there be a need. Did she plan to meet Dupont there? For his mother's sake, and her affection for Miss Delamare's mother, he intended to put a stop to any connection she had with Dupont. Seeing them two nights ago at the theatre, when Dupont had visited Lady Carstairs' box, had increased his suspicions. Had Dupont been passing on some message, as he had waited until he'd had the chance to speak to her before leaving the theatre and setting off on his own journey? Why had she followed him so promptly? He had seen her arrive at the inn the previous evening, and been puzzled. What could she do? Did Sir George Clayton, who lived so conveniently near to the Norfolk coast, have some connection with the smugglers? It would not be unknown for members of the gentry to be involved, if only to provide safe places for storing any contraband. If Sylvie Delamare were in any way helping Dupont she had to be stopped, not only for her own sake, but because of her connection with Lady Carstairs. Any disgrace would reflect on her friends.

He had pressed his mother for information on the reclusive Sir George, but she had been unable to tell him much.

'Once he came to town regularly, when I was a girl. I don't know what happened, but suddenly he was no longer here. He'd never been particularly popular, he was tight-fisted, so people did not make a great fuss, asking what had become of him, as they would have done with someone they liked.'

'Did he travel much? Go to France?'

'He did the grand tour when he was a young man, and I have a slight recollection that he bored everyone with tedious descriptions of Versailles, talking as though none of us had ever been there.'

If he had been a fervent Royalist, Randal decided, it was not likely he would be plotting with Napoleon's men. But he could be in league with smugglers. The hint that he was a miser tended to favour that view. Most smugglers operated from the south coast, but there were others who found the revenue men less attentive elsewhere. He would suggest a close watch be kept on Clayton Court.

The curricle was waiting by the door of the inn when he led Sylvie out.

'A pleasant morning for a drive, is it not?' he asked blandly.

She did not reply, but she permitted him to assist her into the curricle.

He swung up beside her and gave the horses the office. His tiger climbed on behind, and they moved smoothly off.

'A passable pair of nags,' he said cordially. 'The best the inn could provide. They should take us to Clayton Court without any problems. Tell me, when did you last see your great-uncle? Did he visit you in Bath?'

'He is too old to travel far,' she replied after a slight pause.

'Your guardian, I take it?'

'No! He is one of my trustees.'

'Oh, I see. So now you are of age you come to take charge of your inheritance?'

'I fail to see what business it is of yours, sir!'

'None whatsoever,' he replied, intrigued by her edginess. There was some mystery here, unconnected to the man he was trailing. Perhaps, when they saw Sir George, it would be explained.

★   ★   ★

It was a beautiful spring morning, and Sylvie felt herself relaxing as the miles went by. Sir Randal kept up an innocuous stream of chatter, comments about the countryside, and the new agricultural methods which were being introduced, largely thanks to some of the Norfolk farming gentry. When he asked questions about how she had enjoyed her few days in London she was able to reply easily. She eyed him surreptitiously. If he were not of such a managing disposition, she decided, she could have liked him. He was tall, with broad shoulders and narrow hips, and his clothes were clearly made by a master, they fitted him so perfectly.

The bones of his face were strong, but not overpoweringly so. Unlike his cousin Aubrey, who had a softer, almost feminine face, his was decidedly masculine. His eyes were of a pale but piercing blue, and now, as he drove, they were narrowed against the glare of the sun. His mouth was sensitive, the lips well-shaped and not too full. She disliked full lips on a man, and had done ever since one of her father's friends had insisted on kissing her cheeks when she was barely five years old. She shivered at the recollection, and Sir Randal immediately asked if she were cold.

'There is another rug under the seat.'

'Thank you, I'm not cold,' Sylvie said.

He gave her an amused glance, but said no more. She felt gauche, and to distract herself from those feelings began to wonder how she might evade him once they reached Clayton Court. Somehow she suspected he would not be content just to deliver her to the door and drive away. Simple civility would insist on his being asked in for some refreshment. Even her great-uncle, recluse though he was, would not be able to dodge such basic hospitality. Then she sighed. It was doubtful if her great-uncle had even normal instincts of civility to guests. If he tried to refuse her admittance she might need to depend on Sir Randal to insist. That could be one advantage of having accepted his help.

As they drew nearer to Clayton Court, though, her feelings changed. Much as she wanted to confront her great-uncle, she felt very alone. If only she dared confide in Sir Randal, and he would remain to support her, she would feel much more confident of discovering the truth. If Sir George simply denied everything, and presented her with explanations she simply could not check, about how her inheritance had dwindled to almost nothing, what could she do?

She twisted impulsively in the seat, wanting to say something, but at that moment Sir Randal lifted his whip and pointed.

'Those must be the chimneys of Clayton Court. It was built in the time of Elizabeth, was it not? Those twisted chimneys are so distinctive.'

'I — I think so,' she said slowly. She could not recall coming here before, and if she had visited she'd have been too young to be interested in architectural details. She sighed. The impulse to confide in him had gone. She realized she would have to depend on herself.

They drove alongside a low wall, falling down in places, and overgrown with moss and ivy. Her great-uncle did not, it seemed, believe in spending money to keep his estate in good order. Had he lost whatever fortune he had, she wondered suddenly? Had the same calamity which had destroyed her inheritance also affected his? If so, her hopes of regaining something more than the forty pounds he said was hers seemed to be vanishing rapidly.

They came to a gateway, flanked by two small houses. Only one seemed occupied, with smoke coming from the chimney. Panes of glass in the single window of the other were broken. The gates were open, and so overgrown with rank grass and scrambling weeds they could not have been shut for years.

No one appeared to welcome them, and clearly there was no need for a gatekeeper. Someone had tried to make a garden in the patch of ground surrounding the occupied house, but only a few straggling winter cabbages had survived amongst the rampant weeds.

Sylvie stole a glance at Sir Randal's face, wondering what he was thinking about her relative, but his expression was neutral. He slowed the curricle and turned into the driveway. This was overgrown with weeds, and badly rutted, but fortunately not long.

Within two minutes they came through the belt of trees and drew up on a half-moon patch of gravel in front of a small, but exquisite house. It had been built over two centuries ago, in the typical Elizabethan style, and did not look as though it had been touched since.

Sir Randal drew to a halt and sat looking at the house. Sylvie waited for someone to arrive, grooms to take care of the horses, perhaps a footman to open the front door to the visitors, but all was silent.

The tiger had run to the horses' heads. He looked round and shrugged.

'The stables'll be round the back, guv,' he said.

'Yes.' Sir Randal leapt down and held out a hand to help Sylvie descend. 'Take the nags there. Come, we'll hope someone is at home,' he said, but Sylvie thought he sounded doubtful.

He kept hold of her hand and trod up the two steps to the front door. She took a deep breath and went with him. What awaited her on the far side?

5

Ten minutes later Sylvie acknowledged that, had she arrived on her own, she would still have been standing on the front steps. The untidy old man who had eventually responded to Sir Randal's continued knocking on the door had insisted Sir George saw no one. He was ill, they were told, resting, forbidden by his doctor to see anyone. Only Sir Randal's persistence had eventually overborne the servant, and he had grudgingly admitted them.

The room to which he showed them was clearly unused. It was cold, the atmosphere frowsty, and Sylvie jumped as what she was certain was a rat scuttled across the room and through an open door. She drew closer to Sir Randal, who was looking uncommonly grim.

'Do you wish to see your uncle alone?' he asked. 'I will come with you if you would find my presence helpful.'

Sylvie, her antagonism towards him quite vanished as she saw the careless manner in which her great-uncle lived, looked at him gratefully.

'Yes please. I suspect he won't answer my questions,' she admitted. 'Besides, you will know better what to ask, and whether he is telling the truth.'

Sir Randal looked at her quizzically. 'Tell me now what you already know. I'm aware your mother had a large estate, and your father was a successful jeweller, and they died ten or so years since.'

Swiftly Sylvie explained about the forty pounds. 'I do not believe that can be all that is left,' she concluded.

'It seems highly unlikely. Your uncle has always been a recluse?'

'As far as I know. He never married, and I don't think he ever visited us at Danesfield.'

'Why did your parents make him a trustee?'

'He was our only relative.'

'Is he the only trustee?'

'No. The other is my father's solicitor, Mr Haines, but I never met him or had any communications from him. Sir George paid my school fees and sent me my allowance, but that stopped when I was eighteen. I earned my living teaching French at Mrs Shaw's seminary in Bath. That's where I met Celia.'

There was time for no more, as the servant returned and grudgingly said Sir George would spare her a few minutes, but she wasn't to tire him, as he was unwell, and

96

she would not wish to cause him a relapse.

Sir Randal took Sylvie's arm and they moved towards the door.

'Not you, sir,' the servant said, standing in their way. 'Sir George said only the young miss.'

Sir Randal smiled, and Sylvie shivered. She would not like to be the recipient of that smile. He let go of her arm and gently but firmly pushed the servant out of their path.

'Miss Delamare wishes me to accompany her,' he said, his tone mild but underlain with steel. 'Now pray lead the way, or do you prefer I should look for Sir George myself?'

★   ★   ★

The room he took them to was large, clean, sunny and well-furnished. From what she saw through open doorways and in the passages they followed Sylvie concluded it was probably the only comfortable room in the house. It appeared Sir George spent all his time in it. There was a curtained bed in one corner, a large armchair drawn in front of a roaring fire, and tables on either side on which, all within reach, were books, decanters of wine and several wine glasses, a tray with a large tankard and a plate containing scraps of meat, and an array of medicine bottles.

Around the walls were chests and bookcases, the former covered with heaps of paper, the latter bulging with books stuffed in higgledy-piggledy.

The man in the chair glared at them and waved a hand dismissively. 'I said only the girl, sir! I don't know who the devil you are, and I don't care, but you intrude!'

Sir Randal smiled. 'I know, and my identity is unimportant, but if you imagine I am going to permit Miss Delamare to go anywhere in this unwelcoming house on her own you mistake, Sir George.'

'Well, you needn't think I'm going to discuss her affairs in front of a pesky interfering stranger. If that's what she's had the impertinence to come for. Besides, there's nothing to discuss. The damned trust's been wound up. I have no more to do with her affairs, thank the Lord!'

'That is where you mistake. There is the matter of why a substantial inheritance has dwindled to forty pounds!' Sylvie said, all her earlier fury returning at this evidence of his intransigence. 'Also, by what right do you presume to withhold even half of that amount from me? Especially if you say you have no more interest in it.'

Sir George glared at her. 'I'm not answerable to you, miss! I looked after what your parents left, and that's all there is to it.'

Sir Randal shook his head. 'No, I think not. The courts can be asked to look into how you, as a trustee, have carried out your duties. I will ask them to do that the minute I return to London.'

'What's it to you? Were you hoping to marry a wealthy woman?'

Sylvie gritted her teeth. This was even worse than she had imagined it could ever be, and Sir Randal was being abused for his efforts to help her. She felt ashamed for her great-uncle. But Sir George's rudeness made her more determined than ever that she would remain here until she had answers to her questions.

'What happened to Danesfield?' she asked. 'If you sold it, by what right was it yours to dispose of? Or the London house?'

'I didn't sell them, and whoever has told you that tarradiddle needs his head examined.'

'Then they must still belong to me. So why have you not told me so?'

'They don't belong to you, miss, but I didn't sell the damned houses. Women can't understand finance.'

'Then what happened?' Sir Randal asked. 'If you refuse to tell us the courts can find out,' he reminded the obstinate old man.

Sir George's bombast suddenly left him, and he shrank back into his chair, gasping and reaching for one of his medicine bottles. He uncorked the top with shaking hands and drank straight from the bottle.

'You'll be the death of me,' he muttered.

Sylvie wondered whether he was really suffering. He did look pale, and he was trembling, but she hardened her heart. Somehow he had cheated her, and she was convinced he could play the invalid if it suited him. Sir Randal, when she glanced at him, had a sardonic look on his face. It didn't seem as though Sir George's show of feebleness had any effect on him.

'Before you expire,' Sir Randal said, his voice bored, 'do tell us who sold the houses, with what authority, and for what reason.'

Sir George took another gulp of the medicine. 'They had to be sold to pay your school fees,' he muttered. 'I wasn't responsible. I left all that to Mr Haines. I'm a sick man, I can't deal with such matters. All I did was send money for the school fees with what Haines provided.'

'Haines was the other trustee?' Sir Randal asked. 'Now we are getting somewhere. Sylvie, even though we haven't been asked to sit down, I suspect we are here for some time.'

He pulled forward a chair for her and another for himself.

Sylvie was looking incredulous. 'Either Danesfield or North Audley Street would have paid my school fees a thousand times! And what about my father's business? And my mother's jewels. Where are they?'

Sir George glared at her. 'You're a pesky nuisance with all your questions. Haines should have told you. When that Frenchman died his pathetic little workshop reverted to his partner.'

'What partner? He didn't have one.'

'You don't know everything, miss! How do you think he ran his business while he and your mother played at being landowners? Haines told me the agreement was that if one died the other would inherit the rest of the business.'

Sylvie shook her head. 'I don't believe it! My father would never have agreed to that! He was only too anxious to provide for Mama and me.'

'Your mother had her own fortune, there was no need. But believe it or not. Now you know, so get out of my house.'

'And her jewels, where are they?'

'How the devil should I know? Sold along with the houses, I dare say. If they were worth anything. But being a jeweller no doubt your sainted father could have made glass look like real gems, to impress people.'

Sylvie was furious, and tears of rage came into her eyes. Irritated, she brushed them away. 'How dare you slander an honest man so? My father was honest, which is more than I believe you are! He'd never have cheated anyone with fake jewels, much less my mother, he loved her! Oh, you are despicable, and I'm ashamed to have to call you a relative of mine!'

'I never wanted you to be a relative either. I've asked you to go before. Get out before I have the pair of you thrown out.'

'I think that's beyond your powers, sir,' Sir Randal said. 'I saw no evidence of an army of burly retainers. But we will gladly leave when you have given us a draft for the other twenty pounds you admit belongs to your great-niece.' He rose languidly to his feet and fetched an elegant writing slope from the top of one of the chests. Putting it down on Sir George's lap, he handed the old man a pen. 'Pen, ink and paper to hand, Sir George. An order to your bank to pay Miss Delamare twenty pounds. Or I fetch the nearest magistrate and charge you with theft? You have admitted she is entitled to that.'

Fuming impotently, Sir George glared at him, but in the end shrugged and complied.

Sir Randal read the paper carefully, nodded, and held out his hand to Sylvie. 'Not a totally wasted visit. Now let us see what more progress we can make.'

★   ★   ★

Sylvie was white-faced and shaking as Randal helped her into the curricle. He pulled a flask out of a pocket in his driving coat and held it to her lips.

'Here, a sip of brandy will help,' he said.

They had spent more than a hour arguing. Sir George had offered them no refreshments, and Randal could see that Sylvie was feeling weak from hunger and helpless fury.

She revived a little with the brandy. 'Thank you. Can I really ask the courts to check? I didn't believe him! How could an estate like Danesfield be sold for almost nothing? And my father would not have left his own fortune away from me and my mother! I'm going to Danesfield to find out the truth!'

'First you are going to find an inn and have some food.'

She nodded, and he drove away, his thoughts busy. There was something very wrong here, but he was undecided whether it could be anything to do with Marc Dupont. Sylvie's reason for this journey was clearly genuine. Sir George was undoubtedly a villain where her inheritance was concerned, and there was something they could do about that. With reasonable luck they might be able to recover it, or at least force Sir George to pay recompense if he had used it incorrectly. The man certainly had not spent it on riotous living or even on normal care of his possessions. The house was neglected, the estate, what he had seen of it, run down and in poor condition. Randal decided he was simply a miser, and had stashed away his wealth to gloat over it.

He had serious doubts whether Sir George was involved with the French. The man was old, seemed unlikely to move far from his home, and was far too self-absorbed to care for political ideologies. On the other hand, if he had been offered money, by either the French or local smugglers, for his compliance, Clayton Court was ideally situated for nefarious and clandestine doings. It would pay them to keep an eye on what went on there.

How did Sylvie's connection with Marc Dupont fit in? She had met him that morning in the City. Later they had pretended to be strangers. He had spoken to her at the theatre only a short time before he set out for Norwich. The following morning she had travelled the same road. She had a valid reason for doing so. Could it all be coincidence? When she was less shocked he would question her. First, though, he needed to feed Sylvie, and he drove to the village where he found an inn which looked promising.

It was on a slight eminence and faced the sea. Later he could perhaps spy out the land and take a look at the coast. It would do Sylvie good to have a short walk in the spring sunshine along the shore.

He drove into the yard and handed Sylvie down. She smiled at him and squared her shoulders.

'Thank you. I feel better now. I'm able to think again. Thank you for your support. I doubt he'd have told me even that small detail if I'd been on my own. He seemed to be the sort of man who would scorn to tell a woman anything!'

★　★　★

'Will you take me back to Norwich?' Sylvie asked an hour later. The inn where he had stopped had provided them with simple but adequate fare and she had regained her colour. 'I am feeling much better. I will hire a horse and go to Danesfield and discover what has been happening.'

'I have to return to Norwich,' he replied. 'Of course I will take you there. But it will be dusk when we arrive. You cannot set off today. Meanwhile, I suggest a gentle stroll. The sea breezes will blow away the unpleasant taste of your deplorable relative.'

Sylvie agreed. 'A good notion. I need to take some deep breaths, and striding out along the beach against this wind will help clear my head. Perhaps I won't feel quite so anxious to do something really horrible to Sir George.'

'I used to enjoy running along the beach with bare feet when I was a child, feeling the sand against my toes,' Randal said.

'Yes, I loved that too. It's been years since I've been so close to the sea, but I don't think I dare remove my shoes today. It would be unthinkable.'

He laughed. 'Another time, perhaps.'

'If it were high summer I would like to immerse myself in the sea and wash off all contamination. Unfortunately I think it would be too cold now. We stayed at Brighton once, when I was about eight years old, and I swam in the sea. It was delightful, so different from when I swam in the lake at Danesfield, though I hated the clinging gowns we had to wear.'

A startling image of a naked Sylvie

106

swimming in the sea, rising out of it like Venus, came into Randal's mind. Hastily he suppressed it. He was not in the habit of imagining such scenes, even of the ladies with whom he sometimes enjoyed agreeable connections. He turned to practicalities to distract himself.

'I think we ought to be starting back soon.'

In spite of himself and his suspicions about Sylvie's involvement with Dupont, he felt obliged to help. She was brave, and had, it seemed, been treated abominably by Sir George and the other trustee.

★   ★   ★

Sylvie felt more relaxed as they set off towards Norwich. She appreciated how much she owed Sir Randal, not only for supporting her against Sir George's hostility, but his care of her afterwards. And the draft for the other twenty pounds, she thought, smiling to herself. Her entire fortune, doubled. She was more ready to confide in him.

'Where exactly is Danesfield?' he asked, after they had been driving for some time.

'A few miles south of Cambridge.'

'A day's journey. I have to see some people in Norwich tonight, then I plan to go back to London. I suggest we stay at the inn, then I

107

will escort you to Danesfield on the way. You cannot travel on the common stage again.'

'But, I don't want to ask more of you,' Sylvie protested, though she admitted to herself that his company and support would be very welcome. She thought of the inn-keeper she had berated, and knew he would be insolent and uncooperative if she returned alone to his inn.

'It is almost on my way, and if you receive the same sort of welcome as at Clayton Court I may be of assistance.'

'Then thank you. Your presence certainly helped me today.'

'And afterwards, you will return to London, to Lady Carstairs?'

Sylvie nodded. 'I will need to discover what happened to my father's business, and see the lawyer, Mr Haines.'

'I can ask my own lawyer to find out what happened to your father's business,' he said. 'He ran it under his own name, I assume?'

'Yes, and I know where.' She told him the address, and saw him frown.

'So that is why you were in the City that morning, looking for it?'

'But it was not there, I'm sure.'

'Someone else in the area will be bound to know what happened.'

Sylvie sighed with relief. 'I feel that with

your help I shall discover the truth. I am so grateful to you. Why are you helping me?'

'My mother knew yours,' he said after a slight pause, while he negotiated a narrow gap left by a farm wagon standing on the road, being loaded with logs of wood cut down from a belt of woodland. He wasn't really sure of his motives himself. 'Besides, I took a strong dislike to your great-uncle!'

Sylvie chuckled. 'So did I!'

★   ★   ★

She fell silent, planning how she could approach the new owners of Danesfield, and ask them how they came to buy it. She had little knowledge of what powers trustees had over the estates they administered, but thought it would be unusual for them to sell an estate which had been in a family for several generations, unless there was an overwhelming need for cash. The only expenses they would have needed to cover were her own, and surely her mother's income, from the estate and what she had invested in the funds, would have been more than enough for school fees and her allowance, which had not been lavish. Even without her father's business it should have been ample.

'I need to see some people,' Sir Randal said, as he drew up in the busy yard of the inn. 'I will order dinner for later in the coffee room.'

Sylvie retired once more to the small room under the eaves. She tried to ignore the sly looks cast her by the landlord and the chambermaid he summoned to serve her when she walked in with Sir Randal. At least the wretched man did not comment on their previous clash. He would not dare in front of Sir Randal. She lifted her head high. No doubt they thought there was some intrigue, but the very idea was laughable. Sir Randal was so much older, and she was far from beautiful. If they were conducting some illicit liaison they would scarcely be staying openly at one of the busiest coaching inns in Norwich. Nor would they be dining in the public rooms.

She tried to dismiss the notion, but a small part of her mind insisted on wondering what it would be like if her relationship with Sir Randal had been different. He was handsome and attractive, as well as rich, and Sylvie recalled Lady Carstairs' comments that he was pursued by all the debutantes. More important, from her viewpoint, he was helpful and kind. But that was all. He was doing what he did from a sense of duty, partly through chivalry, partly because his mother had known and liked hers. And no doubt he had been prompted to help by the dislike he had discovered for Sir George. She was glad of his help, but he would have done the same for any girl in a similar situation.

★ ★ ★

Randal found his contacts at another inn near the cathedral. They greeted him with shaking heads.

'Nothing to report?' he asked, sitting down on the bench opposite and calling for wine.

'We followed him all day. He went to Cromer, so he lied saying he was going only part of the way. He spent the whole morning walking round the town, gazing at the houses, and spent at least an hour in the church,' the senior man said in disgust.

'And after he'd gorged himself on crabs he spent the whole afternoon sitting outside an inn, enjoying the sunshine,' his companion said. 'I managed to fall into conversation, and he said he was a student of architecture.'

'He spoke to no one else?' Randal asked, puzzled.

'One of the vergers, the innkeeper, and a couple of shopkeepers. Oh, and the waiter back here in Norwich at the inn where he ate

111

a meal an hour ago.'

Randal frowned. 'Our information was firm. There was a ship off the north coast, a French ship, and he was planning to come here. It was obvious they were connected.'

'The French ship's left. It was reported halfway back to Holland.'

Randal digested this news. Here in Norfolk it was much more likely to be smuggling Dupont was concerned with than agitation. There were no mill workers to stir up into revolt. Yet the smugglers' boats going to Holland could also be taking messages, from French spies, and bringing back instructions. Was this Dupont's function, as a go-between? But he'd been seen in Manchester. Perhaps he had a dual role.

'Where is he now?'

'He set off along the London road after he'd eaten. He told the ostler he meant to spend the night at Newmarket.'

'Is he being followed?'

'Yes, he'll be tailed all the way back to London. We put someone he doesn't know on to him.'

'This is another time he's taken a journey for no apparent reason, just the excuse he wants to see more of the country. What the devil is the man up to?'

'Could he be deliberately misleading us?'

'A decoy, you mean, while someone else we don't suspect does the real work?' Sir Randal shook his head. 'I don't think that's likely. It's too complicated. There's been no suggestion he knows we are suspicious. But we'll keep a closer eye on anyone he makes contact with. You're sure the innkeeper and the others who seem to be innocent really are? Innkeepers near the coast might well be involved with smugglers. If only to get cheap brandy.'

'It would be worth making discreet enquiries. Dupont's behaviour is suspicious.'

'The information we have on him from New York tells us he has revolutionary sympathies.'

'Many Americans have felt sympathy with France.'

Randal nodded. 'Well, I'll report back, and thanks for your help.'

'We'll keep an eye on that innkeeper, too. That might tell us something.'

He went back to the inn deep in thought. Had they got it all wrong? It looked as though Sylvie Delamare was innocent. Her visit to Clayton Court had been genuine, and she had made no attempt to see anyone else, had seemed glad of his company, which she would not have been if she'd had any clandestine intentions. It seemed less likely Dupont was an innocent traveller, interested in the scenery and the architecture as he claimed. Was any apparent connection between them mere coincidence? He didn't believe in coincidences, but for the life of him could not think of any other explanation.

★   ★   ★

Sylvie wasn't sure whether to be pleased or sorry when they arrived at Danesfield on the following morning and discovered the new owners were not in residence. The servant who answered the door said he was just a caretaker, and the Tempests had taken most of the servants with them. He was not someone Sylvie recognized.

'Who can give you the information?' Sir Randal asked. 'There's an inn in the village. They would know.'

'I wonder if any of the servants still employed are the ones who were here when Mama was alive?' Sylvie said thoughtfully. 'There must be some, gardeners and grooms, who haven't gone with them. I'll ask at the gatehouse.'

They stopped on the way out, but the woman who came to the door said she'd only been there for three years, and as far as she knew all the servants had been hired by the Tempests, or brought from their London house.

'None of the old ones were kept on, from what I've been told,' she added.

'So let's ask at the inn.'

The landlord was new as well, but he told Sylvie one of the local farmer's wives had once worked at the big house. 'Name of Tucker, lives at Hill Farm over yonder.'

'I don't recall anyone of that name, but if she married the farmer that would account for it,' Sylvie said. 'May we go and ask?'

Sir Randal turned the curricle in the direction they'd been shown, and soon they were rolling along a neatly kept lane towards a large, low, thatched farmhouse surrounded by barns and cowsheds. The farm looked prosperous, and the house was freshly painted. In front of it was a small enclosed garden full of bright spring flowers. As they drove into the yard a dozen hens squawked and flew out of the way, and a black and white dog came bounding up to them, barking loudly.

Sir Randal was fully occupied controlling the horses, who took grave exception to this greeting, when Sylvie let out a cry of excitement.

'Maggie! Oh, Maggie, it's you!'

Heedless of the dog, Sylvie leapt down from the curricle and ran towards a small, plump woman who had emerged from the farmhouse and was calling the dog to order.

'Miss Sylvie? Surely it must be! You're the image of your poor dear ma!'

Sylvie suppressed a sob and flung herself into the woman's arms. 'Oh, Maggie, it's so good to see you again!'

'And you too, my dearie! Why, we thought you'd never come back here when the house changed hands. Come inside, do, and let me give you something to eat. And who's the fine gentleman? Your fiancé, is it?'

Sylvie blushed and glanced apologetically at Sir Randal, but he, having calmed the horses, grinned down at her.

'Sir Randal Fortescue is just helping me,' she said hurriedly. 'His mother and mine were friends. I came to see what had happened to Danesfield, why it had been sold.'

Maggie Tucker frowned. 'That were a right mystery,' she said. 'But come in, do, the both of you. Can your lad manage the horses?' she added. 'There's fodder in the old stable.'

Sir Randal's tiger had already unhitched the horses, and he nodded and led them towards the stables she indicated. Then Maggie turned and led the way through a low doorway into a large, cheerful kitchen.

'Maggie was my nursemaid,' Sylvie explained. 'Maggie, where is everyone? They said all the servants are new.'

'They were all turned off, a few months after your ma and pa died, but a few of us had family here and stayed in the village. I married Jed Tucker the year afterwards. But sit down, and try my scones. Fresh this morning they be.'

She bustled round setting scones and newly churned butter in front of them, with a pot of strawberry jam. Then she fetched a pitcher of cider and poured generous tankards full.

'Maggie, come and sit down. There's so much I need to know. When was Danesfield sold?'

'It weren't sold. Not in the regular way, that is. But I don't know the rights of it. From what Jed tells me it were handed over as a gambling debt.'

6

Sir Randal frowned. 'That's not possible,' he said. 'The house was part of an estate held in trust.'

Maggie shrugged. 'I said I didn't know the rights of it, but that's what folk hereabouts believe.'

'Who has it? Their name is Tempest, but who are they?' Sylvie asked.

'Some London merchant, is all I know. They came down here, dismissed all the servants, brought some of their own, and now hardly ever live here. A big fat man, and an even fatter wife, with two daughters it's rumoured they're trying to marry into the nobility.'

Sylvie asked about the other servants still in the area, but by now there were only two elderly men who had been gardeners, who lived with married sisters in the next village. Maggie had lost touch with the others.

After some time Sir Randal suggested it was time they set off. 'We won't reach London before dark. We'll have to put up at an inn somewhere.'

Maggie immediately offered them rooms,

but he declined. 'I need to get back to London as early as possible in the morning, but thank you for the thought, and for this hospitality.'

'I'm delaying you,' Sylvie said remorsefully. 'Maggie, thank you, and I hope I'll be able to come back soon and see you again.'

★　★　★

They drove part of the way back towards London, and when it began to grow dark sought rooms at a small inn. All that were available were two rooms in a suite, separated by a sitting-room. Randal frowned. If anyone heard of these arrangements Sylvie's reputation would be irretrievably damaged. It was now too late to drive on and hope there would be more suitable accommodation in the next village.

'We'll eat in the coffee room,' he told the innkeeper.

The man looked surprised, but shrugged. Not for him to query the whims of the gentry.

Randal discovered they were little better off. No one else was staying at the inn, or dining there, so he and Sylvie had the coffee room to themselves. At least the dinner provided was edible and ample, and they were both hungry after a day of driving

119

through a cold wind that felt as though it had come straight from the Russian steppes.

'Did your mother have any more property?' he asked, when they had been served and the landlord and his wife, who seemed to be the sole people running the inn, had retreated.

'There was the London house, in North Audley Street just off Grosvenor Square. When I went there I saw only a caretaker, who said the owners were in the country. Their name was Tempest, so I assume they are the same family who have Danesfield. He didn't know whether the house was owned or rented. She also had a small house on the south coast, in Devon, left to her by a cousin, but that was sold when the wars with France started. She was too nervous to stay there in case of an invasion. I think what she saw in Paris when the Bastille was stormed had a great effect on her.'

'It is hardly surprising. She was not very old, was she?'

'She was only twenty when I was born.'

'And they died in a boating accident, I understand. Where was that?'

'Off the north Wales coast. I think it was a fishing boat from a Lancashire port which ran them down in a sea mist, but I never heard details. Their friends all died too. I had been left with my godmother because I was recovering from some minor illness, a cold, I believe, and they felt the exposure to the sea air would be harmful. Sometimes I wish I had been with them.'

'They would not have wished that, Sylvie.'

'I know, but sometimes, when I'm feeling particularly despondent, I wonder what will happen to me, and why I've been left with all these problems.'

'Did you enjoy being at the seminary?' he asked, swiftly changing the subject when Sylvie appeared to be growing mournful.

'Most of the time. I enjoyed being with the other girls, and I liked learning, though we were not encouraged to strain our intellects too much,' she said, and laughed. 'Mrs Shaw permitted me to use her library, since I convinced her that when I could lose myself in a book I would be less likely to mope for my parents. I'm afraid I took advantage of that.'

'Why not? My mother has always found great pleasure in books. Will you have some more of these baked apples?'

'No, thank you. I am tired, I ought to go to bed. But first, can I thank you for all you have done for me. I would not have achieved nearly so much if I'd had to depend on myself.'

★　★　★

Before Sir Randal delivered Sylvie to Lady Carstairs' house the following day he promised to ask around in the City and find out where the lawyer Haines had his offices, and what new name her father's business now bore. 'I'll come and let you know as soon as I discover anything.'

Why, he asked himself as he drove on to the Ministry, was he taking such trouble over something which did not concern him? Was it just because his mother had known Sylvie's mother? Did he still suspect her of some involvement in French plotting, and want to keep track of her? Or did he simply feel sorry for what struck him as criminal injustice?

At the Ministry he reported on their complete failure to discover Dupont in any dubious activity.

'The French ship has gone,' he was told. 'It sailed away the day before Dupont was in Norwich.'

'So I heard. It's not likely that somehow he managed to send a message, unless it was through someone in Cromer.'

'They could not watch him all the time.'

'True, but they told me they made a note of everyone he spoke to.'

'He could have left a letter. Somewhere in the church, perhaps.'

'But who might he have contacted?'

122

'Would any of the locals be involved?' Sinclair asked.

'I suspect many are involved in smuggling,' Randal said. 'It's a busy fishing area, and the Revenue cannot watch every boat.'

'We just don't know.'

Randal sighed. 'Could it have been information from London he was sending to France? Does he have access to anything sensitive?'

'Only through the military people he can scrape acquaintance with, and the gossip he can pick up through them.'

Sir Randal nodded. 'That should be nothing important or useful. Certainly there's likely to be nothing secret, or critical enough to be a disadvantage to our army.'

Feeling restless, when he left the Ministry he decided to set in train enquiries about Sylvie Delamare's problems, so he drove to the City and visited his own man of business.

'Haines?' Lawyer Kidson repeated when he had explained his interest. 'The old man died almost ten years ago, and his son took over. Wet behind the ears, young John Haines was, barely twenty at the time. Not much better now, I'd say. He doesn't appear to have a great deal of business to occupy his time.'

'Interesting. So he might make a mess of

controlling a trust? Or be paid well for mismanaging it.'

'He's sure to have made a shambles of such work, but I'd never heard he was dishonest. Just incompetent.'

'Thank you. I think I'll pay him a visit soon.'

He drove to his rooms deep in thought. If John Haines was so young and incompetent, and possibly persuadable, that might explain some of the problems Sylvie had discovered. Whether anything could be done about it was another matter. But if anything could be retrieved for Sylvie he would do his best to ensure it.

★ ★ ★

Celia greeted Sylvie excitedly and after she had been welcomed by Lady Carstairs bore her upstairs. 'What did you discover?' she demanded.

Sylvie told her, and brushed aside Celia's exclamations about Sir Randal's involvement. 'I was fortunate he helped me,' Sylvie said, 'or I'd never have been admitted to see Sir George. Oh, he's an odious old man! I'm ashamed to be connected to him!'

'So what do you do now? See this other trustee, the solicitor, I suppose?'

'Sir Randal is going to find out where he has his office. And he will ask what has become of my father's business. Celia, I can't believe my father would ever have given this away. And he never had a partner, I'm sure of that! But what have you been doing?'

A great deal, it seemed. Every hour was accounted for, according to Celia's long list of engagements. When she was not riding or walking in the park, paying calls, attending balls or the theatre, she was having fittings for more gowns or changing from a morning gown to a walking one, a riding habit to an evening dress, and then having her hair cut or curled.

'It's exhausting!' she said, laughing. 'And Aunt Augusta says the Season has hardly begun. But I'm so glad you are back, it's more fun to go to things with you.'

'I can't,' Sylvie protested. 'I'm truly grateful to Lady Carstairs for housing me, but I can't expect her to introduce me to Society. Besides,' she added, as Celia began to shake her head, 'I can't afford all these different dresses you have to have, and I certainly will not permit your aunt to give me more.'

'Then you will have to be the eccentric Miss Delamare who always wears the same gown,' Celia said, undaunted. 'Or at least the same colour. We can do a lot to change the appearance with the addition of a few ribbons or some lace, so you'll have no excuse. Sylvie, there's a big ball tonight, you have to come. Aunt says she means to present me to some of the Patronesses of Almack's, in the hope one of them will give me vouchers. I'm terrified I'll do something to offend, and Aunt will be so mortified if they refuse!'

'Having me there will not increase your prospects,' Sylvie said and laughed. She was intrigued. 'Do you need to go to the marriage mart in order to meet a prospective husband? It sounds as though there are plenty of opportunities elsewhere.'

'Oh yes, there are, but unless one has vouchers some of the old tabbies consider one is not respectable enough to marry well.'

'Do you care what they think?'

'Not really, but Aunt Augusta says their approval counts a good deal with the top families. She's being so good to me, presenting me because Mama cannot, that I don't wish to be disobliging.'

'Of course not. What are you going to wear?'

They became absorbed in discussing gowns, and making some alterations to the ballgown Sylvie had worn before. Sylvie pushed her own problems to the back of her mind. Sir Randal would tell her what he discovered, and until he did there was nothing she could herself do.

★ ★ ★

The ball was crowded. Celia said she despaired of ever seeing anyone she knew, but within minutes Aubrey Fortescue appeared at her side and asked her to dance. Sir David, who had escorted them from Carstairs House, led Sylvie on to the floor, leaving Lady Carstairs chatting to friends.

'My mother told me where you have been, and with whom,' he said quietly. 'You must be careful not to ruin your reputation. It's just not done to go jaunting about the country-side with unmarried men.'

Sylvie looked at him, astonished. 'Is it acceptable to go jaunting with married ones?' she demanded.

'That's not what I mean! You had no chaperon.'

'I didn't intend to go with anyone,' she said, angry at having her actions criticized by a boy so little older than herself. 'I don't need to answer to you!'

'You are staying under my roof; I feel responsible!'

'I am staying with your mother, but I

127

suppose the house does belong to you as head of the family. If my actions offend you the answer is simple: I will remove to a hotel in the morning.'

He looked astonished at her reaction. 'Don't be silly, Sylvie. That would be worse! People would talk. As it is, I don't suppose anyone outside the families knows. Don't take umbrage, Sylvie. It's just that I felt you needed a word of advice from someone older — '

'And someone who considers himself wiser, no doubt! Well, Sir David, you may be my host but you have no authority over me. I will do as I choose, and judge for myself whether my actions are reprehensible or not. If people talk about me that is their problem. Now please take me back to your mother!'

'Sylvie, don't be ridiculous. You can't walk off the floor in a temper! You'll look foolish.'

'Can't I? Because people will talk?' she mimicked. 'I don't think I am the one who will look foolish.'

They were at the edge of the ballroom, near the corner where the dowagers were sitting. Sylvie pulled her hand from Sir David's grasp and stepped aside, then walked steadily to where Lady Carstairs sat with some friends. Breathing deeply to calm herself she stood at the side, while David hovered behind her. Lady Carstairs gave her an abstracted smile and turned back to her friends.

What should she do? In a way she knew he was right. If it became known that she had stayed at the same inns as Sir Randal, and driven with him, alone but for a diminutive tiger, her reputation would be gone, even though it had all been so innocent and there had at the time seemed nothing else she could do. It would have been foolish, besides eating into her twenty pounds — now doubled, thanks to him — to have insisted on hiring her own carriage to visit Danesfield. At least he had allowed her to pay her own shot at the inns. But she was too angry with David to consider apologizing to him. No boy little older than herself had the right to criticize her or her actions.

She was standing, deep in thought, tapping her feet in time to the lively music, when a light touch on her arm made her glance up.

'Pensive, Miss Delamare? Come with me, I have things to tell you.'

* * *

Randal led her to a seat in an alcove. 'I discovered your father's business,' he said. 'I went to see them this afternoon. It is

129

managed now under a different name, but in the same street where you looked.'

Sylvie breathed a deep sigh. 'What happened?'

'Apart from the change of name, not a great deal. There is a new manager, who did not know your father, who was appointed a few months after his death. I understand the former manager, your father's French colleague, was dismissed and he set up on his own account in Brighton. Some of the old craftsmen are still there, but the firm does not enjoy quite the same reputation for quality and design as when your father was in charge. Perhaps that was inevitable, as he was so well regarded.'

'Are you saying there was no other partner who inherited it?' Sylvie demanded. 'That what Sir George told us is wrong?'

'Exactly that. It would appear still to be a part of your inheritance. The profits,' he went on, his voice grim, 'have been paid for the past ten years into a bank account belonging to Sir George Clayton.'

Sylvie blinked, and he saw her cheeks go white and then red. 'You mean he stole them?'

'That is what it seems. I persuaded the man to tell me how much the yearly profits were, and they came to a great deal more than could possibly have been spent on your school fees.'

'Oh! That villain! He'll pay for this!' Sylvie raged, and would have leapt to her feet if Sir Randal had not grasped her hand and prevented her. 'I'm going straight back there!'

'Not so fast, Sylvie! You must not be impetuous. That will achieve nothing. We have to have all the facts first, before we confront him. There is your other trustee to visit first.'

She subsided. 'Yes, of course. Does he know what is going on?'

'Somehow I doubt it. The man who was appointed your trustee died soon after your father, and his son took over. From what I hear he is a weak, ineffectual man. I propose going to see him in the morning.'

'I'm coming with you!'

Sir Randal laughed at her vehemence. 'I thought you might want to. I'll call for you at Carstairs House.'

She nodded, and at that moment Aubrey appeared in front of them.

'Miss Delamare, will you dance with me? And may I claim the supper dance with you?'

He took her card, smiled to see so few dances yet granted, and signed his initials with a flourish, glancing triumphantly at his cousin. Randal eyed him expressionlessly, but when Aubrey led Sylvie away he frowned. The boy was becoming too particular in his attentions, and it would not do, for several reasons. He was too young for her. She might be involved with a man who was almost certainly a supporter of the French. And despite his words to Sylvie, he was not at all confident that he would be able to retrieve much of her fortune for her. A simple sense of justice made him angry at the way she seemed to have been cheated of her inheritance, whatever she was. But she desperately wanted to recover her fortune. If she could not, would she turn to a wealthy man and hope to become rich again through him? He could not condone allowing his cousin to become entangled with someone about whom there were patriotic questions, nor did he want the boy to be trapped by a fortune hunter who cared nothing for him as a person.

He knew what it was like, to be pursued for his fortune rather than himself. When he was no older than Aubrey, before his father had died, he had almost become engaged to a woman he later discovered had been interested solely in his prospects. By what he had eventually considered his greatest stroke of luck, a richer, much older man, twice widowed, who had acquired two fortunes by marrying wealthy heiresses, and no longer needed to marry for money, had swum into her ken. He had been reprieved, and vowed never again to be taken in by a pretty face and beguiling manners. He would make sure Aubrey did not fall into that trap.

★   ★   ★

Sylvie had to confess some of the truth to Lady Carstairs. If she thought Sir Randal Fortescue was paying her attentions, heaven knows what inaccurate gossip and speculations would be circulating amongst her cronies. Sylvie was well aware how impossible it was to quell such gossip. She had already had to endure questions about her father's supposedly aristocratic, even noble, connections in France before the revolution, much exaggerated, and avid queries as to whether any of them had perished under the guillotine.

Her response that her father was no more than a second son of a minor count, and that before the revolution counts were two a penny in France, brought only knowing looks.

'My affairs are somewhat involved,' she told Lady Carstairs at breakfast. 'Lady Fortescue knew my mother, and Sir Randal is helping me sort them out. He is taking me to see my trustee this morning.' And if from that Lady Carstairs assumed his mother had asked him to help, it was not her fault.

David, who had spoken no more than a gruff greeting when he had entered the breakfast-room, looked up. 'I could have helped,' he said, 'instead of involving someone who is nothing to do with our family.'

'But I am nothing to do with your family, apart from my friendship with Celia, and your mother's hospitality,' Sylvie said gently. After their quarrel the previous evening at the ball she was amazed he even wanted to speak to her, let alone offer her any help.

'It would look better, create less comment, if I did it while you are staying under my roof,' he said stubbornly.

Sylvie bit back her retort. He was still concerned people would talk. She had a wild urge to do something which would really set the gossips talking, but calmer reflections told her this would be unkind to Lady Carstairs.

This lady patted her son's hand. 'It's very good of you to offer, my dear, but Sir Randal is much older, he's been in control of his own affairs for years, and is quite up to snuff.'

'Are you implying I am not?' David was enraged.

'Of course not, my dear, but you've been away in the army, of necessity you've had to leave all that sort of thing in the hands of your own agents. Sir Randal has been managing his own affairs for years, and he knows the men in the City, and the sort of tricks they get up to.'

David did not look mollified, but he subsided, and as soon as he had finished eating took himself off.

'Have you any plans for this morning, my dear?' Lady Carstairs asked Celia. She seemed impervious to her son's ill humours. 'I hoped you and David might ride in the Park together.'

'If you don't object, ma'am, I mean to go shopping with Georgina Fortescue. She asked me last night.'

'Young Aubrey's sister? I believe her grandmother is bringing her out this year, isn't she? But she is older than you, I think?'

'She would have come out last year but she had measles. May I go?'

'Of course. Now I'd better go and see Cook about the menu for tomorrow evening. I have some old friends coming for dinner, Sylvie. There is a French woman you will like. She escaped from France the same year the wretches imprisoned the King and Queen, and she married an Englishman, a naval officer, but unfortunately he died at Trafalgar. And Monsieur Dupont is coming. Do ask

Randal to join us if he is free. One of my guests has sent an apology, he has an attack of gout, so I am a man short.'

★ ★ ★

'Have you met this lawyer Haines?' Sylvie asked, as Sir Randal negotiated the heavy traffic heading towards the City.

'No, that's a pleasure to come. From what my own man tells me he is not highly regarded. But I doubt even an incompetent clown could lose all your inheritance in just ten years. There has been criminal activity, but whether both he and Sir George are involved we have yet to see.'

'What shall I do about the profits from my father's business? Surely Sir George will have to pay them back?'

'Yes, even if it means selling Clayton Court. I've set in motion, through my own lawyer, your claim. But it could take years,' he warned. 'There should be no question about future profits being paid to you directly, and the manager will already have received instructions to do that. You will be able to rely on some income. He seemed an honest man, and will no doubt be horrified when he learns the truth.'

'You are doing a great deal for me, and I

am most grateful.'

He smiled down at her. 'I hate injustice, and besides, I would have to answer to my mother if I did not help the daughter of a woman she was once fond of.'

Sylvie subsided into silence. She was so fortunate to have acquired someone like Sir Randal who was willing to help her. She had no doubt that in the end she would have discovered all these things for herself, but having him, with all his knowledge and contacts, to help, would speed up the process, so that she no longer depended on the generosity of her friends.

Sir Randal had taken the precaution of sending to make an appointment with John Haines. He inhabited a small suite of rooms in Gray's Inn, with an elderly clerk his only staff. This clerk showed them into the inner office without knocking, and Sir Randal ushered Sylvie in before him. Glancing round at the dusty, unkempt room he took out his handkerchief and ostentatiously wiped the seats of the two chairs which stood facing the large, empty desk, before guiding Sylvie to one of them and taking the other for himself.

Sylvie suppressed a laugh. The lawyer facing them had sprung to his feet on their entrance and was hopping from one foot to another. He was pale and thin, in his early thirties, with an indeterminate blob of a nose in a squashed-looking face. He looked terrified, and kept twisting his hands together.

'Sit down, man, we're not about to assault you, even though you perhaps deserve it. Let us get straight to business.'

He waited while Haines subsided into his chair. Sylvie had not previously had any dealings with lawyers, but she thought he must be one of the least prepossessing of the whole tribe. She would certainly not wish to entrust any of her affairs to such a man.

'Your father was one of the trustees appointed to deal with the estate left by Monsieur and Madame Delamare,' Sir Randal went on, and Haines nodded anxiously. 'When your father died you took over that task.'

Mr Haines gulped. 'Yes, but, that is, I wasn't the only trustee. Madame's uncle, Sir George Clayton, had been appointed with my father. He knew much more about it than I did.'

'You must be aware of the actions of the other trustee. Can you explain why Madame's home, Danesfield, was illegally appropriated?'

'Illegal? Danesfield? You mean the house near Cambridge? No, you've got it wrong! It wasn't appropriated! Not at all.'

'It seems to be owned now by a family called Tempest.'

'No, of course not! They rent it. That's what Sir George told me. You would hardly expect responsible trustees to leave the place empty when there was no one in the family to use it. Miss Delamare was at school.'

'Can you show us the rent books? And the accounts?'

'I don't have them. Sir George dealt with all that. He found the tenants, and made all the arrangements.'

Sir Randal sat back in his chair, and grasped Sylvie's hand warningly. She had been on the verge of speaking, but now looked at him and subsided.

'Do you mean you have nothing to do with the trust you are paid to administer?'

'I see the accounts. Really, this is normal practice. We can't both be involved in day-by-day decisions. As Sir George was related, after my father died, it was only sensible to allow him to continue looking after the property. He knew all about it, and besides, he lived nearer to it than I do, here in London.'

'A debatable point. You are, however, within a stone's throw of the jewellery business, and of the North Audley Street house. Has that been sold?'

'I — of course not! Sir George deals with it also. As for the jewellery business, I'm not a

139

businessman. I can't be expected to run such a business. Sir George appointed a manager.'

'What has become of my mother's jewels?' Sylvie asked, but by now she was not expecting any sensible answer.

'Jewels? I suppose Sir George has them, or has deposited them with his bank. I never had anything to do with them, and I'm sure my father knew nothing about them.'

Sir Randal rose to his feet. 'You're neither a businessman, a good lawyer, or a responsible trustee! I acquit you of being a fraudster, I think, though I reserve judgement on that. So far you appear to be merely a gullible fool!'

Mr Haines, looking as though he expected to be attacked, pushed back his chair and leapt to his feet. He cautiously remained behind his desk. 'Sir! You insult me! I — I demand satisfaction! Or an apology.'

Sylvie stifled a giggle. He looked so frightened at what he had just said, and backed away from the desk to the wall behind him.

Sir Randal went on inexorably. 'Would it surprise you to be told that Danesfield has apparently been given to the Tempests in payment of a gambling debt? We can discover nothing about the London house, except that a family called Tempest live there. The same family who occupy Danesfield, we presume.

140

Sir George tells us the jewels were probably sold by you or your father, to pay Miss Delamare's school fees. Did you know the profits of the Delamare jewellery business are paid into a private banking account belonging to Sir George? And he told his great-niece all that remains of her inheritance is a mere forty pounds? I think, sir, as a joint trustee equally responsible to Miss Delamare for her inheritance, you have some explaining to do!'

7

Randal looked around the drawing-room at Carstairs House, where the dinner guests were assembled, and frowned. Marc Dupont was standing by one of the long windows talking to Sylvie. Just as he had begun to think she had nothing to do with the man suspected of being a French agitator, here they were, heads close together, and all his suspicions returned.

At that moment Dupont moved away and Aubrey Fortescue took his place. Sylvie smiled at him, and Randal found he had a new worry to contend with. His cousin was becoming too close to the girl. Aubrey was too young for a serious attachment. If it looked like becoming one it would be his duty, somehow, to step in and put a stop to it.

Before he knew what he was doing he found himself strolling across the room towards Sylvie. When she turned to him and smiled he felt a little jolt. She was far prettier than he had at first thought, beautiful, even. Perhaps it had been worry over her inheritance that had dimmed her looks previously. Now she looked radiant. Was she concerned solely with possessing a big fortune? He told himself not to be cynical. Anyone unjustly deprived of what they considered their own had a right to feel cheated. That did not prove that Sylvie was on the catch for a rich husband. Yet most girls were. He had been avoiding them for years, ever since that first disastrous entanglement just after he left Cambridge and began to work occasionally for the Ministry.

The butler announced dinner, and Randal had to leave Sylvie to be taken in by Aubrey. Sir David escorted Celia, and he wondered whether Lady Carstairs was promoting a match between her son and niece. Dupont, he noticed, had been paired with his compatriot, Mrs Warrilow. He was taking in one of Lady Carstairs' friends, another widow, and he somewhat wryly wondered whether he was considered too old and staid to interest any of the younger ladies. He knew none but the most optimistic or naïve of the debutantes even considered attempting to attach him, and for a moment felt a pang of regret. For years he had tried to remain aloof, petrified of being trapped into marriage, a state he had convinced himself was not for him. He had an heir, Aubrey, so that was not a consideration. If he wished, there were any number of barques of frailty willing to entertain him, and part from him with no regrets. His own parents had led separate and, as far as he could judge, contented lives. Most of the *ton* seemed to exist in the same fashion. There must be some other way, and for the first time he began to consider seriously what it might be like to be married to a woman he could respect, with whom he might have rational conversation, and with whom he might make a welcoming and comfortable home for their children.

Briskly he shook off these introspective thoughts and devoted himself to his dinner companion. They were seated on the opposite side of the table to Sylvie, and he found his gaze kept straying to her. She was between Aubrey and Dupont, but he could catch only a few words of their conversation, being fully occupied with his widow and Celia, on his other side. It all sounded quite innocuous, dealing as it did with the various entertainments on offer. Then he caught a few hurried words.

'Miss Delamare, may I drive you out tomorrow?'

Sylvie cast a quick glance at Aubrey, then smiled at Dupont. 'That would be most enjoyable, sir.'

All Randal's suspicions flooded back. If they were conspirators, they now had no need for clandestine meetings. They had met socially, and it was perfectly normal for them to walk or drive together. He found his teeth grinding together, and unclenched his jaw as he turned to the widow.

'I beg your pardon, ma'am? What did you say?'

★ ★ ★

Assured of an income from the jewellery business, Sylvie was able to indulge herself buying new clothes. She was still cautious, buying lengths of muslin and making them up herself, but she was able to spend on two ball gowns, new slippers and gloves, and a delicious hat she simply could not resist.

She was wearing this and her new pelisse a few weeks later when she drove in the Park with Marc Dupont. Celia was walking with Georgina Fortescue, who had become a good friend, and Sylvie saw them stop to talk with David and Aubrey.

The two young men had been away for a few days at the races at Newmarket, and must just have returned to London. Then as Dupont's phaeton swept on she forgot them. He had been away for a few days himself, visiting Canterbury, and he was describing the cathedral to her.

'You like cathedrals, I understand,' she said. 'Haven't you visited the one at Norwich?'

'Oh, yes, and several more. England has so many old buildings, something we do not have in America. I would dearly like to visit the cathedrals in France, but while this war continues that will be impossible. I will have to return to New York in a few months, but I hope I might come back once the wars are over, and visit France.'

Sylvie sighed. 'The wars seem to have been going on for ever.'

'So sad. I expect Sir David will be returning to his regiment soon. They are in Spain, I believe?'

Sylvie nodded. 'I'm not sure exactly where. But his doctors will not allow him to go yet.'

'He looks well enough.'

'I think some wound has not healed fully, and they are afraid that undue exertion might reopen it. Really, I am not a doctor and I don't know the details.'

Secretly Sylvie suspected Lady Carstairs had some influence over the doctors and was persuading them to declare her precious son unfit. She was, Sylvie was now convinced, trying to promote a match between him and Celia, and for this to succeed David had to be kept at home.

'Such a waste of lives, this war. I pray it will be over soon,' Dupont said. 'I do not even care which side wins. The revolution was deplorable, but Napoleon has in some ways been good for France. If only he could be persuaded against his dreams of conquering the world!'

'Would you live in France if you could return safely?'

'I think not. New York has much to offer, even if it does not have old buildings. I can travel to Europe to indulge my taste for them.'

★　★　★

Celia was still out when Dupont took Sylvie back to Berkeley Square, but David and Aubrey were in the drawing-room, standing near one of the windows.

'Ah, there you are,' David said, and Sylvie frowned at the curt tone of his voice. 'We've been waiting for you. Come and sit down. I have something to say to you. Did you have a pleasant drive with your Monsieur Dupont?'

'He is not mine, and yes, thank you, it was pleasant,' Sylvie replied, refusing the chair he indicated and remaining near the door. 'Did you have a pleasant time at the races?'

'It was pleasant until we stopped at the

Black Bear,' he said. 'What we heard there gave us cause for concern. We are hoping you can explain.'

Sylvie took a deep breath. The Black Bear was the inn where she and Sir Randal had spent the night on their way back to London. 'Explain what?'

'A disturbing and rather disreputable story we heard there. When the landlord heard one of our party call Aubrey here Fortescue, he asked if he was related to Sir Randal. Then he said he admired the woman he'd had with him when he stayed there. He described you.'

'And naturally you believed the worst!'

'You had better explain then, if you can prove his suspicions were wrong. After all, when an unmarried couple share a suite of rooms, however they try to make it seem respectable by dining in public, what else are people to think?'

'What evil-minded people think is not within my control! For some reason, Sir David, you have never approved of me, and would love to spread scandal about me. I am not answerable to you for my actions, so you can wait for any explanation! You will wait a long time.'

She turned and almost ran out of the room. She was furiously angry, and half inclined to pack her bags and leave. She could now afford to stay in a hotel until her affairs were sorted, and the question of her inheritance settled. When it was she might even have a house where she could go and live.

She was standing in her room, indecisive, when Celia knocked and came in. Her friend immediately saw something was the matter, and demanded to know if she had quarrelled with Dupont.

'I saw you driving with him, but you seemed to be having a serious conversation. Has he offended you?'

'It wasn't he who offended me!' Sylvie told her, too angry to consider whether she ought to complain to Celia about her cousin. 'David has the impertinence to criticize my conduct, and I won't endure it. He's no connection of mine, and if he objects to what I do the answer is simple. I'll leave his house and then he will have no fears that his wretched reputation will be smirched. All he cares about is that people don't talk about him!'

Celia demanded details. As Sylvie had already told her all about her visit to Norfolk, and how she had been forced to stay in the inn with Sir Randal, Celia was unconcerned.

'David is behaving like a stuffy old dowager,' she said. 'Really, I cannot imagine him as the dashing cavalry officer Aunt

Augusta thinks he is. Please don't go, Sylvie. It's so much more fun going to parties with you and being able to giggle about them together afterwards. Besides, it would upset Aunt Augusta to know he has been so rude to you.'

★ ★ ★

Randal left the Ministry deep in thought. They had no further evidence that Marc Dupont was in contact with the French, and were considering reducing the surveillance on him. Randal was still not sure. The man had ingratiated himself with many families, but to Randal's suspicious eyes these seemed to be mainly families with sons in the army, or, like the Carstairs, where soldiers were on leave or recovering from wounds.

He shrugged off his worries. Perhaps they had more important things to do than keep watch on Dupont. He had an appointment with his lawyer and John Haines, to try and sort out Sylvie Delamare's inheritance. It was over two months since his visit to Clayton Court, and nothing seemed to have been achieved except the payment of the jewellery business profits to Sylvie. Haines had visited the old reprobate, but had reported no progress.

'The old man is very ill,' he'd said in excuse. 'I truly believe he is losing his mind. He cannot recall any details.'

Randal was sceptical. Haines was so ineffectual he would not have insisted, and would have accepted the first excuse Sir George offered.

He had, though, promised to try and obtain all the papers pertaining to the trust, and the three of them were planning to go through these to try and discover what they could. Randal had little hope of success. He distrusted Sir George, felt sure his illness was feigned, and suspected that the papers Haines had managed to bring away were but a small fraction of what was needed to sort out the mess.

If nothing useful emerged from today's meeting, he planned to visit the Tempests and see what they could tell him. Sylvie had told him about her visit to North Audley Street, and he had been there himself, but the family had not been in residence. He had intended to go to Danesfield, but a letter from Maggie Tucker had told Sylvie they were not there either, so it would be a pointless journey at present.

He had another important reason for remaining in town. He was still determined to prevent Aubrey from making a fool of himself by offering for Sylvie. Her possible connection with Dupont seemed less important now, especially if they could convict him of nothing more heinous than a love of visiting cathedrals, but Aubrey was too young to be married, especially to a girl like Sylvie. She was too strong, too decided a character for him to live with. Perhaps he could make Aubrey see this by enticing Sylvie away from the boy. If it were to Aubrey's ultimate benefit he had no compunction about doing this.

He had kept an eye on them at the social events of the Season. They did not make a show of any preference for one another, and he assumed they were being discreet. This, he mused, was more likely to be Sylvie's doing than his impetuous cousin's idea. Aubrey asked other girls to dance, drove out or rode with others as well as Sylvie, and she also spread her favours amongst half a dozen young men. Not, however, with David Carstairs. He could not recall seeing her dance with him, or drive out. Had they quarrelled? As she was living in his house it would seem only polite for them to dance at least once at any ball where they were both present. David attended these balls, but after a few duty dances he was usually to be found in the card rooms.

Distracting Sylvie's attention from Aubrey

suddenly seemed a tempting idea. He was bored with chasing an agitator who never seemed to do any agitating, and waiting for elusive Tempests to surface. He could endeavour to show Aubrey that women were fickle.

★ ★ ★

Sylvie accepted every invitation she received, to ride or drive or attend balls and parties. It was one way of distracting herself from the uncomfortable atmosphere in Carstairs House. She had listened to Celia's arguments, and agreed with her that living in a hotel would be far less pleasant than remaining, and could well utterly ruin her reputation unless she hired a duenna. In front of Lady Carstairs she and David managed to be polite, but Sylvie was astounded his mother did not notice their coldness and query the reason.

'You're being too sensitive,' Celia insisted. 'You and David may know there is something wrong, but it's not obvious to anyone else.'

The main problem with riding and driving with several young men was the risk of being thought fast, but again Celia reassured her.

'Aunt Augusta says it's best not to show too open a preference. She is encouraging me to do the same. And yet, she seems anxious that none of them become too particular. I have wondered whether she thinks that if I drive with several it will prevent me from forming an attachment to one. Sylvie, do you think she wants David to offer for me? She seems to be encouraging him to pay me attentions, and she never warns me not to go out with him too often.'

'Do you like him?'

'As a cousin, yes. We've always been friends. But I don't want to be married to him.'

Sylvie nodded. 'I have suspected it,' she said. 'Perhaps you should find more excuses not to go with him.'

She herself was intrigued by the number of times Sir Randal took her driving. He had almost nothing to report about her inheritance, telling her these things always took time. The Tempests were neither in London nor Danesfield. All they could do was wait.

He was an interesting and amusing companion, and she frequently wished some of her younger admirers had his wide interests and sophistication. She supposed it was because he was older and had seen more of the world. He had even travelled to France during the short-lived Peace of Amiens eight years earlier, and she listened eagerly to his

154

descriptions of the country of her birth.

'Oh, I wish I could see Paris,' she exclaimed one day when he was driving her in the park. 'It is so frustrating to have been born there and have no knowledge whatsoever of it, apart from what I have read in books.'

'The wars will not last for ever, and then you will be able to go. By then you will have a husband and he can take you.'

She glanced at him but did not reply. He was staring straight ahead, apparently engrossed in controlling a somewhat fractious horse.

Would she be married? Later that night, as she lay in bed, she considered her prospects. None of the men who were paying her attentions appealed to her as a prospective husband. She liked them, on the whole, but they were either too young, or older, widowed, and looking for someone to manage their houses and bring up their children. The young men were often immature or inexperienced, and she could endure neither for a great length of time. They were amusing enough for an hour or two, but she could not imagine living with any of them. As for the widowers, she could not see herself being content to fill some other woman's place, which could involve being constantly compared with the former wife. Nor did she relish the prospect of being expected to mother children who could well resent her.

Besides, she had always had a romantic view of marriage, probably encouraged by the happiness she had witnessed with her parents. They had married for love, against the expressed wishes of their parents, and never regretted it. Sylvie dreamed of finding someone she could marry for love. Until now, she told herself, she had not met such a person.

She shut her eyes, and saw Sir Randal Fortescue's face, and grinned to herself. He was neither young nor elderly and widowed. He was mature, but not too old. He was experienced. In fact he was the ideal candidate. She liked him, and appreciated the way he was helping her to sort out her inheritance. But did that mean she loved him and would be content to marry him? He was not the marrying kind, and Sylvie recalled all the stories she had heard of how girls had attempted to change his mind, without success. These girls, from the names she'd heard mentioned, were often the most beautiful and alluring debutantes of their years. Several, giving up on him, had gone on to marry men of much higher birth or greater fortune. Even if she thought she loved him, and she hastily assured herself she did not, she would have no chance whatsoever of succeeding where all the others had failed.

★ ★ ★

Another month went by. There was still no development regarding Sylvie's inheritance, and Mr Haines, who had been induced to go to Norfolk again after some particularly cutting remarks from Sir Randal, came back with a few more papers and the news that Sir George seemed to be ill again.

'I really could not press him,' Mr Haines protested, when he, Sir Randal and Sir Randal's lawyer met. 'If you had seen the poor man you would have had sympathy. But I came home by way of Danesfield, and they tell me there the Tempests are due back from wherever they have been in the next few weeks.'

Randal had to accept this. He wondered whether a visit by himself might induce Sir George to hand over more of the papers, but he had no official standing. If his judgement of Sir George was accurate, he suspected the old man would dig in his heels and refuse to co-operate just to be awkward. Progress was slow, but they would win in the end.

Meanwhile he was hoping his strategy of weaning Sylvie away from Aubrey was successful. Scarcely a day went by without him seeing Sylvie to drive or ride with. They met most evenings at one or other of the entertainments of the *ton*. He danced with her at every ball, visited Lady Carstairs' box when they were both at the theatre, and called on Lady Carstairs at least once a week.

It was his mother who brought him up short.

'When do you mean to present me with a daughter-in-law?' she asked one evening when, for once, they were dining alone at the house in Grosvenor Square, which she still occupied while he had bachelor rooms nearby.

'I beg your pardon?'

'I am reliably informed that you are paying unusual attentions to Sylvie Delamare,' she said. 'People are speculating on when you intend to propose. Indeed,' she added, 'I understand there are bets being laid at the clubs, as to how long it will be. Are you at last serious about marrying? You know I would be pleased for you if you have found a girl you can love.'

Randal was speechless. He had not intended it to go this far. Careless of the opinions of the *ton*, he had never considered what might be interpreted from his attentions to Sylvie. He was appalled.

'If you have no serious intentions, my dear, I suggest you draw back before it is too late, and people accuse you of playing with her emotions. I like her, I would find no difficulty in welcoming her into the family, but I do not want her to be hurt. Still less do I want people to call you a hard, cold man. Don't answer me now. I don't wish you to make any decision in haste. Do be careful you know what you want first.'

She went out soon afterwards to a small party with some close friends. Randal had been intending to go to a ball, but instead he stayed in the dining-room, drinking port and considering what she had said. Looking back over the past few weeks he acknowledged she was right to be concerned. His plan to show Aubrey all women could be fickle had made him careless.

Did Sylvie regard his attentions as significant? Did she, as it appeared most of the *ton* did, expect him to make a declaration? Ought he to do so? He went cold at the thought. Nothing had been further from his mind. If he had given her the wrong impression, it was through thoughtlessness, not design.

Then he began to consider, for perhaps the first time in his life, what it would be like to be married. His parents had existed in a state of great correctness and ceremony. Both had appeared content, but he wondered whether they had been happy. Their marriage had been one of convenience, he was sure. His father had been married before, at the age of fifty, and his first wife had died in childbirth a year later, along with the much-desired son. Within a year he had married his second wife. Once she had produced her son, they seemed to have lived independent lives. His father had devoted himself to his racehorses and, Randal was certain, his mistresses. His mother had supervised their houses, and found solace in her children and her studies. He admitted to himself that somewhere he had absorbed the notion this was not an ideal marriage. He dreaded repeating the cold formality if he himself should ever marry.

Marriage to Sylvie, who was lively and intelligent, need not be like that. He pushed aside the thought. He had no intention of marrying her, so he must draw back from the intimacy he now realized they had achieved. He hoped she had not read too much into his attentions, for he had no wish to hurt her. A small worm of a thought crept insidiously into his mind, telling him that the watchers who had been predicting he was at last about to enter parson's mousetrap would perhaps be unpleasant about his failure to live up to their predictions. He would have to endure the sly comments, but hoped he would be able to care as little for them as he did for most of the *ton*'s opinions. He just hoped Sylvie would be spared hurtful innuendos.

★ ★ ★

Sylvie looked in vain for Sir Randal. She had become so accustomed to his presence it was disconcerting to realize he was not at the ball. One or two of the other debutantes, noting his absence, made a point of asking her if he were ill, as he had not appeared. David gave her a rather superior smile, and she gritted her teeth. He was, she assumed, thinking she was disappointed, and revelling in the knowledge. She told herself she was not in the least concerned, and greeted all her other partners with serene friendliness.

When he did not appear for several days she did wonder whether he were indisposed, or had gone out of town. When he had previously left town for a few days he had always told her. But she had no right to expect that. She tried to put him out of her mind.

She was intrigued with what was happening to Celia. Her friend had accepted that her aunt wished to promote a match with David, and was doing her best to resist. At the same time she was becoming more attached to Aubrey. He had been cool towards Sylvie ever since the affair which had provoked her argument with David, and she assumed he also disapproved of her. He had not allowed an open breach, however, but continued to dance with her, and occasionally drive out with her. He was paying far greater attention to Celia, and she admitted rather shyly to a growing liking for him.

'Has he declared himself?' Sylvie demanded.

'Yes,' Celia said, 'but we are both so young. I asked him not to approach my aunt yet. I know Sir Randal will not agree to our marrying for years yet. And Aunt Augusta will be disappointed.'

'Sir Randal controls Aubrey's money, I believe, but I doubt he can prevent his marriage, or at least his betrothal.'

'Aubrey thinks he can.'

'I thought Aubrey wanted to join the army when he finished at Cambridge? And he has been in town for months now. Haven't his tutors asked what he is doing?'

'He says if we are allowed to marry he will forget the army, and we can settle on his estates. As for Cambridge, he never really wanted to be there, so he does not care what they say.'

Sylvie privately wondered what Sir Randal would have to say, but it was not her affair. She wished Celia well. They were young, but would probably confound the cynics and make a success of marriage. Both were pleasant, kind, easy to be with. Neither would be happy wed to more forceful personalities.

It was a few days after this conversation, when Lady Carstairs and the two girls were taking tea in the drawing-room with some callers, that the butler came to ask if Miss Delamare could come to speak to a man who claimed to be her great-uncle's man of business.

Sylvie, intrigued, excused herself and went to the library where the visitor had been shown. He was, as she half expected, Mr Haines.

He was standing by the fireplace, adjusting his cravat in front of the mirror, and swung round nervously when she entered.

'Mr Haines. Have you some news for me about my property?' she asked. She could not imagine why else the man would come to seek her out. Normally he tried to avoid meetings if he possibly could.

'Er, no. Not exactly. That is, Miss Delamare, I have some news for you. Is your hostess in the house?'

'Yes, but she is entertaining guests. Why do you ask?'

'I — well, I think perhaps she ought to be here with you.'

'As a chaperon?' Sylvie asked, and laughed. 'I don't think I or my reputation are at risk in her house, Mr Haines. And kind though Lady Carstairs has been to me, she has nothing to do with my affairs, nor with Sir George. I take it there has been some development? Has he finally agreed to reimburse me for what he has stolen over the years? You are at liberty to tell me.'

Haines gulped and shook his head violently. 'You mistake, Miss Delamare. It is bad news. I heard only an hour ago, and I came here immediately to give you the news. Your great-uncle, Sir George, died of a seizure yesterday. You are his only surviving relative, and as such you inherit his property, and according to his will, which he drew up only a month ago, you are to be responsible for his funeral.'

8

Riding towards Oxfordshire Randal considered what to do. His only objective when he had ridden or driven with Sylvie Delamare had been to detach her from Aubrey. He had enjoyed her company more than he had expected, which had perhaps been why he had not realized how often they had been together.

Was he, as his mother suggested, causing people to talk and speculate about his intentions? If he stopped seeing Sylvie would people assume he had lost interest, or had proposed and been rejected? Either would offend his sense of honour. He did not want to be married, but perhaps he would have to make Sylvie an offer.

He told himself he was perfectly content with his life. His estates occupied much of his time, and he enjoyed experimenting with new crops and breeding better strains of cattle and sheep. When he needed company he could spend time in London with his friends, or invite them to visit him in Somerset. He could hunt and shoot as much as he wished, attend race meetings, dance at balls and

165

assemblies, and visit the theatre. Then there was his work for the Ministry. A wife did not fit into this scenario.

Aubrey was his heir, so he did not need to produce children, the usual reason for marrying. And yet — his thoughts veered towards his older sister. She had been married for fifteen years, and produced three children, a boy and two girls. It was always a pleasure to visit her home, which was warm and welcoming, full of laughter, childish squabbles, and continuous excitement. Alicia herself seemed completely fulfilled, and as much in love with her husband as the day they had married. Was it fear of not being able to achieve the same contentment which made him hesitate? This was a new and disturbing thought which he did not welcome. Could he create the same sort of life with any woman, in particular with Sylvie Delamare?

Cravenly he decided to put off a decision. They still did not know whether she was involved with Dupont, and if she were an offer from him would be disastrous. The new estate he had inherited from his cousin demanded his attention. The elderly steward he had depended on to run it for him had suffered a heart attack, and wished to retire. He must make other arrangements, and he did not know the people there well enough to judge who could be trusted to do the job properly in his absence. He hoped the old steward was well enough to advise him.

★　★　★

Sylvie retreated to her room, her emotions in turmoil. She ought to be feeling sad when the last of her relatives died. But she had heartily disliked Sir George. Now, because he had shown some family feeling and left his fortune to her, she felt guilty, as though she had not appreciated him sufficiently.

She also felt a stab of remorse in case her own actions in confronting him, causing him anxiety and distress, had contributed to his death. She had not fully believed in his ill health. She had been certain he was exaggerating. Perhaps he was not. She would probably never know.

After a while she began to think of this new inheritance. What would it mean to her? At the thought of having to return to Clayton Court she shivered. It was, or could be, a delightful house, but did she want the problems associated with it? It gave her a place to live, but after her encounter with her great-uncle she was not at all sure she could be content there. She would always be recalling their acrimonious encounter.

Did Sir George have money too? Mr Haines had been vague on the subject. He said he simply did not know until he could look at Sir George's papers and talk to his bankers. That would mean his going to Clayton Court and searching for them, and she ought to be there with her own advisers, for her own protection.

He must have money, Sylvie thought. There had been no evidence at the house of his having spent anything for years. There were the profits from the jewellery business for the past ten years which had been paid into his bank. If Sir George had simply amassed the money there would be enough for whatever repairs were necessary. Then there might be some proceeds from Danesfield and the London house, income from rent or sale. What had happened to them was still not known. Now, perhaps, she would discover the truth.

All the evidence pointed to Sir George being a miser, in which case she would be able to recoup some of the money he had filched from her. He had treated her abominably, yet he had left her everything. Had he had a change of heart? She ought to be grateful.

She was not grateful when she considered

his other request, that she arrange his funeral. She had not the slightest idea how to go about it. Her parents had been buried by friends before she was fully aware of what had happened to them, and she had not previously had any close connection with a bereaved person. Thankfully she remembered Lady Carstairs. She would give advice. Had the visitors she'd left in the drawing-room gone? She ought to tell Lady Carstairs immediately what had happened. Sylvie rang for a maid.

★ ★ ★

'You cannot go to Norfolk on your own,' Lady Carstairs stated that evening as they ate dinner.

They had been planning to attend a ball, one of the last of the Season, but Lady Carstairs decreed it would not do for Sylvie to be seen there.

'News of Sir George's death will soon get around, and however bad the situation between the two of you, you will be expected to show proper respect. People would be outraged to think you had been enjoying yourself, and on the very day you hear about it.'

Sylvie accepted that. 'But there is no reason

why you and Celia can't go,' she said. 'You are not related to him, or to me.'

'That is beside the point. You have been my guest for more than three months, and we must show the due observances. Have you any mourning clothes? I will send to my dressmaker and she can come and adapt one of my black dresses for you, until you can acquire some of your own.'

'I will not wear mourning for a man who has cheated me for years. That would be hypocritical.'

Lady Carstairs gasped. 'My dear, you must! What would people say?'

'But he's made it all right now by leaving you everything,' Celia said.

'He has no other relative, and probably no friends, and would be too mean to leave it to some charity. I don't suppose he expected ever to die.'

David, who had been intending to dine at his club, but had been persuaded, as the man of the family, to remain at home, spoke for the first time.

'To return to what Mama says, you cannot go to Norfolk on your own.'

Because people might talk, Sylvie thought, stifling the urge to laugh. David was so utterly conventional, caring so much for the opinions of the *ton*.

'Mr Haines says he must be there to deal with the legal aspects — '

'Then it is even more inconceivable that you, an unmarried girl, should be there alone with him!'

Sylvie was beginning to be angry at his implied criticisms. What did he expect her to do — jump into bed with the wretched lawyer?

'He'll stay at the inn in the village. I won't be there alone with him.'

'Perhaps you could go too, David,' Lady Carstairs suggested, blithely oblivious to the barely concealed antagonism between Sylvie and her son.

David looked horrified. 'That would be even worse! People might talk about Haines being there, but they will not seriously believe an heiress like Sylvie would compromise herself with a lawyer, a tradesman. It would be different with me.'

'My mother married a tradesman, as you have called my father,' Sylvie could not resist saying. 'And are you saying your presence would be enough to compromise me? It doesn't say much for your reputation!'

'Then we will all go.' Lady Carstairs looked pleased at her solution. 'Instead of going to Brighton next week, as we planned, we will all go and help Sylvie. I've no doubt, from what you told us of the house, Sylvie, that a great deal needs to be done to make it habitable. While you are sorting out legal matters with Mr Haines, I can be supervising the servants. We'll take some of the maids from Carstairs House, they can help whoever is there, and we can no doubt hire women from the village. There is a village, isn't there, Sylvie?'

'Yes, half a mile or so away, on the coast.'

'Good. In fact, I will send some people straight away to prepare rooms for us. You say the old man who appeared to be acting as your uncle's butler was unpleasant and is unlikely to be helpful? Then I'll send my butler. Sawyer will soon organize things. And he can set in train arrangements for the funeral. I assume he'll be buried in the village?'

Sylvie was overwhelmed. All day, since Mr Haines had told her of Sir George's death and her obligation to organize his funeral rites, she had been inwardly panicking. She had no idea how to go about it, and dreaded returning to Clayton Court on her own, to face she knew not what. Lady Carstairs' offer was generous and most welcome.

'That would be wonderful, and I thank you from the bottom of my heart, Lady Carstairs,' she said, and made no further demur when her hostess summoned her own maid and

172

bade her go and fetch some of her black dresses so that they could determine which might be made over quickly to fit Sylvie.

* * *

Arrangements were swiftly made. Lady Carstairs had considered sending Sawyer and some maids by the public coach, but when Sylvie pointed out they would need to hire some sort of conveyance in Norwich, for the last part of the journey, she decided it would be better to hire a carriage. They were sent off early the following morning.

Lady Carstairs sent some of their own luggage, hastily packed the previous evening. 'I mean to use my travelling coach, and take my own horses. I never trust hired cattle. So we may have to spend a couple of nights on the way,' she warned them at breakfast.

'I will ride,' David put in. 'Then you will have more room for your maid and the rest of your luggage.'

Everyone was busy, preparing to leave, but Sylvie noticed how quiet Celia was and tackled her about it.

'Are you worrying about leaving Aubrey?' she demanded. 'He won't forget you, and you will be able to come back to London or go to Brighton for the rest of the summer, as you planned, in a few weeks.'

'Oh, no, he won't forget me.'

'Why don't you tell your aunt?'

'Aubrey feels he must tell Sir Randal first, before he makes my aunt a formal offer for me. She might be offended if she thought we were making plans of our own. Especially as I'm sure you're right and she hopes David and I will make a match of it.'

'Then I will invite Aubrey to come with us. He and David are good friends, it will not appear odd, and I can certainly claim that David will be bored with no sport or other entertainment in the country.'

When Aubrey, not having heard the news of Sir George's death, called at Carstairs House the following morning to ask if Celia were ill, as she had not been riding in the park that morning, nor at the ball the previous evening, Sylvie explained and issued her invitation.

'You can help to keep Celia's spirits up, and entertain David,' she said briskly. 'Will you ride with him? There really wouldn't be room for you in the carriage.'

Aubrey looked surprised. 'I was going to Brighton,' he said. 'I was intending to go to Cambridge first, to clear up my affairs there, and then straight to Brighton.'

'You can go to Cambridge, and come on

afterwards to Clayton Court. You'll only take a day longer. Please, Aubrey. I feel guilty that my needs will be depriving Celia of both Brighton and your company.'

He blushed. 'Thanks, Sylvie. You know?'

'Celia does confide in me, I'm her best friend.'

Although Sylvie felt perfectly entitled to invite whomsoever she chose to Clayton Court, she felt it would be more diplomatic not to mention Aubrey's visit until they were there. Lady Carstairs had made the occasional arch remark which indicated she thought he was interested in Sylvie. Really, the lady was not terribly observant. She seemed unaware of the atmosphere between Sylvie and her son, or that David had little interest in Celia.

Aubrey had made rather a cake of himself over Sylvie at first, but had cooled considerably after he had discovered her indiscreet stay at the Black Bear with Sir Randal. Lady Carstairs did not appear to have noticed. Nor had she noticed his interest in Celia. Perhaps he had learned discretion. He had been far less obvious in his pursuit of her. Perhaps when they were living in the same house Aubrey would pluck up courage to talk to Lady Carstairs. His excuse of needing to tell Sir Randal first she dismissed as the uncertainty of the boy he still was. He didn't need Sir Randal's permission to marry, and if his cousin objected they could wait until Aubrey had control of his fortune, or live on his and Celia's generous allowances for the next couple of years. In fact, Celia's parents would most probably make over a large sum on the occasion of her marriage. Sylvie did not know what provisions had been made for her friend, but most wealthy girls would bring a substantial dowry to their husbands.

They set off early the following day, and Lady Carstairs refused to hurry, saying she wished to conserve the energies of her horses. Since they spent most of their time eating their heads off in the Berkeley Square mews, only occasionally being asked to do more than pull her ladyship's barouche for a mile or so around Mayfair, or for a quiet circle of Hyde Park, Sylvie felt they were due for a more invigorating time. As she was reluctant to return to Clayton Court, however, even though her great-uncle was no longer there, she accepted the slow pace of travel. It gave her time to consider at leisure what she might now do with this sudden reversal of her fortunes.

She had already decided she had no desire to keep the house where Sir George had lived in solitary squalor. She would soon, she hoped, recover Danesfield, and she could live there in perfect contentment. If it had been rented to the Tempests, and not sold or otherwise disposed of, she would persuade them to leave. Now she had money, she could give them an incentive. If it had been sold she could, when she had sold Clayton Court, buy herself a small property in the country. She had no need of a London house. If she spent other Seasons in town she would rent a house and employ some respectable matron to be her companion.

Would she marry? Now she had prospects that was a possibility. She supposed she might one day find someone she could live with. Hastily she thrust thoughts of Sir Randal from her mind. He was not a marrying man, however much attention he had been paying her during the past few months. She had a strong suspicion his motive had been to separate her from Aubrey. He was someone else who had not noticed Aubrey's change of allegiance.

Her thoughts were distracted as they arrived at the inn where they were to spend the first night, and David clattered into the yard shouting for ostlers. Over dinner Lady Carstairs demanded to be told all Sylvie could remember of the condition of Clayton Court, and began, in her usual rambling manner, to make plans for what they would need to do first. Then there would be the funeral to arrange.

★ ★ ★

Several days later Randal called at Carstairs House to ask Sylvie to drive with him. He had settled matters at his Oxfordshire estate, appointing the old steward's son in his place, and returned to his rooms late the previous night. His dilemma about whether to make Sylvie an offer had not been resolved, and he hoped that seeing her again might help him come to a decision. He had almost persuaded himself she and Dupont were not connected, but before he spoke, if he decided to, he would challenge her.

One of the junior footmen opened the door to him, and informed him no one was at home.

'Then I will leave a note,' Randal said, handing the man his gloves, and moving past him into the entrance hall.

'They've gone away,' the footman said. 'No one's here to give a note to.'

'Gone away? To Brighton? I understood they were going next week. Have they gone early?'

'No, gone somewhere up north,' he was

told, and could elicit no further information from the man.

Randal drove immediately to his mother's house. She was out shopping, and he waited impatiently in the library for her to return. He was too unsettled to sit down, and paced about the room trying to imagine what could have induced Lady Carstairs to change her plans so suddenly. And where, in the north, could she have gone? Had something occurred to send her back to her Oxfordshire house? The footman's geography might be at fault, and they had gone west instead of north. What might that be? Had David and Celia announced their engagement? Were they planning a quiet country wedding?

The butler came in with a decanter of madeira and poured out a substantial glassful. Randal accepted it with an abstracted word of thanks, sipped it and put the glass down, resuming his pacing.

It was an hour later before Lady Fortescue returned, and Randal was out in the hall before she had entered the house.

'Mother, I need to speak to you urgently,' he said.

Lady Fortescue gave him a steady look, calmly took off her hat and gloves, handed them to her maid, and led the way into the library.

Randal followed and resumed his pacing.

'Do sit down, my love, you are making me feel giddy. What has happened to disturb you so much?'

'I don't know. Lady Carstairs has gone out of town, and all that idiotic footman left behind in Berkeley Square can tell me is that they have gone to somewhere in the north. Do you know why they have changed their plans? They were going to Brighton.'

'Have you not heard? I suppose not, as you have been out of town yourself. Sir George Clayton died.'

'Dead? Then he really was ill, when we all thought he was feigning it to avoid having to listen to us.'

'It would seem so. The news was brought to London a week ago, and Lady Carstairs arranged to go to Clayton Court to help Sylvie. The poor girl could scarcely be left to deal with everything herself. I believe, though I do not know for certain, that the entire family has gone to Norfolk, Sir David and Celia as well. Perhaps that lawyer you've been talking to will know.'

'Why should they all have to go to Norfolk? Sylvie didn't owe the man anything. Surely his lawyer is the right person to clear up the estate?'

'Sylvie Delamare is his only relative, I

understand. I expect she considered it was her responsibility to clear up his affairs.'

Randal nodded slowly. 'That could be the explanation.'

'How did you find matters in Oxfordshire? Stay and have a nuncheon with me and tell me all about it.'

'Forgive me, but not today. I have to visit the Ministry.'

He left, but drove first to Mr Haines's office. There was no one there, not even the elderly clerk. The people occupying the neighbouring suite told him the offices had been closed for a week, Mr Haines had gone out of town and would be gone for some time. The clerk had told them he had been given a holiday and was going to visit his daughter at St Albans.

His own lawyer knew no more. 'This will create more confusion in settling that girl's claims,' he said, frowning.

Randal nodded. There was nothing more he could do so he went to confer on any developments with Peter Sinclair.

'Good, I'm glad you have come back to town. Marc Dupont has gone to Norfolk again. He left yesterday.'

'Norfolk? Norwich, or somewhere else?'

'Norwich, we think, from what he said when he hired the horse. But I have not yet heard from the people there. They did discover, though, he has been seen in the town several times. It begins to look more and more as if he is using smugglers to send messages to France.'

Sylvie Delamare had probably gone to Clayton Court, so near to the coast. Was it significant that Dupont had followed her, so quickly? All Randal's suspicions of collusion between them, which had virtually disappeared during the past few weeks when he had come to know her better, came flowing back.

'I'll go there straight away.'

9

At Clayton Court a few bedrooms had been made habitable by the maids Lady Carstairs had sent ahead. The first thing to be arranged was the funeral, and after breakfast, when David had gone out with the intention, he'd said, of seeing what was needed out of doors, Lady Carstairs sent one of the footmen to the village to ask the Rector to visit.

Sylvie had been relieved to discover that Sawyer had already arranged for Sir George's body to be removed to the village church. She suspected she would never have slept if she'd thought her great-uncle was in the same house. She wasn't afraid of ghosts, she told herself, but her only meeting with him had left such a feeling of distaste she had no desire to view even his dead body.

'You should think more kindly of him,' Lady Carstairs had said once on the journey. 'After all, he has left you his own fortune, as well as what already belongs to you.'

Sylvie had choked back a giggle. 'I am to be thankful for his generosity in leaving me what already belonged to me?' she asked.

'Well, not exactly, perhaps. From what you

have told me it seems your money and his were linked so firmly it would have been almost impossible to disentangle them. Really, he has done you a favour by dying.'

Sylvie hoped Lady Carstairs would not repeat that sentiment too loudly, or she might find herself accused of murdering Sir George. Much as she had sometimes felt like it, she could do without that complication in her affairs.

★   ★   ★

The Reverend Archibald Dawes, a youngish man with thin wispy hair and long thin arms and legs which were clothed in garments too short to cover them, arrived within minutes of the footman's return. They received him in the morning-room, the only room apart from the dining-room which had yet been cleaned. He sidled into the room looking highly embarrassed, and made no attempt to greet them until Lady Carstairs sharply bade him to come closer and sit down. Then he gulped and shook his head, at the same time approaching the chair she indicated.

'Miss Delamare?' he asked, bowing towards Lady Carstairs at the same time as he backed towards the chair and lowered himself on to it.

'I am Lady Carstairs. This is Miss Delamare. She has been staying with me. And this is my niece, Miss Mannering. I understand Sir George's body has already been taken to the church. When will it be convenient to hold the funeral service? I expect there is a family plot in the graveyard?'

He seemed to gain confidence with business to discuss. 'I suggest the day after tomorrow. We do not wish to delay too much. It has been several days since poor Sir George went to his Maker, and — and the weather is hot.'

'Indeed. Shall we say midday?'

'Yes, my lady, that was what I was going to suggest. It will allow people to travel here.'

'People? We do not know anyone in the district. Can you advise me who should be invited?'

Smiling in triumph, he extracted a sheet of paper from his pocket. 'I thought that might be the case, as Miss Delamare has not been in the habit of visiting her relative. So I have taken it upon myself to compile a list.'

Sylvie bit back her indignant protest at the implied criticism. How could she have visited the wretched man without an invitation or money for the journey? But to start such an argument now would be pointless.

'Who are these people,' Lady Carstairs

asked after a swift glance at the list. She handed it back.

The Reverend Dawes pointed to the names in turn. 'First the local gentry. Then the farmers who own their land. Next the tenant farmers. And Sir George's servants. No doubt other villagers will wish to pay their respects too, but I have not enumerated them.'

Sylvie caught Celia's eye and bit back a laugh. 'All in good order of precedence,' she said.

Reverend Dawes smiled and nodded. 'I try to do things correctly,' he said complacently. 'As you do not know these people perhaps I can be of service notifying them of the time?'

'That would be most helpful,' Lady Carstairs told him. 'Now, perhaps, we should discuss the order of the service, which hymns and so on.'

★ ★ ★

'What an impossible man!' Sylvie exclaimed an hour later when the Rector, thoroughly pleased with himself and bowing obsequiously to them as he managed to get out of the room, had left.

'At least he is being useful, telling everyone,' Lady Carstairs said, as they sat down to a nuncheon of cold ham and

186

chicken, and fruit she had brought from London, rightly suspecting there would be none at Clayton Court.

'I wonder how many of these local dignitaries will feel obliged to come? If Sir George was as rude to them as he was to me, I doubt they'll want to pay their respects. Unless they wish to make sure he's well under ground!'

'Sylvie, that is disrespectful!' David chided. 'I hope you will not make such remarks when strangers are present.'

'I'll say what I please, David, and it ill becomes you to criticize me. Talking of strangers, Mr Haines sent to say he is coming this afternoon.'

David insisted he ought to be present when Sylvie was ensconced with Mr Haines, and she felt too weary of fighting him to protest. If he interfered or became too obnoxious she was sure she could get rid of him.

Lady Carstairs announced she would set about organizing Sir George's small and demoralized group of servants, along with two women Sawyer had recruited from the village. He had also found a carpenter who began to repair some floorboards in neglected rooms in the east wing, where broken windows had allowed the wind and rain to create considerable damage.

187

'If you are to get a good price for the property, Sylvie, you need to have it in good repair,' she said. 'You do mean to sell, I presume? You will have your own house at Danesfield restored to you now.'

'That depends on what evidence Mr Haines can discover that the house is only rented. Even so, it may have been rented on a long lease, which could mean I cannot move there for some time, unless I can persuade them to give it up,' Sylvie said. She sighed. 'There is so much to do here! I had not realized before how very dilapidated it is. I only saw a few rooms then.'

'Don't worry about that, dear. Apart from the east wing, it's mainly dirt and general neglect. We will soon put it to rights. You may need new curtains, and covers for the chairs, as no one thought to cover them up, but the furniture is good, and will polish up well.'

David, ignoring Sylvie's earlier rebuff, spoke. 'What do you wish to do about the second gatehouse? The woman who lives in the first one tells me it used to be inhabited by the head gardener, but he died a few years ago and Sir George did not bother to employ another. The two men who are still working in the gardens spent most of their time growing vegetables, and as far as I can judge, they sold them too. I had a look at the kitchen garden. It's in a far better state than any other part of the grounds.'

'We'd better repair the other gatehouse, I suppose, and if we are to get the grounds into good condition I'll need more than one extra gardener. The grass has not been cut all summer and is like a hayfield. When we drove in yesterday I noticed several dead trees. They ought to be cut up for firewood. And the stables are a disgrace. I was ashamed to ask your grooms to house your carriage horses there, Lady Carstairs. Which reminds me, I think we ought to purchase some riding horses, and perhaps a small trap that I can drive. I cannot be using your travelling carriage and coachman to go to the village.'

★ ★ ★

When Aubrey Fortescue arrived just before dinner, after Sylvie had spent an unsatisfactory afternoon with Mr Haines trying to make sense of a mass of documents he had brought with him, and others they retrieved from Sir George's room, Lady Carstairs looked surprised but soon recovered.

'I suggested he came, as company for David,' Sylvie explained, feeling guilty. She had put off telling Lady Carstairs of her invitation.

'Yes, dear. I see,' Lady Carstairs said slowly

and smiled, and Sylvie felt even more guilty. She clearly thought Aubrey had followed Sylvie, and had no inkling of the real situation.

'David will be very bored here,' Sylvie hastened to say. 'It's very good of him to offer to help me with Mr Haines, but really, there is nothing he can do, and if he is so concerned about my reputation, one of the maids can sit with us. There is plenty of mending for her, the bedlinen is in sore need of attention.'

* * *

Randal paid a swift visit to his rooms to alert his valet. This time he would take the man with him, as well as his tiger. He would need to visit Sylvie at Clayton Court, and might become involved in some social occasions. He would find an inn closer to the coast than Norwich, perhaps in Cromer, so that he could keep an eye on Dupont.

He went to his desk to write a swift note to his mother informing her of his movements, and found there a letter which had been hidden under a new packet of writing paper he had ordered. He recognized Aubrey's untidy scrawl, and wondered what his cousin had to say to him. He had not been due to go to Brighton for some days, and could have expected to see Randal that day or the next. They had both been invited to a picnic at Richmond.

He opened the folded note, and frowned as he scanned the few lines.

Randal, I expect you have heard of Sir George Clayton's death. Sylvie has gone to Clayton Court to sort out his affairs. Lady Carstairs, David and Celia have gone with her, and Sylvie invited me to join them. Yours, Aubrey.

'Confound the boy!'

As if he had not enough to worry about with Dupont's possible activities, and his connection with Sylvie, here was his love-lorn cousin chasing after the girl when he was half thinking of making her an offer himself. He'd thought the affair had cooled somewhat, especially since he'd been paying Sylvie attentions, but it clearly hadn't. Well, that made it even more imperative he made haste to Norfolk.

★　★　★

Sylvie, in deference to Lady Carstairs, consented to wear one of the black gowns that had been made over for her on the day of the funeral. David and Aubrey would represent them at the service, and the ladies would wait in the hastily cleaned drawing-room for the mourners to return after the interment.

'Though who on earth will want to come?' Sylvie asked. 'We have provided far too much refreshment.'

Lady Carstairs shook her head. 'There is nothing that will not keep for another day if we have overdone it. My dear, I doubt if many of these people have visited Sir George in the past few years, if he was unwelcoming, but they will be agog to see you. They will want to know if their wives may call, and whether you mean to live here.'

Sylvie shrugged. 'I want to be rid of the place as soon as that incompetent Mr Haines has sorted out Sir George's affairs. The way he has been dithering the past two days it will take months.'

If only, she could not help thinking, Sir Randal were here to chivvy the man into some sort of efficiency.

'The carriages are coming up the drive,' Celia said. She was standing beside the window overlooking the front lawns. 'Goodness, there are at least a dozen, and several men on horseback, even some people following on foot.'

Sylvie groaned and went to look. There were two large, cumbersome old travelling carriages, several curricles and gigs, a governess cart, and a barouche.

'You were right, ma'am,' she said, as she returned to her seat beside Lady Carstairs. 'We have become the latest source of entertainment for the neighbourhood.'

'It will not last long,' Lady Carstairs consoled her. 'They will be expecting us to have the will read, and none of them has any interest in that. They will surely have the tact to leave once they have paid their respects.'

'But we already know about the will. Mr Haines had to tell me so that I might arrange the funeral. Which I would not have done if Sir George had not left me my own fortune,' she added.

Sawyer was already at the front door, admitting the first arrivals and formally announcing them as he directed them into the drawing-room. David, taking it upon himself to act as host, stood just inside to greet them, and introduce the ladies.

Sylvie soon abandoned any attempt to remember names. The first comers, who seemed to be the local squires, took the proffered glasses of sherry or Madeira, and after having murmured conventional words of

193

condolence to her, congregated by one of the windows to talk amongst themselves, Others, by their dress of a lower social stratum, looked less confident and made their own group, near the fireplace. Sir George's menservants, who had attended the service, disappeared to their duties. Aubrey hovered beside Lady Carstairs, looking uncomfortable.

It seemed as though everyone was there, and Sylvie began to hope they would soon begin to take their departures, when Sawyer appeared once more in the doorway.

'Sir Randal Fortescue.'

He stood there looking at the assembled company, an inscrutable expression on his face. How elegant he looked, compared with the rest of the men in the room, was Sylvie's first thought, and then she felt a wave of thankfulness. Now, perhaps, Mr Haines would be persuaded to do what he was being paid for.

★ ★ ★

Randal's emotions were mixed. He had driven to Norfolk as fast as possible. Passing through the village he had seen the funeral cortège wending its way out of the church to the tomb which had been opened to admit Sir George's remains. Watching from the road outside he had seen Aubrey walking alongside David, apparently the chief mourners, though neither of them had any connection with the man they were burying.

He wondered how Sylvie's affairs stood now. Would they have even greater problems to sort out, in order to regain her inheritance? Mr Haines, chest thrust out pompously, was walking behind David, and Sir Randal looked forward to that encounter.

He waited until everyone had left, and then followed them at a leisurely pace to Clayton Court. Rather to his surprise, recalling his previous visit, he found the front door standing hospitably open and, when he saw Lady Carstairs' butler inside the entrance hall, understood why.

'Good day, Sawyer. Are you in charge here now?'

'Sir Randal. I have that honour. Does your tiger know where the stables are? It will be rather crowded there, I'm afraid, but he will find some ale provided. This way, sir.'

He paused inside the drawing-room and glanced swiftly round. Sylvie, looking pale and solemn, dressed in unrelieved black which did not at all become her, sat with Lady Carstairs and Celia in an isolated group close to the door. He sent her a swift smile, then frowned as he saw Aubrey standing in what looked like a proprietary attitude behind her. He hoped Aubrey had committed no folly, but he would deal with his cousin later. He was surprised to find so many people present, for he doubted Sir George had been a gracious or convivial neighbour, and then he grinned slightly. They were understandably curious to view the people who were now in control, wondering, if they did not know, what would happen to the property. He doubted whether any of them even knew of Sylvie's existence previously.

He took one of the proffered glasses and moved across to greet the ladies. 'Sylvie, I only heard two days ago. I won't prate insincere condolences. Are you left with settling matters here?'

'With Lady Carstairs' help,' Sylvie replied. 'She is a tower of strength, I am fortunate to have her support.'

He nodded. 'I see Mr Haines is present. Is he being his usual fount of wisdom and expertise?'

Sylvie chuckled. 'What else? Sir Randal, are you — that is, are you staying in the village? Did you come just for the funeral?'

'I came to see if I could help, amongst other things,' he added. 'I have a room at the inn in the village. Aubrey. It is a surprise to see you here.'

'Sylvie invited me,' Aubrey said. 'I can help, too.'

Sylvie seemed to breathe a sigh of relief. 'If you really do mean to help, we can accommodate you here. The maids have been scrubbing the bedrooms, and I am sure we can find one fit for use.'

'Thank you. I'll send for my gear from the inn.'

'Of course,' Lady Carstairs said, 'and I have no doubt Sylvie will be glad to have your assistance. David has been trying his best, but as he knows little of the previous situation, he is rather handicapped when it comes to forcing Mr Haines into creating order out of what seems to be utter chaos.'

David, who had abandoned his post by the door, overheard this. 'Really, Mama, I am quite capable of persuading that man to do his job.'

'Of course you are, dear, but if Sylvie has Sir Randal to help, you and Aubrey can be supervising the men in the gardens and on the home farm. Heaven knows, they need it.'

★ ★ ★

Early the following morning Randal found Mr Haines had set himself up in the library, and spread all his papers out on a big table.

197

He and Sylvie were picking them up, casting a quick glance at them, and trying to allocate them to separate piles. A rather embarrassed-looking maidservant sat near one of the windows surrounded by a pile of sheets and tablecloths.

Sylvie looked up at him and smiled. She did have a most attractive smile, but now she was looking harassed. Had the funeral been too much for her yesterday, entertaining all the local squires and farmers who had descended on the house afterwards? She must have felt very much on display. He had overheard a few comments which seemed to imply Sylvie had been neglectful of the old man, and he had no doubt she had been subjected to a few similar remarks. He surprised himself by wishing he could have done more to assist her through what must have been a considerable ordeal.

'It looks as though you have a heavy task sorting through those papers,' he said, drawing up a chair beside Sylvie. 'Tell me what I can do to help.'

Mr Haines sighed. 'They are in total confusion,' he said fretfully. 'We have retrieved all we can find in Sir George's own room, where he seemed to keep everything. There were old papers here in the library, but whether they are relevant I have yet to decide.

198

There is no order. Old receipts, farm accounts, letters, all jumbled together. Miss Delamare and I are trying to sort them into categories, and then we can perhaps begin to make sense of them.'

After another two hours they had several neat piles of papers.

'Now we can go through and sort them into date order,' Mr Haines said.

'Is there anything relating to Danesfield, or Sir George's bank accounts?' Randal asked.

Mr Haines shook his head. 'There are no deeds, and unless we discover anything in the correspondence, we shall know nothing more.'

'Then we cannot have found all the papers. Sylvie, have you any idea where more of them might be hidden? You know the house a little better after the past few days.'

'I thought we had searched everywhere in his own room. There are a good many chests and bureaux in other parts of the house, and we haven't looked in those. But most of them looked as though they had not been opened for years, judging from the layers of dust on them. Could there be some secret place in here, perhaps? I've heard of false book spines and cupboards hidden behind them. Or even bookcases that swing out.'

Randal stood up and stretched. 'Can I

suggest we have something to eat, and then Haines and I will search in here while you, Sylvie, look in any chests in the rest of the house.'

★ ★ ★

Sylvie was glad of the break. They reported their lack of progress to the others, and David looked scornful. He and Aubrey, it appeared, had been visiting the two tenant farmers and the manager of the home farm.

'The park and the immediate surroundings of the house have been atrociously neglected,' David said, 'but you will be pleased to hear, Sylvie, the farms are in better condition. The farmers clearly value the land, and I think all of them show a profit most years, unless there are bad harvests like they had last year.'

'That is something to be thankful for, then,' Sylvie said. 'I suppose they were able to pay their rents?'

'They had to, or they said Sir George would have evicted them. He seems to have been a hard landlord. I have been discussing some improvements they could make, and they were grateful for my advice.'

Sylvie happened to glance at Sir Randal, and caught a sardonic gleam in his eye. She choked back a laugh. David was so very pompous. She was grateful for his help outside the house, as she and the other ladies had enough to do inside. Indeed, she was thankful that this occupation kept him from interfering in sorting out Sir George's other affairs.

Lady Carstairs was preoccupied with domestic details, another task Sylvie was happy to hand over to someone else. She was talking about which rooms needed painting first, once they had been thoroughly cleaned.

'Or do you think it would be wiser not to spend too much money, in case the people you sell to have different ideas?' she asked Sylvie.

'I certainly don't want to have delicate Chinese wallpapers put in,' Sylvie said, laughing.

'No, of course not, I would not suggest such extravagance,' Lady Carstairs said.

Sylvie smiled at her. 'Until we have looked through the papers and found details of the bank account I have no idea what money I have available.'

'The rooms you have already had cleaned look far better than when I brought Sylvie here before,' Sir Randal said. 'In fact they have come up much better than I feared. Perhaps not using the rooms has helped to prevent more than surface deterioration.'

'I wonder if we need to employ a different cook?' Lady Carstairs went on. 'Mrs Standish seems competent with plain fare, but she has not been accustomed to catering for a large number of people, or providing the sort of variety men expect.'

'If she needs help in the kitchen, we can find someone,' Sylvie said firmly. 'She has looked after Sir George for twenty or more years, and I am sure the men will excuse any deficiencies. It would hurt her too much to feel she was being pushed aside.'

'If you think so, my dear. After all, while you are in mourning you will not be entertaining.'

Sylvie was thankful to escape back to the library. Glad as she was of Lady Carstairs and David's help, she was feeling overwhelmed. If only they could get the papers and the financial matters sorted out soon, she could think about what to do next.

10

'Well, have you sorted out Sylvie's affairs?' David asked, as they sat at dinner.

Mr Haines had departed to the inn where he was staying. Sylvie had considered long and hard whether she was obliged to give him a room. After all, there were plenty of bedrooms at Clayton Court. Feeling uncharitable, she nonetheless told herself she saw enough of him during the daytime, and deserved some respite in the evenings.

He had taken it upon himself to read Sir George's letters, which she would have liked to have seen. Irritatingly, he kept reading out occasional paragraphs or sentences, and commenting on them. These interruptions broke her concentration on the miscellaneous heap of papers which had fallen to her lot, while Sir Randal, as the most experienced of them, tried to make sense of the various financial papers.

'There is insufficient detail here to give us more than a fraction of what we need,' he said when he had been through them all.

He repeated this to David's query. 'There must be other papers, but Sylvie found nothing in any of the bureaux, and though we went over every shelf in the library there were no hidden compartments.'

'I'm surprised you thought there might be,' David said, and Sylvie looked astonished at the barely concealed sneer in his voice. 'Surely hidden cupboards and secret rooms belong to the fanciful novels women like reading?'

'Well, no,' Sir Randal replied. 'My own house in Somerset has a disguised compartment behind one of the bookshelves.'

David looked startled for a moment, but Celia begged for more details. Sir Randal smiled at her enthusiasm and explained how one shelf filled with real books swung out to reveal a shallow cupboard buried in the wall behind.

'It's not a secure hiding place,' he added. 'It's too easy to find, and we've shown many visitors the secret. Alicia and I used to hide our more precious toys there when we were young.'

'Alicia is your sister, Countess Frankley, is she not?' Lady Carstairs asked. 'I don't think she comes to London a great deal now.'

'No, she prefers to spend her time at home with her family.'

He smiled reminiscently, and Sylvie wondered whether he envied Alicia her family. If he did, she told herself firmly, he had it in his own hands to start creating one. But he was either very particular, or against marriage, to have resisted the lures of so many years' worth of debutantes.

David began to describe his own day, repeating much of what he had told them earlier, and calling on Aubrey to corroborate what he had said to the farmers he'd visited.

'If you take my advice, Sylvie, you will find another manager for the home farm. The man is insolent, refusing to listen to good advice, and having the impudence to tell me he knows better than I do what sort of crops to grow.'

'I expect he does,' Sir Randal said quietly. 'The soil here is very different from that in Oxfordshire, and I understand he has been at the home farm for over thirty years. Experience counts.'

'How do you know he's been there for so long?' David demanded. 'Have you been pok — going round visiting them too?'

Sir Randal shook his head, seemingly amused. 'I've been reading the farm accounts, and his were more complete than any other set. I can see by the profits he makes that he knows what he is about.'

David took a deep breath, and Sylvie expected him to make some other cutting remark, but instead he changed the subject to talk with Aubrey about their plans for the following day.

'We ought to go and see the village,' he said. 'From what the farmers told me I believe Sir George owned several houses and the inn. I suppose you've been reading the rent rolls as well?' he demanded, turning again to Sir Randal.

'They seem to be missing. I have not come across them so far.'

Sylvie was thankful when the meal ended and Lady Carstairs led the way to the drawing-room. Sir Randal, rather than stay with the two younger men drinking port, said he would spend more time trying to make sense of the papers they did have. She couldn't imagine what had got into David to make him so objectionable.

Celia was clearly as embarrassed by his behaviour as she had been, but Lady Carstairs had smiled indulgently at him throughout the meal, nodding occasionally when he looked towards her after making what he clearly felt was an unanswerable point. His mother, widowed tragically early, had probably pampered her only child until he felt he could do no wrong.

She slipped away after a while and went to the library, intending to apologize to Sir Randal. She found him standing in front of one of the bookcases, leafing through one of the volumes. He turned and smiled at her.

'If it would not be impertinent of me to give you advice, Sylvie, I suggest you have an expert to catalogue and value these books. Your uncle was an avid collector, at least in his younger days.'

She chuckled. 'Thank you, I will. I came to say David's behaviour at dinner was unpardonable, and I hope it will not drive you away in disgust. I really value your help.'

'I'm not disgusted,' he said. 'In fact, he gave me an idea.'

★ ★ ★

He would say no more, and they went back to the drawing-room just as the tea tray was brought in. David and Aubrey appeared, but settled in a corner for a hand of piquet. Sylvie, tired after a day of hard concentration, soon went to bed.

There were no more papers, so Mr Haines announced on the following morning he intended to go to London and talk to Sir George's bankers.

'Perhaps after that we will have a clearer idea of how you stand financially,' he told Sylvie.

Sir Randal took himself off in his curricle,

and Sylvie joined Lady Carstairs and Celia in the morning-room where they were engaged in mending linen. She was threading a needle for herself when she raised her head quickly, listening. Then she jumped up and went across to the window.

'Oh, dear. I think the local squirarchy approve of us. There's a barouche with two very fashionably dressed ladies approaching. Are we at home?'

'I think we had better be,' Lady Carstairs said. 'We don't want to offend anyone. Quickly, let's move into the drawing-room. In future perhaps we should leave some ladylike embroidery there, so that we are not caught turning sheets side to middle!'

They went to the drawing-room, feeling like conspirators, and suppressing giggles.

Sylvie picked up a book which had been left on one of the tables and opened it at random. 'Do you think we have been accepted? Their husbands approved of us at the funeral?'

Lady Carstairs nodded. 'It would seem so.'

At that moment Sawyer threw open the door and announced Lady and Miss Acton. Sylvie inspected her first visitors. Lady Acton was a woman in her fifties, her daughter mid-twenties, both fair-haired and pale-complexioned. She rose to greet them, and ushered them to seats facing Lady Carstairs.

'My dear Miss Delamare, it is such a pleasure to meet you at last. Even though the occasion is a sad one after the death of Sir George. We live at Acton Manor, a few miles west along the coast.'

Sylvie introduced Lady Carstairs and Celia, and the older ladies soon discovered they had acquaintances in common. Sylvie and Celia began to talk to Miss Acton, asking her about society in the area.

'Oh, you won't know, as you never visited,' Miss Acton said.

'No, I was at school in Bath, and was actually never invited to visit my great-uncle,' Sylvie said, determined to put an end to the growing opinion in the area that she had neglected Sir George. 'My great-uncle was a recluse, as you must have known. Did he ever entertain the local gentry, do you know?'

'Well, no, but he was a very ill man.'

'Yes. But tell me, although I cannot attend assemblies while I am in mourning, what entertainment is there in the area? If I sell Clayton Court I will need to tell any prospective purchaser about this.'

'You are going to sell? What a shame. We were hoping there would be another family in the area. It is woefully lacking in congenial company.'

'I have my own home, I do not need this house,' Sylvie said. 'Is Cromer the nearest town? What is it like?'

She and Celia were soon involved in discussing what was, or in Miss Acton's opinion, what was not available in the area. She despised Cromer because of the many invalids who flocked to it to take the sea bathing cure. Norwich was provincial, with no interesting company to be found there, nor fashionable shops. Nowhere else within easy reach had anything to commend it.

'I much prefer London or Brighton,' Miss Acton said.

'Oh, I don't recall seeing you in London these past few months,' Celia said, with such an innocent air Sylvie was hard put to stop laughing.

Miss Acton gave her an unfriendly glance. 'We avoid the big affairs,' she said. 'I can't abide crushes where simply everyone attends.'

'By which we infer she is not invited,' Celia said when the Acton ladies had departed.

'Little cat!'

'Oh, Sylvie, if she is typical of society here, you will be thankful to escape. I do hope you can recover Danesfield.'

'So do I. And if I do, you shall be my first visitor.'

It was late afternoon when Randal returned. He had spent most of the day in Cromer, without finding any trace of Dupont. He had watched with interest the fishing boats, and decided there was so much activity it would be impossible to identify any particular boat suspected of smuggling. Soon he would go to Norwich to make contact with the Ministry men there, to see what information they had. He could not allow his private concerns, his determination to help Sylvie, interfere with finding and stopping contact with France.

He found Sylvie in the library, listlessly going over the papers they had searched before.

'I hoped there might be some reference we had missed,' she explained.

'Forget that now. Come with me. I want to have another look in Sir George's bedroom.'

'But we have all searched everywhere.'

'Perhaps not quite everywhere. Do you remember I said David had given me an idea?'

'Of course, and you were odiously superior, refusing to say what it was.'

He grinned at her. 'Patience, child. How old is this house?'

Sylvie gritted her teeth. 'What has that to

211

do with anything?'

'Quite a good deal, if I am right. It was built in the late sixteenth century, in the time of Elizabeth, wasn't it?'

'Yes. So I have always been told, and the style of it is typical of that time.'

'A time of religious persecution, when Catholic priests travelled the country in secret, and the houses which sheltered them provided secret places to hide them in case of need.'

'A priest's hole, here?'

'Why not?'

Sylvie was frowning in concentration. 'Sir George seemed to live only in that one room, and he had all he needed there with him. So if there is a priest's hole and he knew of it, and used it to hide things, it must be in that room.'

'Good girl. Can you find a couple of lamps? It will be dark in there.'

'Have we time to search before we need to change for dinner?'

'We can start.'

'Wait for me! I'll get some lanterns from the kitchen.'

She found him in Sir George's room, which had not been changed since the old man was alive. Sylvie had not been able to order it to be stripped, and the others had not wanted to do anything to it without her express command.

'If it's anywhere, I suspect within the chimney breast,' he said. 'It's unusually wide. You take that side and tap the panels, twist all the knobs. I'll try this side.'

They concentrated, carefully exploring every inch of the panelling and the ornate carving between the panels. Then Sylvie gave a gasp as one of the panels moved under her searching hand.

'I think this is it!' she whispered.

Randal went swiftly to her side. He lit one of the lanterns and held it through the gap. The glow it cast was feeble and showed only a small space a few feet square. To one side was a gaping hole, and the top of a ladder stuck up above it. Sylvie's gaze was drawn to the other side of the space, where a large chest sat against the wall.

'That's it!' she exclaimed, and began to scramble through the hole.

Randal caught her arm and pulled her back so that she fell against him.

'Be careful! There is often no way of opening these hiding places from inside. We must not get trapped.'

Sylvie nodded, and moved away from him. He was only then aware that he had been holding her in his arms. He took a deep breath.

'Let's find something to wedge the panel open. Here, this footstool will do. Then we can lift the chest out and look at the contents in greater comfort.'

The chest was large and heavy, and Randal wondered how the old man had managed to install it. He would presumably not have asked for help, if he wanted to keep the hiding place secret. Perhaps he had been much younger, and fit. And it would have been empty. They eventually managed to lift it into the room, and Randal closed the panel.

'Aren't you going to see where the passage leads?' Sylvie asked, and she sounded disappointed.

Most girls, Randal thought in some amusement, would have been eager to shut up the hole. They would not have wanted to venture into it.

'Not now. It must be almost time for dinner. Let us have a quick look, and come back after dinner to search properly.'

'It's probably the deeds of Danesfield,' Sylvie said. 'Oh, how I hope it is.'

There was no lock on the chest, and Randal lifted the lid carefully. Sylvie knelt beside it, and gasped as the contents were revealed. There were several rolls of documents, some the size of letters, others large enough to be maps. In amongst them were dozens of soft leather bags, folded over or with drawstring necks. She lifted one out and carefully unrolled it. A soft cloth was wrapped round the contents, and Sylvie carefully undid this.

Randal watched her, guessing what they would reveal. He was not, however, prepared for the sheer brilliance of the diamond necklace Sylvie, speechless, held in her hands.

She looked up at him, and there were tears in her eyes. He felt a sudden urge to clasp her in his arms, to share the joy which emanated from her.

'They must be my mother's jewels.'

★ ★ ★

She touched more of the rolls and bags but did not unwrap any, just gazing at the diamond necklace and blinking away the tears.

'Sylvie,' Randal's voice was serious, 'can we lock this room?'

She nodded. 'You think they may tempt someone?'

'I suggest we don't tell anyone else they are here, until we have had an opportunity of listing them. Then we should find a safe place to store them. Perhaps, when we know how much space they will occupy, the carpenter

215

working in the east wing could make a strong box, with more than one lock.'

Sylvie sighed. 'I could trust Lady Carstairs, but we don't know all the servants, do we? It's frightening.'

'Just a sensible precaution. We none of us know how we might be tempted if given the opportunity. Yet,' he paused, 'Sir George's servants could not have known about the chest, or the hidden room. They have had the opportunity since he died, but by the dust on it the chest had not been disturbed. I think all your jewels are safe.'

'There are the documents, too.'

'Yes. We had best leave them here for the time being, until Mr Haines returns from London, or we would have to explain where we found them, and have everyone rushing up here to see.'

'Like eager children.' Sylvie laughed. 'We'd best go and dress for dinner. Sir Randal, I am so grateful to you for solving this mystery.'

She lovingly wrapped the necklace in the cloth, replaced it in the bag, and put it back in the chest. Then she stood up and took the key of the room from the inside of the door. Going out, Sir Randal by her side, she locked it behind them, and hesitated. Should she ask him to keep the key?

He forestalled her, putting his hand over

hers. 'No, you can only trust yourself. It's too big a key to wear round your neck, so find a secure place in your room to hide it.'

'When can we make a list? Later tonight, after dinner?'

'If we disappear together people will be suspicious. They know we have no more papers to read in the library. Can we get up early tomorrow morning? I will bring writing materials.'

'There is some in the room,' Sylvie reminded him. 'When you made him give me my twenty pounds. Twenty pounds! It seemed such a huge amount to me then, half my entire inheritance, yet that necklace must be worth many times that sum. Its value to me, though, is that my father created it for my mother.'

'Hush,' he said, and put his fingers to her lips.

Sylvie felt a frisson of delight course through her, and could not determine whether it was from his touch or the thought that her mother's jewellery had been found.

'Oh, my tongue will betray me!'

'Or your bright eyes! Do try not to look so cheerful, it will give us away.'

★ ★ ★

Several times during the rest of the evening Sylvie saw David glancing at her suspiciously. She tried to subdue her high spirits by thinking serious thoughts, but every few minutes the memory of the diamond necklace in her hands made her want to smile.

She had been too young to know much about jewellery, but she could remember the delight she'd had in watching the bright, sparkling necklaces and bracelets her mother had worn. Whenever they were going out in the evening, her mother had come to her bedroom to say goodnight, and Sylvie had touched and twisted the jewels, making the colours glitter in the candlelight. Occasionally she had been allowed to wear one of the bracelets for a time, and her father had made some small ones for her. They must have been semiprecious stones, she thought now. Suddenly she wondered where they were. In the misery of knowing her parents were dead she had not cared about finery. She could not recall ever seeing them afterwards. Perhaps whoever had been looking after her had decided they might be lost if sent to the seminary with her. Perhaps she would find them amongst the others in the chest.

Dinner was almost over when Sawyer brought a note for Sir Randal.

'My apologies, ma'am,' he said to Lady

Carstairs, 'but the messenger said it was important Sir Randal had it immediately.'

Randal scanned the note swiftly, and stood up. 'My apologies also, my lady. I'm afraid I must leave at once. I expect to be gone just the one night.'

He ignored the anxious questions — Lady Carstairs trusting it was not bad news about his family, Celia exclaiming what a pity he had to go — and gave Sylvie an apologetic shrug.

'I'll be back as soon as Mr Haines, I expect, and we can continue looking through your papers. He will undoubtedly have some more.'

She knew what he meant, and her spirits drooped. She could, however, make a start herself on cataloguing the jewels, and she would have the documents in the chest ready for him to read when he returned.

★ ★ ★

Randal drove to a village some miles west of Clayton Court at a fast pace. The message had reported that Dupont had been there for several days. Today he had hired a boat and put out to sea before Jones and Roberts, the two men watching him, could intervene. Jones had followed in a second boat, while

Roberts awaited Sir Randal at one of the inns.

He was inclined to blame them for negligence. Surely, if they had been keeping a close enough watch, they would have seen him talking to the fisherman or whoever he hired the boat from, and guessed his intention. They would have had sufficient cause to arrest and question him. It would have revealed their interest in him, and probably ended his usefulness to his masters, but better that than he escape them altogether and they have no chance of discovering what he knew.

A room at the inn had been booked for him, and he and Roberts retreated there with a flask of wine. 'Have you any further information?' Randal asked. 'What has the man being doing the past few days?'

'We didn't discover he was here until late yesterday. From what we've been told it all seemed quite innocent. He has been riding out into the countryside, always in a different direction, as though exploring it.'

'He'll have met innkeepers and waiters where he stopped for meals or a drink, and ostlers, presumably, if they tended his horse. Any of them might be in league with smugglers and able to pass on messages.'

'We can't discover exactly which inns he

stopped at,' Roberts said.

'Of course not. And it would probably be a waste of time trying. It just demonstrates what difficulties there are in keeping a close enough watch on the wretched man. We'll have to hope Jones can prevent him from boarding a French boat, if that is his plan.'

They waited for another hour, and then there was a knock on the door and Jones appeared.

'Well? Did you lose him?' Randal asked.

Jones shook his head. 'He hired this boat and set out, but when they were a few hundred yards offshore they just followed the coast. They went past the village by Clayton Court, and after a little time they just sailed on to Cromer. He went to an inn there and told the ostler he would be leaving very early in the morning. I can't imagine what he was doing. It seemed so pointless.'

Randal frowned. 'I don't think this man does anything without a reason. Were you seen?'

'They must have wondered what I was doing, following. When he turned back and we did the same it was obvious.'

'A pity, but it can't be helped. Roberts, he's probably going back to Norwich. I suggest you follow him, then, in the morning, and Jones can show me which boats were used.

221

They don't know me, so I can fall into conversation with them, and perhaps find out something. Many of the people who come here for the cure might enjoy a short pleasure cruise. I'll see you in Norwich in a few days, and then I think I will have to go back to London.'

★ ★ ★

Sylvie woke early, feeling restless. After tossing for a while she decided to get up and make a start on cataloguing her mother's jewels. No one else apart from the maids would be up yet. She could make sure they did not see her, lock herself in Sir George's room, and begin the task.

As she let herself in she could not prevent a shudder, recalling her visit to the old man and his unconcealed antagonism. Why had he left her his own fortune? Had he suffered some kind of remorse? It didn't make sense to her.

She locked the door after herself, and looked across the room at the chest, then the innocent-looking panel which concealed the hidden room. For a moment she was tempted to look inside, and perhaps venture a little way down the ladder, but she had no lantern today, and it would be stupid to try in the

222

dark. When Sir Randal came back she would insist they explored.

She opened the chest and decided to remove the papers first. Carefully she laid them all on the bed, glancing at some as she did so. There was no time to read them now, but those she looked at seemed to be letters or accounts, and the large sheets plans of the Clayton Court farms and estate. Nothing she saw seemed to be connected with Danesfield. When Sir Randal returned they could take these papers to the library and add them to the others. Perhaps some were from the incomplete sets of accounts they had already seen. Then she turned to the jewellery. She lifted out the bags and rolls and laid them on one of the tables which had been next to Sir George's chair. She placed paper and pen and inkwell on the other table, and set about her task.

She had thought, earlier, that she could not recall particular items of her mother's collection, just remembering the general glitter that always seemed to surround her mother when she was dressed in her finery to go out, or receive guests. As she unrolled the wrappings, though, she found she did know many of the more distinctive pieces. Here was the emerald necklace Lady Carstairs had mentioned, dozens of tiny stones set in patterns of leaves. Next she found the heavy rope of pearls which, her father had told her, came from a far-distant land, she thought India.

She had filled three sheets of paper with brief descriptions of the jewels when she came across two of the small bracelets her father had made for her. One was of coral, the pieces encased in delicate cages of gold filigree. The other contained almost every jewel colour imaginable, and Sylvie was sure some of the stones were precious ones, rubies and emeralds, diamonds and sapphires, tiny pearls and opals and amethysts. In between were others she could not name, but which she thought were less precious. The whole gleamed and sparkled, and Sylvie could recall wearing it and twisting it all ways to enjoy the reflection in the candlelight. It was too small now for her to wear, but she vowed that if she ever had a daughter she would give her this treasure.

Blinking back tears she finished the task, then gathered the jewels together and looked for a safe place to store them for the time being. They could carry the chest to the library with all the documents, and explain where they had been found, but for now the jewels had to be hidden elsewhere.

In the end she mastered her repugnance at

touching Sir George's clothing, and laid the jewels out in a drawer where he kept his cravats. She was intrigued to see he had several dozen, and they all seemed to be freshly laundered and starched. She hadn't noticed his dress when she visited, and somehow the thought of a recluse being so particular in his attire made her feel sorry for him. She removed all but a few of the cravats, to make room for the jewels, put back some to fill the drawer, and stuffed the rest of them in the cupboard where the shoes were kept.

Listening carefully, she let herself out of the room, relocked the door, and reached her own bedroom just before the maid came with her morning chocolate.

'What a lovely morning,' she said cheerfully. 'I woke early and decided to go for a walk.'

Which was not a lie, she thought. She had walked to another room. If the maid chose to think she meant she'd gone outside, so be it. As she drank her chocolate slowly, she wondered when Sir Randal would return.

11

At breakfast David was full of suggestions about what Sylvie ought to do in the village. 'The inn could attract visitors staying at Cromer who wish to drive out into the country,' he said. 'After all, taking the sea bathing cure cannot occupy much of their time, and what else is there to do in this flat, boring countryside. But the inn serves very limited fare.'

'I imagine it serves what its customers want,' Sylvie said with a barely concealed sigh. She was becoming thoroughly irritated by David's constant criticism and suggestions for what he considered improvements to the estate.

He was oblivious. 'Besides, it has almost no wine, though there is plenty of ale and brandy — the latter no doubt smuggled. You need to stop that, Sylvie.'

'You can't prove the brandy is smuggled.'

'Perhaps not, but most of the brandy in coastal areas, and beyond, is known to have paid no duty.'

'Well, I really don't see what you think I can do about it! Should I patrol the coast all night and try to catch the men on my own?'

'There is no call to be sarcastic when I am trying to help you. Inform the authorities, and they can watch.'

'So I inform, without proof, on one of my great-uncle's people, get him arrested and have no one to run the inn so that my rents fall, no doubt alienate the entire village as well, probably, as all the local gentry. Thank you, David, for that suggestion.'

'Sylvie, dear, David is just trying to help you,' Lady Carstairs intervened. 'He is a man, and older than you.'

'Being a man does not make him more intelligent. I am grateful for the reports on the farms, but it is my responsibility to decide what to do.'

'You own the place, it's up to you to improve it,' David went on. 'You also own several cottages in the village, and from what I saw the tenants are a surly lot. Their rents are probably too low, and because your uncle was ill for so long they no doubt think they can get away with all sorts of things.'

At this Sylvie lost her temper. 'I am not interfering in the innkeeping business, something I know nothing about, and neither, I may point out, David, do you! And if I know Sir George the rents are probably far too high. As to the tenants being surly, I don't

227

blame them, when an impertinent Londoner who has nothing to do with the estate comes along and starts interrogating them about their own affairs!'

Lady Carstairs began to protest, but Sylvie cut in. She stood up and with immense care folded her napkin and laid it beside her plate.

'I apologize to you for this, Lady Carstairs, and if you think I have been rude, I am sorry. But I will not brook any more interference. David, you are welcome to remain here, so long as you understand that I want no more suggestions which sound, I must say, more like orders.'

She swept out of the room, and found she was trembling with fury. She shut herself in the library but could not concentrate on anything. An hour later Lady Carstairs entered, and Sylvie gave her an apologetic smile.

'I'm sorry, I shouldn't have lost my temper.'

'You are somewhat overwhelmed with all your new responsibilities, my dear. I understand, but I'm afraid David has taken offence. He and Aubrey have left. They are going to Cambridge to visit some friends.'

'I'm sorry!'

Part of her was glad, thankful to be rid of David's irritating presence, but she was sorry to have hurt Lady Carstairs, who had been so good to her. Sylvie tried to express her thanks, but Lady Carstairs shook her head and persisted in believing Sylvie was just unable to cope with all the changes that had happened to her. By the time she took herself off, saying she needed to tell Cook there would be two fewer for meals, Sylvie felt like screaming.

Then she thought of Celia, deprived of Aubrey's company, and felt the first genuine remorse for her outburst.

Where was Sir Randal? He seemed the only sane, strong person about her, and she would be so thankful when he returned.

★　★　★

The rest of the day passed with the three ladies, for the most part, keeping cautiously apart. When they met at meals they were carefully polite, choosing innocuous topics of conversation, Celia kept out of Sylvie's way, and by the time they went to bed Sylvie was seething with frustration.

She was angry with herself that her loss of temper had driven Aubrey away from her friend. During the day she had tried to suggest to Lady Carstairs that as her affairs seemed to be almost settled, she could take Celia to Brighton as they had originally planned, but Lady Carstairs had rejected the notion, and Sylvie felt she had only made matters worse when the older lady had accused her of not wanting her. It had taken time and patience to reassure her, and many protestations of gratitude for her hospitality during the Season, but Sylvie knew they would never again be on the same easy terms.

When Mr Haines appeared just after breakfast the following day, Sylvie greeted him with relief, something she had never expected to feel in his presence. It gave her an excuse to retire to the library to talk about what he had been doing in London.

She wondered whether to tell him of the discovery of the chestful of documents, but decided that could wait until Sir Randal returned. To her immense relief he arrived just before they were about to break for a nuncheon, and the presence of the two men made the meal relatively normal. Neither of them asked where David and Aubrey were, probably assuming they were riding out and had taken some food with them. Sir Randal explained he had been delayed on some private business, and Sylvie immediately felt guilty again, this time for keeping him away from his own home.

He managed to speak to her quietly as they left the table. 'Have you told Haines?'

'Nothing. I wanted you to be here.'

'Can you go and fetch the documents to the library? We'll just say we found a hidden cupboard.'

'I can't carry the chest.'

'No, but we don't want to have to explain to Haines where we discovered that, I think.'

Sylvie collected one of the old sheets they had been repairing, let herself into Sir George's room, made sure the door was locked behind her, and piled the documents into the sheet. It made a bulky, awkward bundle, but she managed to carry it down to the library without anyone seeing her. Lady Carstairs and Celia had been persuaded to go out for a drive, and the maids, apart from the one who had been deputed to sit in the library as chaperon, were all in the servants' hall eating their own meal.

Sir Randal had prepared the way. The men had cleared space on the big table, and Sylvie deposited the bundle on it.

'First, though, Mr Haines, please tell me about your visit to London. Are there problems?'

Mr Haines smiled at her. 'No, indeed. Sir George has a substantial amount in his bank account, much more invested in the funds, and it will be transferred to you in due course. Things are improving. And when we have investigated these new documents Sir Randal tells me you have discovered, I hope everything will be clear.'

They started again, first separating the papers into piles. This time it was easier, as Sir George seemed to have kept them in some kind of order. By dinner time they were ready to read them through and put them together with the ones they had already read. Sylvie invited Mr Haines to stay for the meal, knowing his presence would help to lighten the atmosphere. She told Sir Randal that David and Aubrey had gone to Cambridge, and though he gave her a searching look she did not elaborate.

Afterwards, when Mr Haines had departed, Sir Randal challenged Sylvie to a game of chess, and under cover of this she told him she had temporarily hidden the jewels.

'They take up one drawer, not too big,' she murmured.

'Good, then you can order a box to be made. First, though, I want to explore that passage. Are the lanterns still there?'

'No, I took them back to the kitchen in case they were missed. I can get them again, but not until tomorrow.'

'Then we can give Mr Haines the slip and explore tomorrow afternoon. Do you wish to come with me?'

'Of course I do! It's my house,' Sylvie said. At last she was going to satisfy her curiosity.

★ ★ ★

Randal wondered what they would find there. He had spent much of the previous day talking to fishermen and boatmen who plied for hire along the coast. The one who had taken Dupont had been willing to talk when he'd been softened with ale and a coin was slipped into his hand.

'Odd sort o' fellow,' he said. 'Kept asking where the best landing places were. He were dead keen on finding one near Clayton Court. That a big 'ouse along the coast, one old man livin' there on 'is own. Dead now, I hear. Well, that'll make things easier fer some.'

He'd refused to say more, realizing he had been indiscreet, but the hint was enough for Randal. Dupont probably had connections with smugglers. Smugglers needed safe places to store their contraband. One such place could well be Clayton Court, isolated, near the coast, and occupied by a reclusive old man who may or may not have known about the use to which his land or buildings were put.

The more he thought about it, the more likely it was that the secret passage held some clue. Sylvie had not been at Clayton Court before, so she could not be involved. Besides, she was too eager to explore the passage, and she had not known it was there. He had, without thinking much more about it, decided she was not in league with Dupont, and their meetings had been pure chance. That he was using people near where her great-uncle lived must be coincidence. No one could have known Sir George would die and leave Sylvie the house.

He forced himself to concentrate on the documents the following morning, and found there all Sir George's more recent dealings. There were rent books, farm accounts, letters to and from his bank, maps and deeds of Clayton Court and the properties he owned in the area, including many of the village houses, but there was nothing that mentioned or pertained to Danesfield.

'I suppose I will have to go there,' Mr Haines said. 'Really, I can't do it for at least ten days. I have other clients and they are demanding my attention.'

'I'll go,' Sylvie said, 'but how can we be sure they are at home? Should we write first?'

'There is no need for you to make the journey, Miss Delamare. I will send a letter asking them to make an appointment to see me, either in London or at Danesfield. Then we can ascertain the true facts.'

'Which is probably that the house was sold,' Sylvie said with a sigh. 'Was there enough money in Sir George's bank account to indicate it had been sold?'

Mr Haines shook his head. 'Not if what I think the value of the property will be, from what you have told me. Nor would it cover the sale of the London house.'

'Then it is still a mystery, and perhaps I will never know the truth. If the Tempests did buy it, would I be able to buy it back, when this house is sold? I would so much prefer to live there than here.'

'I will enquire. I'm afraid I must set off for London this afternoon, but at least matters are much clearer now than they were before you discovered these new papers.'

★ ★ ★

Lady Carstairs, once more her normal cheerful self, assumed that Sylvie and Sir Randal were continuing their perusal of the documents in the library, so they were able to slip away and meet in Sir George's room. Sylvie had changed into one of the old dresses she had worn at the seminary.

235

'Don't mock me!' she said, as she saw his surprise at her unfashionable gown. 'I'm not wearing a good dress to go crawling through cobwebs.'

'The mob cap should take care of most of them,' he replied, and she saw his lips twitch.

He was wearing only breeches and a shirt, open at the neck, and Sylvie swallowed hard. He looked even more handsome now, with muscles rippling under the fine fabric of his shirt. She forced her gaze away from him and turned to the business they were here for.

She opened the secret panel and Sir Randal propped it open, making absolutely sure it could not close behind them. He lit the lanterns, and in their light they could see the ladder, consisting of metal rungs fixed into the brick of the wall, descending down what felt like a wide chimney.

'I'll go first, to test the rungs,' Sir Randal said. He slung one lantern on his belt, and with a length of rope fashioned a belt for Sylvie to which her lantern could be attached.

As he slipped this rope round her waist Sylvie was breathlessly aware of his nearness, the male scent of him, a spicy waft of sandalwood, and concentrated on not allowing her trembling to show. Why on earth was she permitting herself to become attracted to this man who seemed so averse to marriage?

When, satisfied the lantern was firmly fixed, he moved away, she took a deep breath. To control her own emotions she must keep her distance.

He swung himself over the drop, and Sylvie kilted up her gown to give herself greater freedom of movement. She wished she had been able to acquire breeches, but she would manage somehow. She wanted to see where this passage led. When Sir Randal gave the word she followed him, feeling carefully for each rung and hanging grimly on to the one above her.

She counted thirty-five rungs, all of them about the height of the main staircase steps, which took them well below the ground floor. As she reached the bottom Sir Randal's hand guided her, and he held up his lantern to illuminate the narrow passage in which they stood.

It stretched away into the distance, dark and mysterious.

'This points towards the back of the house,' Sir Randal said. 'Sir George's room was in the south west corner, so this goes beneath the west wing. If it were once a priest's hole I would expect it to have an exit somewhere away from the house, either into some buildings or the open.'

'The stable yard is behind the west wing. It

must exit there. The ground in between is too open, just a drying ground, and any sort of doorway or opening would be too visible.'

'Unless the passage turns, but that would bring it out either into the open park or the kitchen courtyard. Well, we shall soon see. Are you happy to go on? At least it is dry and there is some fresh air entering from somewhere, the atmosphere is not as foul as it might have been.'

He moved forward, holding his lantern high in one hand, and grasping Sylvie's hand with the other. She had unfastened her own lantern and held it so that they could see all around them. The passageway was narrow, but was high enough for them to walk upright. The walls were of brick, roughly laid but solid. Stout wooden beams supported the roof, above which they assumed were the rooms of the west wing.

'We'd best not speak too loudly,' Sir Randal said, bending close to Sylvie's ear so that his breath touched her cheek. 'We're under the rooms that are most used, and if there are airholes inside their chimneys, perhaps, our voices might be heard.'

They walked on cautiously. The floor was rough hewn, but easy enough to walk on. It seemed like miles to Sylvie, but she told herself they were walking slowly, and it was unlikely they would emerge on the seashore.

At last they came to a flight of steps, ending in a wooden trapdoor.

'The stables, I expect,' Sir Randal said, and set down his lamp on the highest step. He pushed the trapdoor, but it did not move. He set his shoulder to it, but could only lift it a fraction. When Sylvie added her weight they still could not move it.

'We'll have to search for it from the other side,' Sylvie said. 'Can it be bolted, or is it just something heavy piled on top?'

'We'll find out.' He bent to examine the floor at the foot of the steps more closely. 'Look, Sylvie, there are what look like rings here in the dust.'

She bent down to look. 'Barrels? They are the right size. So this is probably used by smugglers to store their haul, until it is safe to carry it away.'

'In Sussex there are large gangs, and they use pack ponies, taking the entire consignment away at once. It would not be so easy to do that here. They probably use one or two horses and take a few barrels at a time. Which indicates, I think, that the people who use it are fairly local.'

'David said the inn in the village had plenty of brandy.'

'The innkeeper is almost certainly involved,

if only by purchasing brandy, but I suspect someone else is the organizer. One of the landowners, perhaps.'

'Could it have been Sir George?'

'It's possible. It's odd there are no barrels here now. If there had been any, the rest of the gang would probably have moved them as soon as he died.'

'He was far too ill to climb down that ladder.'

'He might have visited the stables. We can ask. But he would not need to be personally involved, so long as he received his money, and that could have been passed over openly. We should ask what visitors he received regularly. That old man, the one who let us in when we called, is he still here?'

'Stott? Yes, he grumbled when Sawyer took over as butler, but when he saw how much there was to do with all of us here he became content to sit in the kitchen sharpening knives, washing the glasses and polishing the silver.'

'Then, if you permit, I will talk to him.'

'I'd be glad if you did. He won't talk to me. I think he blames me for Sir George's death, muttering about upsetting him and giving him shocks.'

'Do you blame yourself?'

'I did, a little, at first. But as it's impossible

to know I tell myself it's stupid to worry.'

'Good girl. If anyone were to blame it would be me, for I bullied him.'

'On my behalf!'

'And in the interests of justice. Come, we ought to go back. Let's count our steps so we have some notion of where to begin searching in the stables.'

★ ★ ★

They reached Sir George's room and closed the panel. Sylvie looked down at her dress, which had dust on the hem but was otherwise still looking respectable. She tore off the mob cap and shook out her hair. Sir Randal's hair had a cobweb decorating it, and she let out a peal of laughter.

'You need to make yourself tidy before facing the others.'

She peered into a mirror at her own face while he went across to the dressing-table on which Sir George's hair brushes still rested, and brushed his hair. Sylvie pulled out a couple of the cravats she'd stowed in the boot cupboard and handed him one.

'A pity there is no water, but these will get rid of the dust on our hands. It's taken longer than I expected. I'll go and wash and change, but first let me show you the jewels. What sort of box do you think I need to have made?'

They were looking at the bags containing the jewellery when there was a knock on the door. Sylvie froze and looked in panic at Sir Randal. Whoever it was rattled the handle, but then, after another pause, footsteps could be heard going along the corridor outside.

'Gently. Let's put these away first,' Sir Randal said quietly. 'The size you suggest would be right. Tomorrow you can ask the carpenter to make it.'

Ten minutes later Sylvie quietly unlocked the door and opened it. As she looked to see if the corridor was empty the door was pushed back and she almost fell, saved only by Sir Randal catching her round the waist.

David Carstairs stood glaring at them. Aubrey, looking embarrassed, stood a little behind him.

'So,' David said, and Sylvie recognized the gloating in his voice, 'we catch you, do we? Not only is your reputation in tatters, Miss Delamare, you dare to carry on your intrigues when you are living under my mother's protection. We'll see what she has to say about this.'

12

They were all in the morning-room. Sylvie was still in her old gown. Sir Randal had picked up the coat he had discarded on the back of Sir George's chair, and slipped it on while David stood watching, a complacent expression on his face. Then, taking Sylvie's arm and giving it a comforting squeeze, he had walked calmly past David and Aubrey and led the way to where Lady Carstairs and Celia were engaged in mending the household linen.

Lady Carstairs had looked up in astonishment as they entered.

'My dear, have you been doing some housework? Why are you wearing that dreadful old dress? And Sir Randal!'

Words clearly failed her when confronted by a gentleman in a state of undress.

He suppressed a grin. 'I apologize for appearing in front of you in such a manner, my lady, but your son somewhat imperiously required our presence without delay. We had no time to wash and change. We have been exploring the secret passage. That is where we found the new documents, in a chest which

Sir David did not spare the time to look at when he interrupted us.'

'Oh, so there is a passage,' Celia said in excitement. 'Can we all go and explore it?'

David was less impressed. 'Secret passage! Pah! That does not excuse your being alone with Sylvie, and in a bedroom too. How she can desecrate her great-uncle's memory by putting his bedroom to infamous uses I don't know.'

Randal began to speak, but Sylvie, pale with rage, spoke first. 'David Carstairs, your mind is filthier than a midden! You'll apologize immediately to Sir Randal, or leave my house at once. I don't know why you have come back anyway when you are not welcome here.'

'I've been in Cambridge,' he replied, still looking maddeningly superior. 'The story of your tryst at the Black Bear is all over the town. In London, too, they tell me, though for shame that you are associated with my family I did not go there to test the truth of it.'

'Gossip! You demean yourself by listening to it,' Sylvie said.

David shook his head. 'You and Sir Randal are the ones who are demeaned, and you have compounded your fault by carrying on the intrigue here where my mother is meant to be your guardian.'

'There is no intrigue,' Sylvie said. 'Please leave.'

'Not so fast. It is now common knowledge your reputation has been ruined. You will be ostracized by everyone.'

'As if I care for what gossip-mongers think! I know we have done nothing wrong.'

'You may not care, but your actions reflect on my family, particularly on my mother. They will also affect Celia, possibly ruining her chances of a good marriage since most people will associate her with you and believe she is tarred with the same brush.'

'Oh, David, no!' Lady Carstairs said. 'Surely you don't hold it against Celia that Sylvie has been a little imprudent?'

Sir Randal, standing leaning against the window, decided to let them fight it out. Was Lady Carstairs afraid her plan to marry off her son to Celia would collapse? If the pompous young ass behaved like this in his early twenties he would be intolerable in a few years. Celia would be well out of it if the match did fall through.

'Sylvie is ruined, and largely by the actions of this rake! She is young and heedless, but must bear some of the responsibility. She has been taught what is acceptable behaviour by ladies of breeding, but she has chosen to ignore it. I demand, Mama, that you and

245

Celia pack immediately and return to London with me. If you go on to Brighton, or preferably somewhere quieter, the scandal will have died down by next Season.'

'Oh, dear, David, I ought not to leave Sylvie alone here. Matters are not fully sorted out, and she cannot leave just yet.'

'I am not suggesting she comes with you. What she does is her choice, but the only way to save her reputation is for Sir Randal to put right his culpable behaviour and marry her.'

Randal had been expecting this, and fighting off the panic sweeping over him. He was not ready to marry. He knew there had been no wrongdoing, at the Black Bear, or just now in that accursed bedroom, but he knew his world. People would not believe them. He would soon be forgiven. Men were. Sylvie, however, would have to bear the brunt of Society's disapproval, and her chances of a respectable marriage were virtually nil.

He smiled somewhat grimly towards Lady Carstairs, who was looking bewildered. 'Ma'am, I accept Society will misconstrue events, and that cannot be helped. I am willing to do what I must, but I beg the indulgence of being able to propose to Sylvie in private.'

'No! There is no need,' Sylvie said, her voice faint.

He turned to her. 'Of course there is, but we won't discuss it here. Come, let us find a place where the atmosphere is free of venom and malice.'

★ ★ ★

Sylvie was scarcely aware of being led along the corridor to the library. The maid, having no one to chaperone, had gone, and Sir Randal locked the door before guiding Sylvie to one of the deep window seats. He poured a glass of brandy from the decanter placed there by a solicitous Sawyer, who firmly believed that reading dry old documents was a task which called for plenty of stimulation.

'Drink this,' he said, and Sylvie gratefully began to sip at the fiery liquid.

'I expect this is smuggled,' she said, and began to laugh. 'David is an unmitigated pest! He's interfering with the estate, the village, and now trying to dictate whom I marry. Well, I won't have him in the house a moment longer, and if he won't go I'll bring in the gardeners and have them throw him out. I can hardly expect Sawyer to do it, as he is his own butler.'

'Sylvie, don't get hysterical.'

She looked at him in amazement. 'Hysterical? Oh, I thought you were different from most men, who accuse us of hysteria when we offend them.'

'Very well, I won't. We need to talk seriously, my dear. God knows, this is not how I would like to propose to my future wife, virtually with a gun pointed at my head, but however firmly we know we have done nothing wrong, the world, especially aided by David Carstairs, will view it very differently.'

'I don't care what they say, and you will scarcely be damaged by the gossip of a silly boy.'

'But I care for your reputation. Sylvie, don't you see, there is nothing else for it, we have to marry to silence lying tongues.'

She stared up at him, and her heart lurched. She was attracted, she was beginning to think she loved him, but he clearly felt nothing for her. This was not the proposal of a man in love. It was grudging, impossible to accept. If she did marry him, and later he found he loved someone else, it would be a disaster.

She shook her head. 'I honour you for asking me,' she said, forcing herself to speak calmly. 'You don't love me; you would never have thought of asking me if that wretched David had not lain in wait outside the bedroom. I cannot accept.'

He pushed his hands through his hair and

came to stand in front of her. 'Sylvie, you must. Just imagine what David will do if we don't. I don't care what he says about me. It's true, men are forgiven more easily than women, and the *ton* will soon forget. It's even possible my standing amongst certain people will be enhanced, if I am portrayed as a rakish seducer who got away with it. They won't forgive you, though. You are a woman, an unmarried girl whose reputation has to be spotless before any respectable man could even think of offering for you. For another thing, you are not well known as I am. Your family will have been forgotten, but it will soon be held against you that your mother married against the wishes of her family. They will say blood tells.'

Sylvie held her hands over her ears. 'Stop it! I don't want to marry just because that worm tells me I have to! Besides, you clearly don't love me, and I won't marry someone who offers out of a foolish sense of duty.'

'Then how will you withstand the disapproval of the *ton*?'

'I tell you, I don't care a toss about the *ton*! I don't need to mix with people who put so much store on gossip. I can live here, or at Danesfield, quite contentedly on my own.' She gestured at the books all around them. 'See how much reading there is for me to do.

It will take years. And though we have been cleaning the house, there is far more to do. I might occupy myself embroidering several dozen chair seats and a few fire screens. If I can get Danesfield back, that might also be in sad disrepair, giving me years of occupation.'

He stepped closer and took her hands in his, pulling her to her feet.

'Sylvie, don't be ridiculous. Of course I didn't want to make an offer like this, and I understand you are upset, even, perhaps, insulted. We need not marry until you are ready, and we can get to know one another better during that time. But we must be betrothed.'

She shook her head, trying to pull away, but he clasped her hands more firmly and, as she began to speak, lowered his lips and captured hers.

Sylvie went rigid with astonishment. No one had kissed her on the lips since she was a child. His lips, instead of being hard as she'd imagined, were soft, but far from gentle. She felt them exploring hers, and the strangest sensations coursed through her body. She wanted to pull him closer, and if he hadn't been holding her hands in his she would have flung her arms round his neck. His kiss deepened, and Sylvie felt as though she would swoon. Then, abruptly, he released her and she collapsed back on to the window seat.

'Sylvie, we can have a successful marriage. I must wed one day, and you must wed me. Please forget how it has come about, and accept me.'

She was dreadfully tempted. She could, perhaps, make him love her. But he had offered only because he felt he must. She shook her head, her eyes lowered so that she did not have to look at him.

'No, I cannot. Please go. Leave me alone.'

★　★　★

Sylvie watched Sir Randal drive away, his valet sitting stiffly beside him in the curricle, and the tiger standing behind. Miserably she wondered if she would ever see him again. She was aware that what David had said was true: her reputation was ruined. She could not even blame David, for he had not spread the story of their stay at the Black Bear. How naïve she had been to think no one would ever discover it. Somehow scandal always found an audience.

She did not wish to meet anyone, and was tempted to order dinner in her room, though she wondered if she would be able to swallow anything, but eventually pride helped her.

251

She would not allow David to triumph. This was her house — she wanted David out of it, and would make sure he went before dinnertime. He could do his worst. If Lady Carstairs deserted her, then so be it. She was grateful for all that lady's kindnesses, but pandering to David's malice just because she liked his mother was more than she could endure.

Why had he taken her in such dislike? She thought back over the time since they'd met. At first he had been welcoming to her as a friend of Celia's, but their first argument had been at the ball, after he had discovered she and Sir Randal had stayed at the Black Bear together. Was it really because he disapproved of her just for that which made him so antagonistic? It didn't seem reasonable. It was clear he'd been thoroughly pandered to all his life, so perhaps the mere fact that someone disagreed with him offended his dignity. Lady Carstairs said he managed their estates, with the help of an agent, but an employee would take care not to dispute with him. He had come to Norfolk and started to behave in the same overbearing way, thinking he could manage her estate too. When she had objected, he had taken offence, but it really was incredibly childish of him to react so badly.

She took a deep breath and left the library, feeling as though she was leaving a safe refuge and entering a battlefield. She found Lady Carstairs alone in the drawing-room.

'Well, Sylvie dear, is it settled? I see Sir Randal has left. Is he going to inform his mother, or perhaps prepare his home for you?'

'We are not going to marry.'

'Not? But my dear, you must! David is quite right, you will be ruined otherwise.'

'I am not prepared to marry any man who feels compelled to offer for me. He doesn't love me — '

Lady Carstairs was aghast. 'What has that to do with it? He's ruined you! How many men and girls love one another when they marry? It's a foolish, romantic notion. Marriages are business arrangements, and if a couple can live together in harmony, that is enough.'

'Was it enough for you? I had the impression you loved your husband, otherwise, why not marry again to provide David with a father?'

With a father, she thought, David might not have been such a bombastic creature, with an inflated sense of his own importance.

'I deeply respected David's father,' Lady Carstairs said with dignity. 'I had no need to marry again for financial security, and nothing else in the married state appealed to me.'

For a fleeting moment Sylvie recalled Sir Randal's kiss, and the implied promise of further delights. Were they not as delightful as she'd imagined she'd glimpsed? Various comments she had heard, whispered confidences between young married women she had met during the Season, had alerted her to the notion that married intimacies were not necessarily welcomed by every woman. She could hardly pursue the topic with Lady Carstairs.

'I accept the world will think I am ruined. If you wish to leave, and disassociate yourself from me, I shall be sorry, but I will understand. I'm afraid I shall have to ask Sir David to leave in any case. He has been deeply offensive, and I cannot any longer entertain him in my house.'

To Sylvie's horror Lady Carstairs began to cry, deep racking sobs which shook her slight frame. 'I can't help feeling this is all my fault,' she gasped. 'I should have been firmer with you, not permitted you to visit Sir George on your own, sent a maid with you. Then you would never have been trapped into that wretched man's power. Oh, Sylvie, do forgive me!'

'There is nothing to forgive,' Sylvie said, feeling helpless. 'Sir Randal was very helpful, and without him I'm sure I'd never have been able to see my great-uncle. Nor would I have found those documents.'

She was about to add that neither would she have recovered her mother's jewels, but a belated sense of caution restrained her. No one else must know. Lady Carstairs would not be able to resist telling David and Celia, and somehow the secret would be revealed. Until she had the box made and the jewels safely locked away no one else must know.

Lady Carstairs was still sobbing into a minuscule handkerchief. 'Please, Sylvie, can't you forgive David? He was only doing what he considered his duty. Celia is your friend, and would be so upset if he were made to leave her.'

Sylvie marvelled. How could someone be so blind to what was going on around her? Celia had never shown a preference for David, and she and Aubrey had become so close Sylvie had expected the young man to make a declaration at any moment. How would David's mother take that?

She knew she was beaten, at least for the moment. Somehow she would get rid of David, but for his mother's comfort she had to allow him to stay.

'Very well, I will not insist David leaves at once. Please can you make him understand, though, that I will brook no further interference in my affairs. Now I must go and change.'

She escaped, but before going to her room she went to find the carpenter who was working in the east wing. She told him what she wanted, gave him the measurements for the box, asked him to fix two strong locks, and said she wanted him to stop all other work until this was completed. He seemed a sensible man, and promised he would find some hard wood that could not easily be broached. Satisfied that she would soon be able to make her mother's jewels more secure, she went to her room and rang for hot water so that she could soak in a bath and wash away all the emotions she had undergone in the past few hours.

★ ★ ★

Dinner was a difficult meal. Lady Carstairs, recovered from her weeping, was smiling happily. Celia was nervous, casting anxious glances at David and Sylvie. Aubrey said little, concentrating on his food. David was ostentatiously silent, and Sylvie worried, suddenly recalling that in the shock of being discovered by David in Sir George's room, she had not locked the door.

As soon as the meal was finished, Sylvie excused herself and ran up the stairs and along the corridor to Sir George's room. The door was shut, but the key was still on the inside. Locking herself in, she went straight to the drawer where she had hidden the jewels. Breathing a sigh of relief, she saw they had not been disturbed. This time, she made sure the door was locked and the key safely stowed in her own room, beneath her own shifts.

She sat down on her bed. Without Sir Randal she felt aimless. She now had money, Clayton Court and her mother's jewels. She did not appear to have Danesfield, and she supposed she must wait for Mr Haines to discover what the situation there was. There was the mystery of the secret passage, and what it was used for, whether smugglers used it and whether her great-uncle had been involved. Perhaps she could focus on that, and in so doing try to forget she could have accepted Sir Randal's proposal.

No, she could not, she told herself. He didn't love her, and would soon have resented her if she had accepted his offer.

She ought to go down to the drawing-room and rejoin the others. David for one would probably accuse her of sulking if she remained in her room. Well, let him. She had

had quite enough of listening to David's opinions. From now on she would do precisely what she liked, and if he did not like it, that was his problem.

On the following day she could search the stables for the exit from the secret passage. Perhaps she could discover clues about how recently it had been used. And it was time she visited her tenants. If, as she suspected, David had made enemies of them, she needed to try and repair the damage. If she could not recover Danesfield, she would have to live here, and she had no wish to be at odds with her people. She would visit the villagers too, and the inn, and try to judge whether the innkeeper was indeed in league with smugglers.

Planning the next few days, she managed to drive to the back of her mind Sir Randal's very unsatisfactory offer. Without going back downstairs she made ready for bed. She would endure David's presence, but would speak to him as little as possible. She would refrain from quarrelling with him. On that resolve she fell asleep.

★ ★ ★

Celia and Aubrey were the only ones in the breakfast-room when Sylvie went downstairs the following day. They were looking somewhat abashed, and Sylvie immediately asked what was the matter.

'Nothing,' Celia replied, but Aubrey shook his head at her.

'Will you congratulate me, Sylvie? Celia has done me the honour of accepting my offer. We hope to be married soon.'

'Oh, Celia, I'm so pleased for you! You too, Aubrey.'

As she kissed her friend and shook hands with Aubrey, Sylvie was wondering what Lady Carstairs would say. She obviously still nurtured hopes Celia and David would make a match of it, and would be very disappointed.

Sir Randal, she considered, would probably be furious. From remarks he had passed on several occasions, both about Aubrey and other young men, he clearly thought Aubrey was too young and volatile to be married, but he could not prevent the match.

'Will you be married in London? I expect Lady Carstairs will want to organize the wedding.'

Celia shook her head. 'I'd like her to help me, but we want to be married at Aubrey's home. Sylvie, you will be my bridesmaid, won't you? I'll ask Aubrey's sister too. You are my best friends.'

'And I'll ask Randal to support me,' Aubrey said, with a distinct air of bravado. 'He can't forbid the match. Afterwards, I'm taking Celia on a long voyage, we'll visit her parents in India. By the time we come back I'll be five and twenty, or near enough, and in control of my own fortune.'

'Have you told Lady Carstairs,' Sylvie asked.

'No. It only happened late last night,' Celia explained. 'You vanished, and we assumed you'd gone to bed. David went out, down to the village, we think. Normally he'd expect Aubrey to go with him, but I think he wanted to be alone. He was rather upset when you refused Sir Randal's offer. Lady Carstairs went to bed early too, and she thought I had, but when Aubrey asked me to wait downstairs a while I did. Then he asked me.'

'So David doesn't know either?'

'What don't I know?'

It was David, looking as though he was suffering a severe hangover, and less tidily dressed than usual, entering the room.

'Celia and I are to be married,' Aubrey said. 'You'll wish me happy?'

'That is the wrong marriage we ought to be celebrating today,' David said, glaring at Sylvie. He clearly had no intention of forgiving her. 'I suppose you know what you want. If you are sickeningly in love, as Sylvie appears to demand from any prospective husband, then of course I wish you well. Does Mama know?'

'Not yet. She is having breakfast in bed this morning. I think yesterday's upsets were rather tiring for her,' Celia said, and Sylvie silently applauded the firm tone in Celia's voice, indicating she would not tolerate his bad humours.

David shrugged. 'Sylvie, I've been thinking. We ought to make certain this secret passage is blocked. If it has been used by smugglers, we do not want them to have an open entrance into the house.'

Sylvie marvelled. Here he was, after all the upset he had caused, and the arguments she had had with him, trying to order her about again.

'Oh, can we see it?' Celia demanded. 'I've always wanted to explore a secret passage, they sound so exciting.'

'In the first place, David, there is no way to open the panel from the passage. Sir Randal and I went to the far end, and the exit there was blocked, too.' She did not tell him she meant to search for it. If she did, he would insist on taking charge of any search, and she had had enough of arguments with him. She thought rapidly. The jewels were safely hidden. She could show them the opening into the passage. Perhaps that would satisfy Celia's curiosity. She could not imagine her wanting to descend into the depths down that difficult ladder. And perhaps if David and Aubrey knew there was nothing but an empty passage they would not be interested enough to explore.

In the latter expectation she was disappointed. While Celia shuddered at the dark hole revealed, both men reverted to young boys and insisted on going down the ladder. David was about to go to the kitchens to demand lanterns when Sylvie stopped him.

'None of the servants know about it,' she warned. 'It must be kept secret.'

'Yes, I quite see that; you don't need to tell me. But someone must know about the exit if smugglers have been using it.'

'Yes, but they cannot get into the house. If the servants suspect where this entrance is, who knows whether any of them would admit outsiders? I don't know Sir George's servants, which of them can be trusted, and they have no reason to show any loyalty to me.'

Reluctantly David admitted the sense of this, and Sylvie promised to acquire a couple of lamps later in the day. 'You can go down late this afternoon,' she promised.

They had to be content, and Sylvie, abandoning her plan to search the stables until their interest had waned, had the horse she had bought harnessed to a small trap and set out to visit her farmer tenants.

★ ★ ★

For the first few miles as he drove away Randal cursed himself and David Carstairs in equal proportions. David had precipitated the whole affair by his accusations and innuendos, but he had made a mull of his proposal. There was little he could do about it now, but he was well aware he had left Sylvie in a most unenviable position. She might insist she did not care about the *ton's* opinion, but she would find her life very circumscribed if she had to spend all her time in the country.

She did not like Clayton Court, even though it was a charming house. This was entirely due to the unpleasant behaviour of her great-uncle when she had called on him, and he quite understood her aversion to the place. She would be much more content at her old home, and he wondered anew what had happened to Danesfield.

An idea struck him. He could never retrieve the situation his clumsy proposal had created, but perhaps he could still help Sylvie.

He would call at Danesfield and see the Tempests if they were in residence. At least he could discover what the situation was, and let Mr Haines know. Then he must concentrate on Dupont. If the man were passing information to France, he had to be stopped.

He spent the night at Norwich, catching up on information Jones and Richards had gathered. This was not much. Dupont had returned to London, and was being watched. There was no more information on the smugglers. Despite having told some people he intended to go to Brighton, he had not yet done so. As most of the *ton* had now left town for their country estates or the pleasures of the seaside, this was odd. Randal could make innocuous contact with the man when he reached London himself. Meanwhile, he would visit Danesfield.

13

Sylvie spent the next few days visiting her tenants and making herself known to the villagers. As she suspected, David had made enemies, and it took her a great deal of time and tact to reassure them that he had no authority, and was not acting on her behalf.

'But we thought 'e were your intended,' one of the farm wives said.

'Did he say that?' Sylvie demanded, horrified.

'Not in so many words, but when my good man asked if he'd be livin' at the Court, 'e daint say no.'

'His mother is here to keep me company, as I have no family. I asked him to stay for her sake, but you can take it from me he'll be going just as soon as I can manage it,' Sylvie said, and the woman chuckled.

'That's a relief. Sir George was hard, screwed every penny he could in rents, but 'e daint interfere like that one wanted to.'

On the second day of her round of visits Sylvie was driving along the village street when she saw the Reverend Dawes. She hadn't particularly liked the man when she'd first met him, and the sermons he had preached on Sundays had not impressed her. They sounded, and Lady Carstairs had agreed, like those contained in books of sermons, read out without sense or feeling. However, she ought to stop and speak to him.

He greeted her warmly and, when he discovered she was on her way to meet some of her tenants, offered to escort her and introduce her.

She didn't particularly want his escort, but it was difficult to decline.

'Sir George owned about half of the cottages,' he explained. 'As well as the rectory there are four good houses, all occupied by retired tradesmen or their widows from Cromer. They were not, of course, on calling terms with Sir George, as he received no one, but they do mix with the local gentry. Perhaps not on intimate terms, but they are invited to large parties. There is a dearth of polite society here. But you won't be entertaining while you are in mourning,' he added, and glanced meaningfully at the dark-green gown she was wearing.

'I don't feel obliged to wear mourning for a man I met only once, who cheated me of my inheritance, and was exceedingly unpleasant on the only occasion we did meet,' Sylvie declared.

'He left you his fortune, though,' Reverend Dawes said, shocked. 'Surely that entitles him to some respect?'

266

Sylvie pulled on the reins and drew the trap to a halt. 'Sir, I have no desire to argue about my conduct, with you or anyone else. I think I will visit my tenants on another day. Goodbye.'

He began to speak, stammering slightly, to chide her for her attitude, but she cut in ruthlessly, 'Please do not let us quarrel, sir. I am not prepared to accept criticism from anyone, especially someone I hardly know and will probably rarely meet, since I plan to sell Clayton Court as soon as possible.'

He subsided, and clambered out of the trap. Sylvie, inwardly fuming, drove on. She was thoroughly tired of the men in her life presuming to dictate to her on her conduct. Sir Randal had not criticized her, she thought bleakly as she drove back to Clayton Court. With him she could have proper discussions and he listened to her opinions. Oh, why did he not love her! If he had shown that he did, even a little, she could happily have married him.

★ ★ ★

The atmosphere in the house was tense. Sylvie suspected Celia and Aubrey were anxious to go to his estates where they could begin to plan their wedding, and, of course,

Lady Carstairs would have to go with them. David contrived to ignore her as much as possible. He and Aubrey had satisfied their curiosity by exploring the secret passage, but they had not worked out where the exit might be. Nor had they seen the telltale rings on the floor which indicated recent use. David tended to scoff, saying it was clear no one had used it for a long time.

Then the morning after Sylvie's encounter with the rector, Aubrey announced he was off to London.

'I must tell Randal of my engagement,' he said a little defensively. 'And ask him to support me. I hope to be gone no more than two nights, I'll be able to do the journey in a day, but I must see my man of business too. Is there anything I can get for you while I am there?'

Lady Carstairs went away to write a list of things she said were absolutely essential, and David laughed. 'If you meant to ride, you won't be able to carry it all back in saddle-bags.'

'I'll manage; I'll go post from Norwich. But it might help if you met me with the trap when I come back. Save the post boys the extra journey out here. Would that be all right with you, Sylvie?'

Irritated though she was at the assumption

268

he could commandeer her vehicle, she was delighted at the idea that she might be rid of David for a few hours. Since she had banned him from visiting her tenants he had occupied himself in wandering all over the house and making unwelcome suggestions about its future decor. While he was gone she could begin her search of the stables for the other entrance to the passage.

Aubrey departed. Sylvie went to see the carpenter, who had been to Norwich the previous day to obtain, he told her, better locks than were available locally. The chest she had ordered was ready, beautifully finished and polished to a high sheen, and she admired it, saying it would one day become an heirloom. It was heavy, but had carrying handles, and she was able to take it to her room. She would move the jewels there, and for the moment hide the chest in the bottom of an old armoire. She had just finished, and was locking the chest, when a maid came to tell her she had a visitor.

'Who is it?' she asked, hoping it was not Reverend Dawes coming to either apologize or continue his arguments.

'Don't know, miss. A gentleman. Sawyer didn't say.'

★ ★ ★

269

Sylvie tidied her hair and went down to the drawing-room. A tall, stout man with grizzled hair, weatherbeaten face, and fashionable clothes stood by a window looking out. He didn't look like a tradesman, nor quite like a country squire. She could not recall seeing him at the funeral. He turned round as she entered and surveyed her with sharp, intelligent eyes.

'Sir. I am Sylvie Delamare. I understand you wish to see me.'

'Yes, Miss Delamare. I only heard a day or so ago about Sir George Clayton's death, when Sir Randal Fortescue called on me. I came to offer my condolences in person, but there is more. We have some tricky business to deal with. I'm Joseph Tempest.'

'Tempest? From Danesfield?' Sylvie felt as though all the breath had been knocked out of her. She groped for a chair behind her and sat down. 'Please, sir, do sit down. I am so glad to meet you at last. Would you care for some Madeira?'

She rose to her feet again and rang for Sawyer. Until he came back with the tray, neither of them said anything. Then when Mr Tempest was sipping appreciatively at the wine, and Sylvie, declining the ratafia Sawyer offered her in favour of Madeira too, had sipped at hers, she took a deep breath and spoke.

'You live at Danesfield?'

'I do, and have done for eleven years now. It's your family home, I understand?'

'You've been away. No one has been able to contact you, there or in London, since Sir George died.'

'We've been in Bath. My wife is an invalid, and we hoped the waters would help her.'

Bath. Sylvie wanted to laugh. Of all places he might have been, the one where she had been living seemed the least likely.

'You knew my great-uncle, I suppose, as he was my trustee after my parents died?'

He laughed. 'Indeed I did. I knew George Clayton very well indeed. But it's a long story, goes back thirty years.'

He paused, and Sylvie waited. At last, it seemed, she was going to hear something of her great-uncle's life from a man who seemed to have known him well, from the way he spoke.

'George was quite a lively spark about town thirty years ago. Then he fell in love with my sister, Mattie.'

Sylvie controlled her surprise. She could not imagine that dour old man ever being in love. But perhaps he had been different in his youth. 'What happened? Did she die? He was never married, as far as I know.'

'I'd better explain our family. We were

merchants, my father was quite well to do. We lived down by the docks east of the City, and I increased what he left me. Mattie — her real name was Matilda — ran away to be an actress. My father disowned her. He thought all actresses were no better than whores, and we were a respectable family.'

Sylvie was trying to come to terms with the notion of Sir George in love with an actress, and after a pause Mr Tempest went on.

'That's how he met her. I'm not sure if she was a real actress, or just one of the dancing girls. He wanted to marry her.' He laughed. 'All the older people he knew were thoroughly scandalized, while the young men thought he was being very dashing. She came back home and my father forgave her. He was puffed up that she was going to be a lady, after all he'd said against her. George and I became friends. I had ideas above my station, and enjoyed being introduced to all the young men he knew. We went to bare-knuckle fights, and cock fights, played cards, gambled on everything, and spent too much time at the theatre. Sometimes he took me to places where I could mix with the *ton*, dance with the girls, and I had ideas of marrying into the quality myself.'

He laughed, and shrugged. 'That was an idea above my station, then. For me. But it's part of the reason of how I got Danesfield. In the end I married the daughter of another merchant, and inherited his business too, as he had only the one chick. But that's getting away from the story.'

'What happened to Mattie and Sir George?'

'She jilted him. She ran off with a Frenchman, a sea captain.'

'So that's why he disliked the French? My father was French.' This explained a great deal.

'He never got over it. He left London, never came back. But he and I stayed friends for a while, and I visited him here, once or twice a year. Sometimes I could persuade him to go out to a cock fight, but mostly we played cards. I think I was the only person he kept in touch with from the old days.'

Sylvie was beginning to feel sorry for Sir George, an odd sensation. When he had defied Society to actually plan marriage with his actress, instead of making her his mistress, as most men would have done, it must have been galling to have her reject him. Perhaps she had been a calculating girl playing for high stakes, a title and wealthy respectability, and then discovered true love with her Frenchman.

Mr Tempest went on. 'Then I married

myself, and it was more difficult to visit, and after a while I stopped coming.'

Sylvie glanced at the clock and saw it was time for their normal midday meal. 'Mr Tempest, there is clearly much more to be told. Will you stay and eat a nuncheon with us?'

'With pleasure, Miss Delamare.'

'Can I ask you not to mention what we have been talking about? I will say you are an old friend of Sir George's. Did you give Sawyer your name?'

'As a matter of fact, I didn't. Call me Mr Joseph.' He grinned at her, and she found herself responding. Even though he had possession of her home, and she did not yet know under what terms, she liked him.

★   ★   ★

Randal arrived in London just in time to escort his mother to Brighton. He remained with her for a couple of nights before returning to London. At the Ministry he discovered Peter Sinclair pacing up and down dictating urgent messages to a secretary. He waited patiently, and when the man had been sent away to dispatch the messages Peter turned to him and grinned.

'We have him,' he said with satisfaction. 'At

least, we have firm evidence against him.'

'Dupont? How?'

'He has been attempting to persuade the stocking knitters in Nottingham to break their new machines. He has been claiming that installing them is a plot by the French to put them out of work. One of our men who knew him was there and overheard him. He was arrested.'

'So that is over.'

'Unfortunately, no. While they were bringing him to London he escaped, somewhere near Leicester. But he will have to leave the country now, so we are expecting him to use his smuggling contacts to be taken across to the continent. The north Norfolk coast would be the obvious place to make for, and we are sure he has friends there.'

'So you wish me to go back there?'

'You can stay at Clayton Court, be on the spot without causing suspicion if Dupont discovers you there.'

Randal did not reply. He could not go back to Clayton Court now, though during the past few days he had found himself thinking a great deal about Sylvie, and wishing he had used more address when he had made his proposal. He wanted to see her again. He thought rapidly.

'There isn't a problem, is there?' Peter asked.

'I suspect smugglers use Clayton Court,' he said slowly, and told Peter about their discovery of the secret passage. 'I would prefer not to be there, in case my presence alerts them, and they find some other hiding place we don't know about. If I stay at some small inn nearby I can keep watch on both Dupont and the smugglers.'

'If you think it best. We'll send more men to spread out along that coast, to help Jones and Roberts and the coastguards. We should be able to cover all the likely small harbours where there are fishing boats.'

They discussed tactics for a while, then Randal went home. He considered dining at his club, but felt an aversion to making conversation. Most of his friends would have left town, and who knew what bores might be left, anxious to latch on to anyone they could. He would eat at his rooms, have an early night, and set out for Norfolk again early the following day.

It was not to be. Before he was dressed the next morning his valet came to say his cousin was demanding to see him. What had brought Aubrey here so early?

'Show him in.'

Aubrey was dressed particularly carefully, Randal noted with amusement. It was clearly some favour he had come to beg.

'Sit down, join me for breakfast.'

Aubrey said he was not hungry, but he did accept a cup of coffee, and then absently began nibbling at a roll. Randal piled his own plate with slices of ham and beef.

'Well,' Randal asked, when it was clear Aubrey was not going to start the conversation, 'what is it?'

Aubrey gulped, then burst out, 'I'm going to be married!'

Randal lowered the forkful of ham he had been about to eat. Suddenly he did not feel hungry any more. Had the fool, thinking to save Sylvie's reputation, offered for her, and had she accepted him? A wave of anger against both of them caused him to shake so that he was unable to lift the coffee cup his hand had strayed to.

'I want you to wish me well,' Aubrey went on. 'And also, I want you to support me. We'll be married quietly in Staffordshire, as soon as possible, and then we'll go to India to see Celia's parents.'

It took a few moments for Randal to absorb this. He closed his eyes and sighed deeply. 'Celia?' he asked, and coughed because his voice sounded hoarse. 'I thought it was Sylvie you wanted.'

Aubrey looked embarrassed. 'Well, yes, it was, at first, but she — ' He halted and blushed.

'She has a sullied reputation, is that it?'

'No, no, of course not! I'd begun to prefer Celia a long time before — well, before we heard about the Black Bear. That had nothing to do with it. It's just,' he went on, lowering his voice, 'Sylvie is such a managing female!'

Randal almost choked with laughter. 'I agree she'd never suit you. Celia is much more pliable and gentle. Well, Aubrey, if you are quite sure, I wish you well.'

'Sylvie and my sister will be bridesmaids. Now I'd better go and see my grandmother. She is still in town, is she?'

'Yes, but I believe they were planning to go to Brighton soon. Best hurry. Then I suppose you'll be going back to Clayton Court?'

'Yes, it's a confounded nuisance, as we can't leave Sylvie on her own, and we want to go to Lichfield to start preparations.'

Randal was no longer listening. He would see Sylvie again. He would be able to judge whether his feelings of dismay were because of his inept proposal, or because he did, after all, feel more than a dutiful obligation towards her.

★ ★ ★

In the afternoon Sylvie took Mr Tempest to the library. She was amused that Lady

Carstairs did not insist on sending the chaperoning maid after them. Either she thought Mr Tempest was too old to be a threat to her virtue, or Sylvie was so depraved it no longer mattered whether her reputation could be damaged further. 'How did you obtain Danesfield?' she asked.

'Eleven years ago, my sister died, and I had business in Norwich at the time so I came to tell George. I felt he should know. Well, we found we still had a great deal in common, even though he'd become more reclusive. I had made a lot of money by then, and I said I wanted to find good husbands for my girls, with titles, if possible. I was planning to buy a country house so that we could move in the right society, but I was not at the time wealthy enough to buy the sort of property I had in mind, so I would have to lease for a while. George scoffed. He still liked a wager, so he made me an offer. My girls were nine and ten years old at the time. He offered me the lease of Danesfield, and of the house in North Audley Street, for ten years, with an option to buy them if I had by then married one of the girls to a title.'

'Did you know Danesfield belonged to me, and he had no right to sell it?' Sylvie asked, suppressing her anger.

'It belongs to you now,' Mr Tempest said,

looking puzzled. 'Sir George left it to you.'

'It was my mother's home, but when my parents died Sir George was appointed a trustee. He had the right to hire it out, and the ten years he suggested would have taken the lease up to my twenty-first birthday. He had no right, and never did have, to sell it or promise it to you.'

Mr Tempest was looking aghast. 'The cunning old devil! When he wrote to me and said he was unable to sell and so offered me a further year to fulfil the wager, I thought he was being generous. Why would he do that when you should have taken possession?'

Sylvie told him. 'He said all that was left of my inheritance was forty pounds, and refused to answer any questions. He blamed the other trustee, a lawyer, for mismanaging the trust, and the lawyer, a silly young man, said he had not been involved after his father, the original trustee, died. I don't know, but I expect he was going to wait and see whether I accepted what he told me. If I had done so, he would have felt safe to sell Danesfield to you.'

'That was wicked! He had clearly changed from when I knew him.'

'He had plenty of money, according to what is in the bank. He charged his tenants high rents, but he does not appear to have spent it. He was a miser.'

'Well, I came to realize after we'd agreed the rent for Danesfield, that he was charging far more than I need have paid for a similar house. But I had no idea at that time of the rate, and a bargain was a bargain. He'd been badly treated by my sister, and I could afford it.'

'You are very generous.'

'Now I know the situation, will you be willing to sell me Danesfield, and the London house, of course? I will give you a good price.'

Slowly Sylvie shook her head. 'It was my home, and I have dreamed of going back there. I was planning to sell Clayton Court, which I do not like, and ask if I could buy Danesfield back from you. That is, if you owned it.'

'Then you want us to move.' Mr Tempest was silent for a while. 'I quite understand, but I have a different suggestion. Oh, we will move, as soon as we possibly can. But would you let me buy this house?'

'Clayton Court? You are not doing this simply to be kind, are you?'

He laughed and shook his head. 'Indeed not. When I first came here, as a young man, I vowed I would one day own something like it. I was enchanted by it. It is unspoilt, and just the kind of house my wife has always said she liked. But it has other advantages for me.

My wife, as I said, is an invalid, and it has been suggested that she take the sea bathing cure. Here, so near to Cromer and its facilities, she could do that whenever she needed, instead of making long journeys to some resort and having to stay in lodgings, which we do not like, or rent our own house, with all the inconveniences that entails, taking servants and sleeping in strange beds!'

'It would solve many problems,' Sylvie said, 'but I will have to think about it. Sir George let the house deteriorate. He lived in one room, and the rest has been neglected. At this moment we have workmen repairing damage caused by the weather in the east wing, and when they are done those rooms will need to be decorated. The rest of the house needs refurbishing too.'

He looked thoughtful. 'The rooms I have seen look habitable, if shabby. Forgive my plain speaking.'

'Lady Carstairs brought extra servants and has been supervising some cleaning, but we have had no time to do more.'

'My wife has enjoyed decorating Danesfield and North Audley Street. She has an artistic turn. I hope you will appreciate what she has done, by the way. She would prefer to come to a house where everything needs doing, and it would give her a new interest. And one of my daughters has very strong ideas about gardens, though I would not permit her to make any major alterations at Danesfield. She could have her head completely here.'

'Then perhaps I had better show you round, Mr Tempest. But before I do, where are you staying? It would be convenient for us both if you stayed here, and you are very welcome.'

'That would be far better than the local inn! I'll send my coachman for my valet and luggage.'

'And then we had better tell Lady Carstairs. She will be pleased to hear everything. She is longing to go with Celia, who is getting married soon.'

'You will go with her? Did I catch you here just in time?'

'No, I won't go.'

'But you can't stay here on your own. I cannot leave my wife for too long, so why don't you come to Danesfield and meet my wife and daughters? Then we can discuss all the details at leisure.'

14

Mr Tempest, having inspected the house and walked round the grounds, left for home the following day, saying he would wait for a message to say when Sylvie wished him to send for her. Knowing Lady Carstairs would protest, Sylvie decided not to tell her until it was too late for her to prevent her from going to Danesfield.

She still wanted to find the exit from the secret passage, so the moment David drove away to meet Aubrey in Norwich, Sylvie strolled to the front of the house. Counting carefully, and trying to make her steps the same length as they had been in the passage, she walked along the west wing and past the drying ground. Then she was behind the stable yard. She had to move sideways and continue counting as she crossed the yard, past the dilapidated stalls on her right and the tack-rooms and hay and feed stores on her left. She halted when she judged she had gone the right distance. She had come to the archway which led from this yard into the next, which in the past had been an elegant carriage house and cottages for the grooms and coachmen who had once been employed here. Now the cottages were empty and looked as run down as the rest of the property. This position made sense. A trapdoor could more easily be hidden under bales of hay than in a carriage house.

She glanced round, but there was no one in sight. Her one elderly groom could be heard whistling. He was probably washing the ancient carriage which no one had used, so far as Sylvie could tell, for decades, but which was his great pride.

She had to judge the distance back to the line of the passage, and it seemed to be in the centre of one of the hay stores. She looked around, and frowned. The hay was piled high to both sides, but only a thin scattering lay in the centre of the floor. Surely that was unusual? In all the other hay stores she had seen, on her tenants' farms, they had piled in the hay and then started using it from the front, working back evenly. Also, not a great deal had yet been used. It was only a short time since haymaking, and many of the animals who would be fed hay during the winter were out grazing in the fields.

Sylvie found a broom and began to sweep aside the hay in the centre, and soon uncovered a trapdoor set closely in the floor, at the back of the store, with two strong bolts and a ring almost hidden right at the back, where the trap met the wall. This must be it.

She tried the bolts, and to her surprise, they moved easily. She grasped the ring, and pulled. The trap came up smoothly, and Sylvie peered down at the steps where she and Sir Randal had tried in vain to open it.

It was gloomy, but sufficient light came in from outside for Sylvie to see several barrels and sacks piled up at the bottom of the steps. She gasped. The smugglers had been busy during the past few days. Nothing had been here when David and Aubrey had explored, so the contraband could only have been put there since.

Looking round nervously, Sylvie dropped the trap in place and shot the bolts. Then she scattered hay over the floor until the trap was hidden. Who were they? Were some of her tenants, even some of the servants, involved?

She looked out carefully before leaving the store, and continued through the archway and past the carriage house, as though she were idly strolling round her domain. Then she walked through the kitchen garden and round to the east wing, as if to see what progress was being made there. Mr Tempest had seemed satisfied the work was being done satisfactorily, but this was the last thing Sylvie was thinking of. Why was Sir Randal not here when she needed him? He would have known what to do.

Back in the house she installed herself in the library, telling Lady Carstairs there were papers she wished to read again. Instead she sat and wondered what best to do. Should she tell David and Aubrey when they returned from Norwich? The idea did not appeal. David would immediately take charge, and make such a noise he would alert the entire district. That would not catch the smugglers, which she wanted to do if at all possible, and prevent them from using the passage again. It would need to be filled in. For all she knew, if Mrs Tempest were of a nervous disposition, she might refuse to move to Clayton Court, and that would upset their plans.

She knew no one in the district well enough to know whether they were involved in the smuggling. In all probability some of her tenants were. In any case, they were more likely to close ranks against her, an outsider, to protect one another. Of the gentry, only Lady Acton and her daughter had called on them, and Sylvie did not relish asking for their help. She did not know the local magistrates, and they could well be involved. If they were not, they might be unwilling to take action against what many people regarded as a legitimate activity, evading high duties on goods they felt entitled to buy cheaply.

Then Sylvie recalled the suggestion that the smugglers removed their booty gradually, taking a few barrels away at a time. If she could find somewhere to hide, she might recognize some of them. If she did she would go to Norwich and find a magistrate there. Inland, they were less likely to be involved, and could contact the Revenue for her.

* * *

Randal, driving once more to Norwich, resolved that when this operation was completed, and Dupont captured, he would go to Clayton Court and this time ask Sylvie to marry him in a way that might induce her to accept. The shock and despair he had suffered during the few moments he had thought she was going to marry Aubrey had revealed to him that he cared for her more than just as a pleasant companion. He had never expected to fall in love, had indeed taken great care not to, but Sylvie, without him realizing it, had captured his heart and he was at last willing to admit it.

He had to put aside his own concerns for a while, and concentrate on Dupont. The man had caused trouble, and now they had firm evidence against him. He had to be captured and tried, punished to deter others.

Jones and Roberts had co-ordinated the plans, with the extra men sent from London allocated to the fishing villages along the coast.

'We'll be watching all the boats to see Dupont isn't taken off on them, but that's a huge task. As for the smuggling, we heard there was a run a day or so ago, and they will be wanting to move the goods as quickly as possible. We'll watch all the suspected hiding places, and must hope the smugglers don't notice there are so many strangers about,' Jones said.

'When do you think Dupont will make a dash for it?'

'The usual pattern, so far as we can judge, is for the smuggling boats to go out every few days. They fish normally in between, then they go further, either to Holland, or to meet French boats well out in the North Sea. So we expect them to take off Dupont within the next few days.'

'Let's hope we are in time.'

'I think we are. We've booked you into a room at an inn a few miles inland, as you don't want to be at Clayton Court. But we're watching that place since you warned us about the secret passage.'

'And because Dupont was interested in landing places nearby. He might be heading for there instead of a busier place like Cromer.'

He would go there that night, Randal decided. 'I know the estate, I think I know where the other end of the secret passage ends. Can you supply me with three or four men?'

'Good ones. Yes. You'll take charge there?'

'It will be my pleasure.'

Late that evening, as it grew dark, Randal positioned his men. There was insufficient cover close to the house and stables, so the men were stationed at intervals in the clumps of trees that were scattered about the park. As this had not been maintained, there was plenty of thick undergrowth to conceal them, but they were too far away from the buildings for comfort. Unless they could creep up on the men unseen there was every chance they would get away.

Randal crawled closer, making use of the uncut grass on what had once been parkland closely cropped by sheep and deer. He was grateful now for Sir George's neglect of his property. If he could get close enough to see into the stable yard, where he suspected the secret passage to emerge, he might be able to have good warning of activity there.

It was a warm night, but there was no moon and the sky was cloudy, cutting off any starlight. Randal strained to see, and listened intently, but there was nothing to see or hear. The lights in the house had been doused. Everyone must be abed. He wondered where Sylvie was, whether she thought of him, and whether, when he was able to go to her again, she would listen to him this time. If she did not, he swore, he would not cease trying. Now he had found the woman he wanted to marry, he would not be content until he had won her.

★ ★ ★

Sylvie crouched down in an empty stall on the opposite side of the yard from the hay store. She had pleaded a headache and gone to bed early, then crept out again through the deserted east wing. She had once more dressed in her old grey gown from seminary days. It would merge with the buildings and help her to remain invisible, she hoped.

She dared not take a lantern. There was no moon, and only intermittent starlight when the clouds parted briefly, but she had come this way earlier, in daylight, and knew what hazards might be in her path.

Would they come before midnight? It

would be a long wait, but if she could identify even one of the men involved she would regard this exploit as a success. Then she began to worry they might not use lanterns, and she would not be able to see any of them clearly.

She made herself comfortable on a pile of straw she had placed there earlier in readiness. Surely she would hear something, so she need not stand for hours peering over the half stable door, waiting for them to come. With nothing else to occupy her, she thought about Mr Tempest's unexpected visit. He'd told her he had the deeds of Danesfield, which was why they had not found them amongst the papers here. He also had copies of the agreements with Sir George. Finally, all the puzzles about her inheritance had been solved. She had written to Mr Haines, and expected him to come back to Clayton Court within the next few days. Then she could go to Danesfield, and Lady Carstairs could take Celia to Staffordshire, to begin planning for the wedding in earnest.

She would see Sir Randal at the wedding. How would he treat her? How should she behave towards him? Often since their last meeting she had berated herself for being so stubborn as to refuse his offer. If she had the chance again, this time she would cast aside scruples and accept his proposal.

A long time passed. Sylvie had no way of judging how long, but she was stiff and cold. She scrambled to her feet, moving her arms in an effort to keep warm, and looked out over the stable door. Her eyes were now adjusted to the dark, and she saw two pack ponies standing patiently outside the hay store.

How had they got there without her hearing them? Had she slept? As she watched, a man came out of the hay store carrying what looked like a barrel. He fixed it on to one of the pony's panniers, and the animal moved sideways. Sylvie suddenly realized the hoofs were padded with something to muffle sounds.

Another man came with a second barrel, and Sylvie let out a gasp of surprise and disbelief. It was Reverend Dawes. She could hardly mistake his tall, lanky figure. She was quite ready to believe members of the clergy might accept smuggled brandy, and she had heard some even allowed the smugglers to store the goods in the churches, but to see the rector taking part in the actual movement of such goods was astonishing.

She could now identify at least one of the smugglers. But would she be believed? She could scarcely believe it herself. As two more men emerged from the hay store, this time carrying sacks, Sylvie leaned out in an effort to see more clearly. If she could identify another man perhaps she would be believed. Maybe he would even give evidence to save himself. She had little idea of how these things worked, but she believed criminals could obtain lower sentences if they gave evidence against their fellows.

They were not men she knew well enough to identify. She gave a little shrug of disappointment, and then almost fell as the door she had been leaning against suddenly swung open. She had time to think some unladylike curses about her great-uncle's neglect of his property, before two of the men were across the yard and had her arms imprisoned behind her back and a hand across her mouth.

'It's the Delamare wench,' she heard Reverend Dawes say. 'We'll have to get rid of her; she'll know me. Where's the boat?'

'Not ready until tomorrow night. We can drop her over the side, but not tonight. We have to get this stuff away, and we can't carry her as well.'

'Put her in the passage. She'll be safe enough there. No one will hear her, and we can gag her and tie her up to make sure.'

294

Within minutes Sylvie was bound and gagged. She was dragged across the yard, and thrust down on to the steps below the trapdoor. Then the trap was swung closed, and she heard nothing more.

* * *

Randal caught a glimpse of a lantern in the stable yard, just before it was doused. Then he heard the muffled sound of hoofs. He hooted like an owl and rose to his feet, as the men with him, abandoning concealment at the signal, ran towards him just as two heavily laden ponies were led out of the yard.

The smugglers, caught unexpectedly, hesitated. Two of them set off immediately, running fast, while the others dithered, reluctant to leave their ponies and the goods they carried.

'Get them,' Randal ordered, and he and another man set off after the runaways. The others had the advantage of knowing the ground, but there was no cover for at least a hundred yards, and before they reached the belt of trees they had been making for Randal and his companion had caught them up. They turned to fight, and in a sudden gleam of starlight Randal saw they had knives.

'Take care,' he shouted, and managed to duck as one of the men threw his knife towards him. The momentary pause gave his quarry time to plunge into the shelter of the trees. Randal sprinted after him, unable to see where he was, but following the crashing sounds of a body pushing through under-growth and fallen twigs.

Then the sounds ceased, and Randal halted. He strained to hear, and thought he could detect heavy breathing to his right. He took a couple of paces forward, then swung round and sideways, colliding with a soft body. The man grunted, and aimed a punch at Randal's head. It slanted off his cheek, but Randal grabbed at the arm and yanked the other forward. As the man stumbled Randal hooked his leg round and brought his assail-ant crashing to the ground. Randal knelt on him, twisting the captured arm behind his back, and with one hand managed to drag some twine out of his pocket. The captured man struggled, but he was no match for Randal. His hands were bound together, he was hauled to his feet and marched back to where the others were waiting beside the ponies.

The second runaway had also been caught, and manhandled back to the group. One of Randal's men went to bring the cart hidden a short distance away, and when he came back he hitched the two pack ponies to the back of it.

'No point in leaving them here,' he said, grinning. 'Good evidence.'

Randal took a lantern from the cart and lit it. In the light he was surveying his prisoners. His eyebrows shot up when he recognized the Reverend Dawes, the man he had himself captured, but he did not comment. None of the others was known to him. Rather to his disappointment Dupont was not there, but he told himself it hadn't been likely a mere passenger the smugglers sometimes took with them would be asked to help move the contraband. Perhaps one of them knew where he was to be found and would be willing to supply that information, with a little pressure applied.

'Onto the cart, next stop prison for you lads,' he said cheerfully.

★ ★ ★

Sylvie was lying awkwardly on the steps, terrified of moving in case she rolled down to the bottom. If she did, she knew she risked breaking an arm or worse. Gradually her heartbeat slowed, and she began to consider her plight. She had to get free. If she was still here on the following night she knew they would carry out their threat to take her out on the boat and drown her. They could not afford to let her go.

Slowly, she managed to wriggle round until she was sitting on one of the steps, with her feet safely resting on another below. Her head did not touch the trap, so she estimated she was sitting at least halfway down the short flight. She thought there were ten steps, so if she was sitting on the fourth or fifth one down, and her feet two below that, she had only to negotiate three or four steps to reach the bottom. She would feel much safer there, while she struggled to free herself of her bonds.

Carefully she stretched out, and her feet touched the next step down. Slowly she levered herself off the step where she was sitting and bumped down to the next one. That wasn't too bad, though she would have bruises in unmentionable places.

Three more, and she was at the bottom of the flight, sitting on the second step. She twisted her hands, tied behind her back, and found that in their haste the smugglers had not pulled the rope tight. That was a relief, for she did not think there would be anything sharp enough down here for her to use to saw away at the rope, which was quite thick, the sort used for tethering horses. After a great deal of twisting and easing her wrists, she was able to get one hand free, sliding it out from the loop round her arms. She dragged off the gag, and took a deep breath. Then she untied the rest of the ropes and stood up to flex her muscles, which were cold and stiff.

She had heard the men shoot home the bolts above the trap, so knew there was no hope of escape through there. There was only the other exit, in the house. But that had no means of being opened from inside. She could shout, bang on the panel, make a noise. Someone would hear her. Then there were the air holes, which Sir Randal had said might be located in the chimneys of other rooms. He'd warned her not to make a noise in case they were heard through these. She tried to think what other rooms were above the passage, whether they were used and when. There was the morning-room. If she could not make herself heard at the end of the passage, she could try to estimate where this was and stand below it screaming. They would think it was ghosts.

She gave a slight chuckle. Then she remembered that vertical ladder. It would not be so bad climbing up it in the dark, but she didn't know if she would have the courage to climb down again.

It was time she moved. She had no idea how long she had been struggling to get free of her bonds. The men were unlikely to come back soon, in fact she did not expect them to come back before the following night, when they would come for her. Even if she had not by then attracted anyone's attention, it would be safer if she were in the small room just inside the panelling. They would find it more difficult to capture her at the top of the ladder, where they might fear any noise would bring people to the scene. She would be able to fend them off, as they could only come up the ladder one at a time. She might be able to push them off it, even.

She would be missed. The maid would report that her bed had not been slept in. They would fear some accident, and search. At some point someone would look into Sir George's room. She breathed a sigh of relief when she remembered that, having moved the jewels, she had felt no further need to lock the door. People would be able to get inside. She would hear them, and could attract their attention. Slowly, feeling her way along the walls, she began to walk along the passage.

★　★　★

The prisoners refused to talk. They had been caught red handed with smuggled goods, and resisted arrest. They had no excuses, but they would not give any information or betray their friends. After a while Randal and Jones left them in their cells and conferred in an outer room.

'The rest of the crew will soon discover these four are missing, but Dupont may not know. He'll keep in hiding until it's time for him to board the boat,' Jones said.

'Was there suspicious activity along the coast last night?' Randal asked.

'Nothing at all. It seems, for the moment, to be concentrated near Clayton Court. Dupont may be expecting the boat to be launched near to it, especially if it's the same boat the smugglers used last time.'

'So it's likely he's hiding nearby.'

'Has he ever been to the Court itself?'

Randal thought of his early suspicions that Dupont and Sylvie were in league. At that time, she had never been to Clayton Court, and they could not have anticipated using it. But Sir George had been associated with the smugglers, if only by allowing them to use his land. Surely she could not have been deceiving him all along?

He shook his head and banished the thought. Dupont might have considered trading on their acquaintance, but so far as Randal knew he had never visited Sylvie. After his arrest in Nottingham surely he would not come out into the open. He would guess they would be looking for him near all the little fishing ports and landing places along this coast.

'He knows Miss Delamare, but I don't think he has visited her here.'

'There's plenty of places a man might stay hidden on that estate,' Jones said. 'It's ramshackle, not enough people to keep it in trim, empty barns, and work going on in one part. I looked round one day, and no one even saw me.'

'Then you should organize a search party. You have cause.'

'Will you vouch for me? There isn't time to get a warrant, we've got to catch the devil today.'

★   ★   ★

'But, ma'am, her bed's not been slept in!'

Lady Carstairs put down her coffee cup. 'Are you sure, Phyllis?'

'Yes, ma'am. Jenny, the maid that normally takes the chocolate, came to tell me, and as I've been looking after Miss Sylvie as well as Miss Celia, I went to make sure. Her night clothes were still laid out, but the gown she wore last night was on the chair, as though she'd taken it off in a hurry. I looked to see what was missing and only that old grey gown she had in the seminary was gone.'

'Thank you, Phyllis. I'll come and see. Perhaps she left a note, though I can't think where she could have gone to, if she went last night. Are any of the horses missing?'

'I don't know, I didn't want to make a fuss if you knew about it.'

'Quite right, but send to ask whether a horse has been taken.'

Phyllis backed out of the breakfast-room, and David, who had listened to this exchange with a smirk on his face, laughed.

'Up to her old tricks, I warrant. I wonder who she's found in this benighted place to bestow her favours on? Could he be the reason she turned down Sir Randal's offer?'

'David, that's unfair!' Celia said. 'Perhaps she went outside for a walk, if she didn't want to sleep last night, and has fallen and hurt herself? We must look for her at once!'

'You are so innocent!'

Aubrey stood up. 'That's enough, David. The women can search inside the house, I'm going to organize the men to search the grounds and outbuildings. Are you going to help?'

'I suppose I'd better,' David said and grinned. 'Or I might be accused of doing away with her.'

Lady Carstairs gave him an abstracted smile. 'Thank you, dear. I'll leave that to you, but I'll go and see if she's left a note.'

'Do you have to be so odious to Sylvie?' Celia demanded, as Aubrey left the room and David poured himself some more coffee. 'What do you have against her?'

David looked at her and smiled. 'I accept you have a right to my mother's hospitality, Celia, for you are family. Sylvie is not; she has nothing to do with us, yet she has inflicted herself on us for the past four months or more, taking Mama's attention away from you when she was supposed to be bringing you out. The fact you have achieved a respectable offer is despite her, and thanks mainly to my friendship with Aubrey.'

Celia stared at him in astonishment. 'You are taking Sylvie's hospitality now! I didn't think you were so mean. You're almost as bad as Sir George.'

'Oh, don't be ridiculous. But for her we could be enjoying ourselves at Brighton, instead of mouldering in this mausoleum.'

'You can go to Brighton if you wish!'

'Mama needs me; she needs a man around, or she would be even more put upon than she is already.'

15

The search of the outbuildings for signs for Dupont had been started early in the morning. Randal himself, obeying a sudden hunch, had gone to the rectory. Admitted by a frightened maid who demanded to know where the Reverend Dawes was, he brusquely told her he was in custody, and began to search the ground-floor rooms.

He moved upstairs, but the bedrooms were empty. On the attic floor, where the servants slept, he found one door locked. The maid, who was nervously following him around, told him it was just a storeroom, and she didn't have the key, Reverend Dawes always kept that on him.

Randal put his shoulder to the door, and the flimsy wood gave way. Inside were several barrels and bales of what he supposed were silk, but more interesting was the view of a gentleman's buckskin-clad rear, legs flailing, as he struggled to squeeze through an inadequately sized window.

Randal grinned, and crossed the room. 'You'll damage yourself that way, sir,' he said and took hold of the threshing feet. He pulled, and with a tearing of cloth the body unplugged itself, and Monsieur Dupont fell on to the bed.

'Sir, I protest!' Dupont gasped. 'How dare you mishandle me so!'

Randal laughed. 'I suppose you are an innocent man, fearing being incarcerated by the terrible English. Don't be concerned, you will have a fair trial, on charges of inciting rebellion, and passing information to our enemies, to begin with. I am sure we will have thought of a few others by the time you face the judges.'

'I am an American citizen!'

'With French antecedents and republican sympathies. Never mind, you will be able to explain why you were anxious to escape through a window which leads only to a rather dangerously sloping roof. Not to take the air, I imagine. Come, sir, do you go quietly, or must I bind you?'

Dupont's bombast had gone. He shrugged and said he would go quietly.

'Of course, but just to make absolutely certain, you will not object if I bind your hands together.'

Randal did so, helped his captive into the curricle, and sent him off with his valet and tiger in charge. He himself was anxious to get to Clayton Court.

*   *   *

He found David furiously haranguing Jones on the front steps.

'What the devil do you mean, sir, saying you are searching for smugglers? Do you think respectable householders harbour such villains? Who sent you? I shall complain in the highest quarters!'

Jones turned with relief to Randal. 'Sir, can you explain?'

Randal grinned at him. 'You can call off the men. Dupont was skulking in an attic at the rectory.'

'Well done, sir!'

David spluttered in annoyance. 'Dupont? Rectory? What is all this?'

'We apprehended a gang of smugglers last night, who were using the secret passage to store contraband. One of the men involved was the Reverend Dawes. This morning I caught Monsieur Dupont hiding in the rectory. He is wanted on charges of stirring up sedition and passing information to the French, by way of messages sent with smugglers. We thought he might be hiding somewhere on Miss Delamare's property, hence the search.'

'We'd better take the rest of the goods,' Jones said. 'Where is this secret passage?'

'It comes out somewhere in the stables. I don't suppose they will have put the goods further inside. Come, I think I can locate it for you.'

'What gives you the right to simply march in and take away goods that do not belong to you?'

'Sir David, I don't think the goods belong to Miss Delamare, and we have the right of the law.'

He turned away, went to the corner of the house and started pacing, counting as he went. They soon found the hidden trapdoor, and he left the men taking away the barrels and sacks. It was time he saw Sylvie, explained his presence here, and tried his luck once more.

* * *

Sylvie felt intolerably weary, but she dared not allow herself to fall asleep. There was plenty of space in this small secret room, she was not afraid of falling down the shaft, but she did not want to miss hearing people who might be searching for her in Sir George's room.

So far she had heard nothing beyond the panel. There was no way of telling what the time was. There were no cracks in the panel, to let light through. She began to wonder whether the wood was so thick sounds could not be heard in any case. Then she tried to imagine how a search would be conducted. In all probability people would simply look into every room, perhaps search in the cupboards and under beds, but silently. Would they call out when they could see she was not there? Would they even search in pairs, so that there was a chance of her hearing them talking?

If she could not hear them, she had to make them hear her. She began banging regularly on the back of the panel, and when her fists grew sore from this she shouted. Then she banged again, and this time used her feet, sitting with her back to the far wall so that she could drum on the panel with her heels.

It seemed like hours that she kept up this routine, but to no effect. She was beginning to think she would have to scramble back down the ladder in the dark. The notion terrified her. It had been bad enough climbing up, much worse than when she had the light of a lantern to show her each rung. Going down, with the constant fear of missing a rung and plunging down that shaft to suffer serious injury or even death, was not something she was yet ready to face. If she did summon up the courage to climb down, she would then have to try to guess where the morning-room was so that she could shout and hope the air inlets would let her be heard. Would anyone be there? They would, surely, all be out searching for her.

Then a new thought made her draw back from the shaft in alarm. If a whole night and day had passed, the smugglers might be coming back for her. They could hear her shouts, but she would not have any warning of their approach. Could they hear her now?

She tried to tell herself not nearly so much time had elapsed. She wasn't hungry, and surely, if she had missed two, or even three meals, she would be ravenous. Not in her present state of fear, she decided. She was thirsty, but that could be the effect of her shouting.

Sitting here frightening herself would not get her out of this pickle. She remembered her thought that if the smugglers tried to recapture her, she could fend them off as they tried to mount the ladder. So it did not matter if they heard her. She renewed her efforts, kicking the panel and making as much noise as she could. It seemed like hours, and once more she stopped, giving in to exhaustion. Surely someone would find her soon!

★ ★ ★

The front door was open and no one came to answer Randal's knocking. He stepped inside, wondering where they all were. As he hovered, trying to decide where to look, Lady Carstairs emerged from the drawing-room.

'Sir Randal? Why are all those men in the grounds? Have they come to help?'

'Help? No, they have been searching for Monsieur Dupont. But we have found him now.'

He explained, but she was not listening. She was twisting a scrap of cambric which had once been a handkerchief round and round her fingers.

'Oh, I don't know what to do!'

There was something seriously wrong. He took her arm and guided her back into the room, leading her to the chair she normally favoured. Then he crouched down beside her.

'Tell me,' he ordered. 'What is it? What's happened?'

She gulped. 'Sylvie's vanished! We can't find her anywhere! We've looked in every room, more than once, but there's no trace of her.'

Suppressing his own desire to leap up and begin to search, he forced himself to be calm. 'Tell me. When was she first missed?'

It took time and patience, and by the end he was ready to tear his hair out, but he had the story. 'And there was no letter? No note?'

Lady Carstairs shook her head.

'Has anything happened to upset her recently?'

'Just the opposite! Mr Tempest came, and everything is settled about Danesfield. He was renting it, and he's going to buy the Court.'

Randal spared a moment to congratulate himself that his visit to Danesfield had been fruitful. But that could wait.

'What shoes was she wearing? And did she take a shawl? Has she taken any money?'

Lady Carstairs did not know, so Phyllis was sent for.

'I didn't look, sir. All I saw missing was her old grey dress. And I couldn't say about shoes. Or money. I wouldn't pry into her desk, sir.'

'Well, I'm afraid we must. Show me her bedroom, please.'

Lady Carstairs seemed to take fresh heart now someone else was in charge, and led the way up the stairs. She and Randal stood looking round the room while Phyllis searched through Sylvie's clothes.

'There's nothing I can see missing,' she said at last. 'She changed out of the shoes she'd worn for dinner, these sandals that match the evening gown. She must have put on some walking shoes, there's a pair missing.'

'So she went outside,' Randal said. 'I'm going to ask the men out there to go on searching. Thank goodness we have so many here, they can search the grounds and outbuildings if necessary. I'll be back.'

Jones, just about to send his men home, heard Randal's story with a frown. 'Could the smugglers have caught her? If the lass was walking in the garden last night she might have seen them.'

'We caught all of them. Or so I had supposed.'

'There's other ways out of that stable yard. There could have been someone else who took her away. I'll send a couple to ask the fishermen. They might know something.'

Randal went back indoors, where a tearful Celia was in the hall, being comforted by Aubrey, while David, looking contemptuous, watched them.

'I tell you,' David was saying, 'she's just gone to her latest lover.'

Randal took two strides and grasped David by the shoulder, spinning him round to face him. 'Take that back!'

David wrenched away, and sneered. 'Why should you care? She turned you down, didn't she? Probably found someone more to her taste.'

Before David knew what was coming, Randal landed a punch on his chin which sent him crashing to the floor. Celia shrieked, and Aubrey knelt down beside David, who was holding his chin and groaning.

'You deserved that, old fellow,' Aubrey said. 'I've been wanting to land a good punch on you for some time now. You know what, David,' he went on, as he helped the other man to his feet, 'I think you fancy Sylvie yourself, and couldn't bring yourself to admit it when you thought she had no money. And now it's too late.'

Randal laughed. 'Get him a poultice, Aubrey,' he said, and ran up the stairs two at a time and back to Sylvie's room where he found Phyllis and Lady Carstairs looking at the new chest which had been hidden by a shawl draped over it at the bottom of an old armoire.

Lady Carstairs turned to him. 'What on earth can that be? We didn't bring it with us from Berkeley Square.'

'I think you will find Sylvie had it made to hold her mother's jewels,' he said. 'It looks about the right size.'

'The jewels? But we didn't know where they were. We thought Sir George had sold them or put them in the bank.'

Randal was thinking. 'Has anyone looked

in Sir George's room?'

'Well, yes, we looked everywhere in the house, even the linen closets.'

'Was the door locked?'

Lady Carstairs shook her head in bewilderment. 'Of course not. Why should it be?'

Then Sylvie had removed the jewels, and they were in this chest. 'Did she show you the secret passage?'

'She showed it to the men and Celia.' Lady Carstairs shuddered. 'Dreadful place, it should be blocked up.'

'Has anyone looked there for Sylvie?'

'Why should she be there?'

Randal didn't bother to reply. He strode out of the room and along to that where Sir George had lived during the last few months of his life. He flung open the door and stood listening. Very faintly, he heard a rhythmic banging.

Swiftly he crossed the room and twisted the knob which released the catch of the secret passage. The panel swung open.

★   ★   ★

Sylvie, sitting back with her eyes closed, wearily kicking the door, suddenly found her foot had nothing to bang against. Startled, she opened her eyes, was dazzled by the light

315

coming through the open panel, and hastily shut them again. When she felt arms coming round her she panicked, thinking the smugglers had found her, and began to struggle.

'Careful, love, we don't want to go hurtling down there.'

She was lifted out of the little room and carried over to the bed. When she felt the softness of the feather mattress beneath her stiff body she sighed, then, shielding her eyes with both hands, she opened them cautiously.

'It's you,' she murmured.

Lady Carstairs and Phyllis had appeared, and were exclaiming and asking questions. Sylvie turned away her head. She was too weary to bother.

Sir Randal turned to Phyllis. 'I think what she needs most is a warm bath, a glass of wine and something to eat, then sleep and no questions for a few hours. If I carry her to her room can you see to that?'

Phyllis nodded and almost ran from the room.

'Lady Carstairs, can you go and tell everyone she has been found, and the men outside can go home?'

She started to ask questions, but the look he gave her sent her away.

Sylvie opened her eyes cautiously, and

smiled at Randal. 'Thank you. I really can't bear to have to talk to everyone yet. What time is it?'

'Just after midday.'

'The smugglers are coming back tonight. They were going to take me on a boat and drown me. One of them is Reverend Dawes, I couldn't recognize the others.'

'It's all right, my darling, they've all been caught. You needn't fear them any more. No more talking; we can hear all about it when you've rested.'

He picked her up and carried her to her own room, where several maids were setting up a hip bath, with Phyllis supervising. As he lowered her to the bed he kissed her cheek, and Sylvie grasped his hand.

'You won't leave? I'll see you later?'

'I want to hear all about it, and then go and beat those devils to a pulp!'

She laughed. 'Can I help you?'

★ ★ ★

Several hours later Sylvie woke to find Celia sitting beside her bed.

'How do you feel?'

Sylvie stretched and winced. 'Stiff, and I have some uncomfortable bruises, but much better. Did I dream Sir Randal was here?'

'No, and he's still here. He punched David when he was rude about you.' Celia laughed. 'I think he did what Aubrey and I would have liked to do.'

'That won't make David like me any better. What time is it?'

'Five o'clock. Dinner has been held back, in case you feel well enough to come down.'

'Yes, I'm not an invalid. Please, though, can you help me dress?'

She could not decide what to wear, discarding every dress Celia suggested, and finally deciding on the green gown Lady Carstairs had given her when she first came to Berkeley Square.

Then, with a triumphant smile at Celia, she took out the key to her jewel chest and unlocked it. 'I didn't tell everyone we found my mother's jewels,' she said, delving amongst the rolls. 'Sir George had hidden them in the secret room, along with all those papers we found. We, Sir Randal and I, thought it best not to tell people until I'd had a secure chest made for them. Look, this is the emerald necklace your aunt remembered; she said it was a pity I didn't have it to wear with this gown. Well, now I have.'

Celia was wide-eyed with admiration. 'It's fabulous!' she breathed. 'If the other jewels are half as wonderful you'll have one of the best collections in England!'

'I'll show them to you tomorrow,' Sylvie promised, relocking the chest. 'What has Sir Randal been doing? Has he been chasing the smugglers? Did he say they had been caught? I was so tired I could not understand.'

'He drove to Cromer while you were asleep, said he had some business there, I think to do with the smugglers who had been caught last night, but he's back now. Sylvie, will it be awkward meeting him again? After, well, after what happened?'

'No, I don't think so. You said he knocked David down. Why?'

Celia giggled. 'David was being his usual odious self, suggesting you had gone to a lover you found more to your liking than Sir Randal. It served him right! Then after you'd gone to bed David said he wasn't to come back, he wouldn't be welcome to dinner, but Aubrey told him it was your house, and you wanted him here.'

'So we'd better go down.'

In the drawing-room they found Lady Carstairs talking to David, who seemed to be urging on her something she was resisting. Sir Randal, looking utterly at his ease, was talking to Aubrey. The men rose to their feet and Sir Randal came across to take Sylvie's hand in his. He looked at her closely.

'You look better,' he said.

'I feel normal again, apart from some stiffness,' Sylvie said. 'I'm sorry if I've kept everyone waiting. Is dinner ready?' she asked Sawyer, who had followed them into the room. 'Good, then let's go in.'

Lady Carstairs wanted to know where Sylvie's necklace had been found, so first of all she and Sir Randal had to confess where they had found them and why they had not told everyone. Lady Carstairs nodded.

'You were wise, one can never know when a servant might get tempted, and with these horrid smugglers about, one doesn't know whom one can trust. Some of Sir George's servants are probably related to the wretches.'

Then Sir Randal told them about the smugglers, and Dupont, and how they had been captured, and Sylvie explained how she had been caught and imprisoned. David maintained a grim silence, but the others exclaimed and demanded more details.

'I cannot imagine how a man of the cloth could involve himself in such goings on,' Lady Carstairs exclaimed. 'And Monsieur Dupont, you say he has been trying to incite the mill workers to riot? He seemed such a pleasant man. I shall be glad to get away from this locality, it seems particularly lawless.'

'Now Sylvie has Danesfield to go to, and

everything here is sorted out, or can be left to Mr Haines to deal with, perhaps we can go to Lichfield,' Aubrey said. 'Celia and I want to be married as soon as it can be arranged.'

'Sylvie had better come with us,' Lady Carstairs said. 'She cannot live at Danesfield on her own. Not until she has hired a suitable companion. We can start making plans in the morning.'

* * *

Sylvie was still weary, so excused herself to go back to bed. Sir Randal had sent for his clothes and accepted Lady Carstairs' invitation to stay at Clayton Court. Sylvie had a great deal to think about.

She thought she could remember him calling her 'love' and 'darling', when he rescued her, but everything was so muddled in her mind she could not be sure. He had knocked David down for insulting her, but Celia had said Aubrey had also wanted to do that, so there was perhaps no special significance in it. Any decent man might have done the same.

The puzzles were too complicated for her, and she was soon asleep. When she awoke it was to find Celia sitting beside her.

'Goodness, what time is it? Have I slept late?'

'You must have been exhausted,' Celia said, going to the bell pull. 'Aunt Augusta said you were to have breakfast in bed, so Phyllis will bring it shortly, now she knows you are awake.'

Sylvie found she was still stiff, and her bruises ached, but that would soon mend. She wanted to see Sir Randal, but at the same time was afraid. Had she imagined those endearments? They could have been the soothing words one would use to comfort a terrified child, and her fright when the panel door had opened and he had lifted her out had been an instinctive, childish reaction. Would he, today, be cold and businesslike? Last night he had been friendly, still concerned about the effects of her ordeal, but she had been sheltered by the presence of everyone else. Today she had to speak to him alone.

Their previous meeting, when he had made her an offer, obviously hating the necessity, and she had rejected him, stood between them. He had been doing what he accepted was his duty, what he knew the world would expect, and in refusing him she had insulted him. Society would love the scandal, and no doubt many of the girls and their mamas who had hoped to capture him would gloat at his discomfort. He was proud, a man courted by all the debutantes, one of the most prized catches in the marriage mart. No other girl would have dreamt of refusing him, whatever the circumstances. Indeed, Sylvie suspected some of them would have contrived to trap him into appearing to ruin their reputations, in the hope of forcing an offer.

After she had eaten she sent Celia away, saying her friend must have many things to discuss with Aubrey. She needed time to prepare herself, to give herself confidence. She had to look her best, so after some thought she put on one of her favourite gowns, a new one she had worn only once in London, and not at all since coming to Clayton Court. It was deep gold silk with a panel of dark green embroidery at the hem, and dark green ribbons ruched at the neck and the edges of the small, puffed sleeves. With it she wore a pair of her mother's bracelets, plain gold bands set with emeralds.

She took a deep breath, held her shoulders back and her head high. She would not give the slightest hint of her apprehension. Then she went slowly downstairs. She reached the morning-room door and heard Lady Carstairs and Celia chatting. Suddenly she could not tolerate the thought of all the exclamations and questions. She turned away, wondering where to go for a few moments of privacy before she summoned up the courage to face everyone, and saw Sawyer crossing the hall.

'Sir Randal asked me to tell you he was in the library, miss,' the butler said, and gave her what Sylvie felt was an avuncular smile.

She thanked him. So it had come, and she was not at all sure she felt ready for this meeting. But it was unavoidable. She had to thank him for finding her, when no one else had even thought of looking in the secret passage. She took a deep breath. Best to get it over, and then she could relax and make plans for going to Danesfield and taking up her life there.

Briefly she wondered what it would be like. She knew the *ton* would consider her ruined, for they would all hear how she had spent a night with a man, however innocently, at the same inn. She could never be received by the high sticklers, and it was unlikely any respectable man would offer for her. Others, those attracted by her restored fortune might, but she would not want them. She would have to resign herself to spinsterhood, and suddenly Danesfield, the home she had been devastated at the thought of losing, which she had been fighting to recover, did not seem so desirable. It would not compensate her for the loss of Sir Randal.

Taking a deep breath she walked steadily

towards the library. It was here she had rejected his proposal. It was cruel of him to ask for their final interview in the same room, so full of memories and regrets. She expected he was going to tell her he was leaving. There was nothing more for him here, since the smugglers had been caught and Dupont was detained, on his way to London.

He was sitting on the window seat, but jumped to his feet as she entered.

'Sylvie.'

She gulped. He wasn't smiling, but he didn't look grim. Perhaps this meeting would not be as daunting as she feared. Before she could speak he had crossed the room and taken her hand in his. 'Come and sit down.' He drew her to sit beside him. 'Can you ever forgive me?'

She blinked. What did he mean? 'Forgive you? But you rescued me, you knew where I was when no one else thought of it.' She shivered at the memory of the hours in that small, dark space. 'I was terrified they would come back and find me, and so ashamed of the fuss I made when I thought you were them.'

'It was understandable; you had undergone a frightening experience. But that is not what I meant. Sylvie, my dear, when last we were together in this room I made such a mull of it! I never expected that when I did finally make a girl an offer I would be so maladroit. I was like some ham-fisted booby.'

Sylvie frowned. 'There is no need to apologize, sir. It could not have been easy.'

'I hated being told what my duty was, even though I recognized it. But that is no excuse. Sylvie, my dear, I did not know then that what I felt for you was love. I doubt if anyone has ever made such a botched proposal! Will you forgive me and let me start again?'

She looked carefully into his eyes, trying to see into his soul. Did he mean it? Had he simply decided it was still his duty to marry her, and come again, better prepared this time, well-rehearsed, to make another offer?

He grinned at her and captured her other hand, forcing her to turn towards him. 'I can't blame you for mistrusting me, my love. Sylvie, I have to confess, for a time I distrusted you too, and that prevented me from judging you honestly, and realizing I was falling in love with you.'

She found her voice at these two unexpected notions. She couldn't yet explore the most important one, that he might love her, so turned to the other. 'Distrusted me? Why?'

'You are partly French. I didn't know where your sympathies lay. You met Dupont one morning in the City, at a time and place where I would not have expected a gently reared girl to be, and later declined to greet him as an acquaintance.'

'I didn't want Lady Carstairs to know where I had been that morning.'

'I know that now. But we were suspicious of Dupont, and wondered who his confederates were. There seemed to be a whole network of spies, messages being passed, and sent to France in the smugglers' boats, and Dupont seemed to be using boats from this part of the coast. When we discovered your connection with Clayton Court, it aggravated our suspicions. Of course, I soon realized it was just coincidence, once I had been here with you and met Sir George.'

'I see. My father had no sympathy with the revolutionaries, nor do I.'

'Of course not. But my suspicions made me push away the feelings I had for you. My dearest one, now I will ask in proper form. Will you do me the honour of becoming my wife?'

Sylvie was still trying to absorb the information that she had been suspected of conspiring with a French spy, and she looked up at him with a question in her eyes.

He misinterpreted it, grinned ruefully, and shook his head. 'Don't you believe me? Sylvie, I do most sincerely love you and want you for my wife, but if words don't convince you, let's see what actions can do.'

He put one arm round her waist and drew her closer. With his other hand he tilted her chin. Then, so slowly it felt like endless hours to her, he lowered his face towards hers, finally capturing her lips with his.

At first the pressure was gentle, and she savoured the feel of him, the scent of sandalwood and maleness. Then his lips grew hard and demanding, and he pulled her closer still. Only when they were both breathless did he raise his mouth from hers.

He was smiling, and she could not misunderstand the look in his eyes. He was not making pretty speeches and kissing her so ardently because he felt honour-bound to do so. A sudden wave of joy engulfed her. When she had been thinking she faced life as a spinster, this delight had been awaiting her.

He laughed a little unsteadily. 'Well, Sylvie, was that a more acceptable offer? Will you marry me? I warn you,' he added, 'if you refuse I shall come and ask you every day until you say yes.'

She found herself incapable of speech, but nodded, and once more he captured her lips with his. After an endless time he let her go and she sighed in contentment. 'I can scarce believe it. I thought I had driven you away.'

'My darling! Soon? I want to have you to myself. Do you want a big wedding, from Danesfield, perhaps?'

Sylvie shook her head and laughed a little unsteadily. 'I would hate the sort of fuss Lady Carstairs is planning for Celia! Besides, with all the gossip about us, would it not appear tactless? Can we not have a simple, quiet wedding?'

'As you wish. As for the gossip, afterwards I can show the world that this was no marriage forced upon us by notions of propriety.'

There was another interval of kissing, by which time Sylvie was fully convinced of his love for her.

He held her away at last. 'Shall we escape to Norwich and marry by special licence, and then go straight to my home? We can let Haines do what is needed here, and Aubrey can take his Celia to Lichfield. Later we can go to Danesfield and you can take possession again.'

Somehow Sylvie knew that Danesfield, while always precious to her, was no longer of prime importance in her life. This man and love for him would henceforth occupy all her thoughts.

She sighed, and held up her lips invitingly. 'It seems as though my dreams have come true.'

We do hope that you have enjoyed reading this large print book.

Did you know that all of our titles are available for purchase?

We publish a wide range of high quality large print books including:
Romances, Mysteries, Classics
General Fiction
Non Fiction and Westerns

Special interest titles available in large print are:
The Little Oxford Dictionary
Music Book
Song Book
Hymn Book
Service Book

Also available from us courtesy of Oxford University Press:
Young Readers' Dictionary
(large print edition)
Young Readers' Thesaurus
(large print edition)

For further information or a free brochure, please contact us at:
Ulverscroft Large Print Books Ltd.,
The Green, Bradgate Road, Anstey,
Leicester, LE7 7FU, England.
Tel: (00 44) **0116 236 4325**
Fax: (00 44) **0116 234 0205**